HOTBED

BRYAN CASSIDAY

Bryan Cassiday
Los Angeles
ISBN 9781737628293
Published in the United States of America
First Edition: June 19, 2023

BOOKS BY BRYAN CASSIDAY

Cutthroat Express (Zombie Apocalypse: The Chad Halverson
Series Book 7)
Knot of Fear (Scott Brody Thriller 5)
Threads (Scott Brody Thriller 4)
Electric Green Mambas (Scott Brody Thriller 3)
Horde (Zombie Apocalypse: The Chad Halverson Series Book 6)
Ice in the Blood
Crime Blotter USA
Murder LLC (Scott Brody Thriller 2)
Bolt (Scott Brody Thriller 1)
Riptide of Fear
The Payout
Force of Impact (Ethan Carr Thriller 3)
Dying to Breathe (Ethan Carr Thriller 2)
Countdown to Death (Ethan Carr Thriller 1)
The Bus Stops Here—and Other Zombie Tales
Two Moons Rising
Alien Assault
Comes a Chopper
Zombie Apocalypse: The Chad Halverson Series 1–5
Helter Skelter
The Anaconda Complex
The Kill Option
Blood Moon: Thrillers and Tales of Terror
Fete of Death

Chapter 1

Phoebe felt her marriage was going to pot.

Supposedly it was a dream come true when she married the popular mayor of her small town of Costaguana in Southern California, Jason Albright. He was considered incorruptible by the citizens who elected him—a man who couldn't be bought because he had inherited a fortune from his father Jackson, a real estate tycoon.

Phoebe couldn't believe it when he asked her to marry him. In her early thirties, she came from a solid middle-class background. Her father Sam was a journalist, her mother Lila a high-school teacher. A cynical journalist, Sam was suspicious of politicians, but even he liked Jason and thought the man could do no wrong.

Which made it all the more shocking that she now suspected Jason of cheating on her. He kept going out at night claiming he had business matters to attend to. She couldn't understand why he was working so late almost every night. She knew politicians lived busy lives, but this was going too far.

She started to suspect it wasn't business matters that were monopolizing his time. It had to be something else. Another woman. What else could it be? she wondered. He had to be seeing someone on the sly.

She had to find out the truth.

She was following his new black Mercedes G-Wagen in her turquoise Mini Cooper as he drove through the nightclub-strewn part of town known as the Strip. She tried to hang back far enough that he couldn't see her tailing him. But she didn't want to hang back too far, or she would lose him in the darkness.

He was slowing down.

What kind of business matter could he possibly be pursuing here? she wondered, figuring she knew the answer. A business matter in a skirt.

She saw three streetwalkers in their twenties strolling down the sidewalk. Two of them wore miniskirts. The blue-eyed blonde with bee-stung lips wore a tight black leather one with an even tighter black tube top. The brunette wore a shiny white polyester one with a shocking pink halter holding up her ample breasts. The third streetwalker, a black with peroxide blonde hair with a half inch of black roots, wore a pair of café au lait stretch pants and a see-through white fishnet blouse. Her sapphire eye shadow glittered under the streetlights.

Phoebe's face reddened with fury as Jason's G-Wagen slowed down, pulled over to the curb, and parked next to the blonde in the tight black leather outfit.

Business matters, indeed, she decided. Was she supposed to believe he was citing them for soliciting? Or maybe for loitering? Fat chance.

Craning her neck toward his car, she slammed on her brakes as she all but crashed into the red Jeep Cherokee in front of her. She swore. She had to keep her eyes on the road.

She decided to pull over to the curb before she got too close to Jason's car. He might spot her if she got any closer. Or was he so focused on the blonde streetwalker's boobs that he had tunnel vision?

She tried to calm down. Her father once told her she had a bad habit of jumping to conclusions, thinking the worst of people. Maybe she had inherited it from him, since it was a journalist's job to dig for dirt, expecting to find it everywhere they looked.

Sitting behind the steering wheel tapping her fingers on it, she took a deep breath and tried to bridle her anger.

She watched the blonde approach the Mercedes passenger's-side door, pulling her tube top down an inch, letting Jason see a little more flesh, swinging her hips with carefree abandon, her transparent stiletto heels clopping on the cement sidewalk. Jason powered down the window.

The hooker leaned forward and placed her hands on the windowsill, jutting out her ass under the wash of the overhead streetlight, smiling and leering at the driver.

If he was warning the blonde against soliciting, why was she smiling and leering at him? wondered Phoebe.

The hooker shook her head and strutted away from the G-Wagen, shaking her butt for Jason to ogle, looking over her shoulder at him making sure he was watching the action.

Phoebe relaxed a bit. Maybe Jason had warned her off, after all. He was doing his job as the incorruptible civic-minded mayor trying to keep the streets clear of prostitutes. Phoebe's fingers stopped tapping the Mini's steering wheel. Until . . .

Until she heard Jason whistle two notes—one high, one low—and saw his hand stick out his passenger's-side window clutching a handful of hundred-dollar bills shaking them at the blonde.

Seeing the cash the streetwalker slewed around and returned to the Mercedes, clopping on her stilettos, practically falling out of them in her haste.

"Bastard," said Phoebe, slamming her fist down on the Mini's steering wheel in white heat.

The blonde flung the G-Wagen door open.

Thinking fast, Phoebe whipped her cell phone out of her purse that sat on her Mini passenger seat and snapped a picture of her.

The blonde slid onto the G-Wagen passenger seat and shut the door behind her.

Phoebe couldn't stand watching the whole sorry incident any longer. Gritting her teeth she peeled away from the curb and sped past Jason, averting her head so he wouldn't recognize her, though she doubted he was noticing traffic, his undivided attention trained on the voluptuous blonde sitting beside him.

The son of a bitch. Incorruptible, my ass.

Chapter 2

Now what was she supposed to do? Phoebe wondered in her well-appointed living room in her Craftsman-style house.

She paced around the carpet in jeans, a baggy sweatshirt, and flats, trying to figure her next move. What could she do? Who should she tell?

She didn't want to tell anyone. Having your husband cheat on you was too embarrassing to talk about. His cheating on her made her feel like a failure as a wife. Not something you want people to get wind of.

How was she supposed to figure out what to do? Was there a guidebook for this sort of thing? None that she had heard of. Everyone had to go their own way and deal with it in their own fashion.

Some people she knew hired private detectives to handle cases of infidelity. But in this case what was the point? wondered Phoebe. They hired PIs to find out if their spouses were cheating. She already knew Jason was cheating. She had seen it with her own eyes. She didn't need a private detective to tell her something she already knew.

Should she confront Jason? she wondered. She didn't know if that was the right move. It was uncharted waters for her. She would have to make up her plans on the fly.

She felt too angry to confront him yet. She would go off on a rant if she did. Maybe after a few days she could bring it to his attention. Or maybe she should forget about it.

If she said nothing to him about it, he would go right on doing it with other streetwalkers or with the same one. Maybe the blonde was his favorite.

A common streetwalker, she decided in fury. If he was going to cheat on her, why not pick an upscale call girl? Why a cheap street tramp, who might have VD?

Phoebe cringed at the thought. She hoped he practiced safe sex with his pickups. She didn't want him bringing home one of their diseases and infecting her.

She picked up her cell phone that was lying on the couch. She didn't know why she had bothered. Who was she going to call? Who was an expert on cheating husbands?

She shook her head in confusion.

Maybe she should confront the hooker. That made some sort of sense, she decided. Confront her and scare her away from Jason.

Her life was going downhill again. Things had started looking brighter after she had met Jason. Now this.

When she had first met him, she was depressed from being on the verge of declaring bankruptcy after her start-up had flopped. She had consulted a lawyer about filing for Chapter 7. She had owed creditors over one hundred thousand dollars and knew she would never be able to pay them off. She had thought it was the end of the world. She considered committing suicide.

Then she had met Jason at a friend's party. He had a striking appearance and an impressive resume. He had obtained his JD from the prestigious Stanford Law School. How could she resist him? He had everything going for him. A fine education and a job in the public eye as a successful mayor.

She and he were attracted to each other. They had started dating. When she had worked up enough courage to ask him for a loan to pay off her debts, he had agreed, to her welcome surprise. She had felt massive relief. They got married soon after.

It was an idyllic marriage—except for his nightly disappearances that he attributed to work. She figured something was going on, something he didn't want her to know about. Well, now she knew what he was hiding. A secret life chasing hookers.

Why did he need hookers when he had her? wondered Phoebe. She couldn't understand him. Rich and successful as a popular mayor, but a liar and a cheat at the same time. Did anyone else know about his secret life?

She cared for him. She also felt inferior to him because of his education and his social standing. She must not be satisfying him in bed. Why else would he cheat on her?

Her roller-coaster life was back in the pits with this latest revelation.

She scratched her head in dismay. She didn't know what to do.

She wondered what good confronting the hooker would accomplish. She doubted she could scare the woman off. How could she scare her? Phoebe had no leverage on the woman.

Phoebe couldn't go public with the transgression. It might destroy Jason's career.

At this point, she didn't want to destroy him. She wanted to save their marriage. She racked her brains for a solution.

Maybe she could pay the woman off. Get her to leave town. She wondered if the hooker knew Jason was the mayor. If she did, she might try to blackmail him. How long had this been going on?

There were too many variables to consider. And they were all bad. Her mind was spinning out of control.

Feeling faint she plunked down on her leather sofa. She blew out her cheeks in frustration.

This was what she got for being too nice. She got treated with contempt by Jason. If she overlooked his hooker, she might be giving him a free pass to visit the hooker again and again. How many times had he already seen the tramp?

Jason had no idea she had seen him with the hooker, she decided. Should she pretend she hadn't seen it? If she ignored it, he would keep patronizing the hooker. Even if she confronted him, he might keep patronizing her—unless Phoebe could figure out a way to get leverage over him and force him to stop whoring around.

Phoebe yawned. Her thinking was wearing her out.

He didn't give a damn about her. That much was obvious.

Should she file for divorce? Because of one hooker? She didn't know.

There was a problem with a divorce, she decided. Even though California was a communal property state, where each spouse got half, she had signed a prenup as a condition for their marriage. The prenup stipulated she would receive much less than half. Jason had wanted to make sure she wasn't a gold digger when he married her.

She would end up in poverty if she got a divorce with a bleak future facing her. How would she make a living? Another start-up? Another visit to bankruptcy court?

She didn't want to think about it.

But she had to make a decision—even if every decision she made was wrong and ended up in disaster. Like her decision to marry Jason. It might turn out to be the worst decision of her life.

On the other hand, he was just cheating on her. She guessed things could be worse. At least he wasn't trying to murder her.

She laughed. She couldn't help it. Her life was such a mess she thought she was fortunate because her husband wasn't trying to murder her. What a joke.

She was on her own. Sink or swim.

Maybe she should forgive him and let bygones be bygones.

She flared up. She couldn't forgive him.

If she did nothing, he would go right on betraying her.

She bolted to her feet, determined to do something. She had no idea what.

Chapter 3

She decided to call her friend Meredith, who was a veterinarian. Maybe Meredith could give her some pointers.

Phoebe felt nervous. She didn't know if she was making the right decision by telling anyone about her husband's infidelity. Frankly, it was humiliating to talk about it with anyone. Jason must not find her desirable, decided Phoebe.

Despite her misgivings, Phoebe got out her cell and phoned Meredith.

"I have to get this off my chest," said Phoebe.

"Oh, Phoebe," said Meredith on the other end of the line. "Hello. Long time no see."

"Hi."

"What are you talking about?"

"Jason . . . ," Phoebe trailed off.

She didn't know if she could go through with it. Tense, she bit her lower lip.

"What about him?" said Meredith, sensing something was wrong. "Did he get hurt? Was he in an accident?"

"No, no."

"Then what?"

"I . . ." Phoebe squeezed her cell phone like it was an almost empty toothpaste tube. "I think Jason may be cheating on me."

Actually, Phoebe *knew* he was cheating on her, but she couldn't bring herself to say it because it would make her look like a fool. Saying *think* gave her wiggle room. Maybe he wasn't cheating on her, which enabled her to save face. At least, that was what she wanted Meredith to think—that Jason might not be cheating.

"I see," said Meredith.

"What do you think I should do?"

"I'm not an expert on this. I'm a veterinarian. I prefer the company of animals to that of people."

Phoebe felt her shoulders slump. "You don't have any suggestions?"

"Maybe you should hire a private detective to find out the truth."

I already know the truth.

"Then what?" said Phoebe.

"Then you would know what to do."

"Which is?"

Meredith paused. "Maybe you should talk to a psychiatrist."

"What good will that do? Will that stop Jason from cheating on me?"

"Maybe you should confront the woman."

"And do what?" said Phoebe, all ears.

"Uh, scare her away?"

Scare away a streetwalker? She's the one scaring me.

"How?" said Phoebe.

"Act tough with her. Act like you're not gonna take any crap from her."

"What if that doesn't work?" said Phoebe, figuring it would be difficult to scare away a hard-bitten streetwalker who was used to having cops throw her in the joint.

"Uh—pay her off. She has to be a gold digger. Everybody knows Jason's loaded. He's the mayor for Chrissake."

Phoebe hadn't thought of that. She wondered if it would work. The woman was a common street tramp. She couldn't want that much. Maybe a thousand dollars and a bus ticket out of town would send her packing.

"That might work," said Phoebe, mulling it over.

"How do you know it's a woman? Maybe it's a man he's seeing. These days you never can tell."

"I'm pretty sure I know who the woman is," hedged Phoebe, not wanting to admit she had seen Jason pick up the woman.

She wanted Meredith to believe there was an element of doubt about the woman's identity. Certainty would admit to being a failure as a wife.

She started as she heard Jason's G-Wagen pull into the driveway. What was she going to say to him?

"Gotta run," she told Meredith, and hung up.

12

Chapter 4

A charismatic man in his sixties, Jason walked into the living room.

Why did he feel compelled to go to hookers? she wondered. He could have any woman he wanted. Why pick a streetwalker of all people?

"Finished work for the day?" she said.

"Yeah," said Jason.

He had no compunction about lying, decided Phoebe, watching his expression, which gave nothing away.

"Do you ever think you're working too hard?" she said.

"No, never. If I don't keep working, I don't bring home the paychecks to pay for this house."

His blank expression annoyed Phoebe. Didn't he feel guilt for cheating on her? Apparently not. It infuriated her. She wanted to scream at him that she knew he was cheating on her. She managed to restrain herself.

"What kind of work did you do tonight?" she asked.

"Same old, same old. Meeting and greeting the public. A mayor has to keep in touch with his constituents."

"Is that what you call it?"

He turned on her. "What do you want me to call it?"

"Call it what it is."

"I don't understand."

She shook her head. "Never mind."

"I have to do my job. I can't help it if I put in long hours. If I don't work, we can't live in this nice house any longer."

"What's your definition of work?"

"Putting in long hours as the mayor of our fair city."

"Meeting and greeting the public?"

"I have to assure them I'm looking out for their interests."

Phoebe changed tack. "Do you have something you want to tell me?"

He stared at her with puzzlement. "I don't understand."

"If something's not right, you should tell me. I have a right to know."

"I don't know what you're talking about." He strode to the sideboard. "Want a drink?"

He opened a bottle of Sancerre with a corkscrew and poured himself a drink.

"OK," she said.

He poured another glass of wine and handed it to her.

"Takes the edge off a long day of work," he said, handing her the glass.

"Your job must wear you out," she said, accepting the wine.

"Long hours are part of the job. Being a mayor is a full-time job. Sometimes I feel like I don't have a life."

"Do you want me to feel sorry for you?"

"What? Not at all. I enjoy my job."

"I'm sure you do."

"Is something wrong?" he said with concern.

"Not a thing."

She could lie as well as he could, she decided. *As though screwing a hooker was part of his job.* Did he really expect her to believe that?

He yawned.

"Are you tired?" she said.

He nodded. "This job's a lot of work."

Didn't he ever get tired of lying? Phoebe wondered. She supposed it was part and parcel of his job as a politician. Tell the people what they want to hear, and they'll elect you. Only a congenital liar could be a politician.

"I guess being incorruptible must tire you out," she said.

She wondered if he detected the irony in her statement. Or maybe he truly believed his reputation in the media that he was incorruptible, even though he was committing adultery by screwing a hooker.

Her words drew no reaction from him, other than another yawn.

Annoyed at his lack of reaction, she wanted to wound him. He deserved to be wounded.

"Did you ever work a day in your life?" she said. "You trust fund babies are all alike, born with a silver spoon in your mouth."

He rounded on her. "Are you drunk? Have you spent the whole night drinking while I've been out working?"

"Not everyone's a lush like you."

"What's got into you?"

"Maybe if I'd been born with a rich daddy—can you take a hint?—I'd be a flaming success story like you and would blow hot air for a living."

Jason stared at her, his face livid with rage.

"You want me to feel sorry for myself for having a rich father?" he said. "Too bad. That's not gonna happen. He didn't get to be a real estate tycoon by sitting on his ass all day. I'm proud to say I'm a workaholic like he is."

She took a pull on her Sancerre and laughed. "Right."

"Maybe if you didn't drink like a fish, you might amount to something instead of being a loser."

"Don't you find me attractive?" she said, spilling some of her drink.

"Pull yourself together, Phoebe. I don't want anyone to see you like this. You could ruin my career."

She smirked. "There are other ways to ruin your career."

"What are you talking about? Tell me what's going on."

"*You* tell *me* what's going on. I saw you—"

She caught herself before she let the cat out of the bag.

"Saw me what?" he said.

"Never mind," she muttered, turning away from him.

He waved her off. "I'm going to bed. I've got a full day of work tomorrow."

"I thought you working stiffs never rested," she said as a Parthian shot.

He stalked off in a huff.

Chapter 5

The next day, Phoebe drove her Mini to the skeevy, vice-ridden part of town lined with nightclubs, casinos, and strip clubs known as the Strip. There wasn't as much activity during the day as there was at night. At the moment, only two streetwalkers plied their trade on the sidewalks near the Lavender Whip nightclub casino.

Phoebe didn't recognize them. Jason's tart must take the daytime off, she decided.

She pulled over to the curb near an Asian streetwalker with dyed blonde hair, killed the Mini ignition, and powered down the passenger's-side window.

Wearing white fishnet stockings and an ivory miniskirt, the hooker leaned forward, peered inside the Mini, and smiled at her.

Phoebe motioned for the hooker to approach.

The hooker strutted across the sidewalk in white vinyl go-go boots that reached to her thighs.

"Looking for a date, honey?" she said, bending over, and putting her hands on the Mini windowsill.

"I'm looking for one of your friends," said Phoebe, scanning the sidewalk and not seeing Jason's hookup from last night.

"You don't like me?" said the hooker, pouting.

"I want to talk to your friend."

"I don't have any friends. You're wasting my time," said the hooker, becoming angry and fixing to leave.

Phoebe pulled a twenty-dollar bill out of her purse. "I'll pay for the info."

"I'm listening."

"What's your name?"

"Francine," said the hooker, holding out her hand. "Now give me the twenty."

"I have more questions to ask you."

"Then you'll need more money."

"OK," said Phoebe, rooting through her purse in search of her wallet.

"First, give me the twenty, or I'm outa here."

16

Phoebe handed her the twenty through the open window. A waste of money, she decided. She didn't care what Francine's name was. She wanted the other hooker's name.

"I'm looking for the blonde who was standing here last night," she said.

Francine rolled her brown eyes. "You know how many blondes work this street? I need more details than that."

Her patchouli perfume was so strong it made Phoebe's eyes water.

Phoebe tried to remember what the hooker looked like.

"She's a blonde in her twenties with full lips," she said. "She was wearing a tight leather outfit—a black miniskirt and a matching tube top."

"Full lips. There are a lot of full lips around here thanks to collagen injections. A lot of black leather too."

Phoebe produced another twenty out of her wallet.

Francine looked disgusted. "Five of those twenties might jog my memory."

Phoebe grimaced and produced five twenties.

"Last night, you say," said Francine, snatching the twenties out of Phoebe's hand.

"Right."

"Was she white or black?"

"White."

"Hmm. How old was she?"

Phoebe thought about it, trying to recall, even though part of her didn't want to remember the woman and was trying to push last night's memory out of her mind.

"In her twenties," said Phoebe.

"You like 'em young, huh?" said Francine, with a wink.

"This isn't for me. I mean, I want to talk to her. That's all."

"I doubt she'd want to see you if that's all you want."

"I'm willing to pay her for her time. What's her name?"

"Last night, you say?"

"Yes."

"Was I with her? Do you remember?"

"I didn't see you."

"Then how am I supposed to know her?"

"You must've seen her here at some time. You work the same street."

Francine deposited the hundred dollars inside her bra.

She rubbed her fingers together. "Another five twenties might help my memory, if you know what I mean."

Grudgingly, Phoebe pulled a C-note out of her wallet.

Francine's eyes widened at the sight of the bill.

"It might be Val," she said.

"Val? Where can I find her? Do you know where she lives?"

"That's another question."

Her petite hand with long enameled black fingernails shot through the air like a hummingbird and snagged the C-note out of Phoebe's grasp.

"Tell me the answer," said Phoebe.

"Two more Ben Franklins will loosen my lips."

"*One* more," said Phoebe, decisively.

Francine shook her head no and turned away.

"All right, all right," said Phoebe, digging out two hundreds from her wallet. "Here."

Lucky she had gone to the bank this morning, she decided.

Francine faced the Mini passenger's-side window again and clapped her eyes on the two hundreds.

Phoebe offered her the money, which Francine took.

"She lives in the pink stucco motel on the next block," said Francine. "You can't miss it."

"Which room?"

Francine shook her head. "I can't remember. It's the second floor. Room 203, I think. Best to ask the manager."

Phoebe coughed on Francine's overpowering patchouli scent carried on a sudden breeze into the Mini.

Francine stuffed the rest of the money in her bra and strutted away.

Her eyes bloodshot and watery from the patchouli, Phoebe fired the ignition and pulled into traffic.

Chapter 6

Phoebe drove to the next block, picked up on a flamingo pink motel, and looked for a place to park on the side of the street.

The two-story motel needed a paint job.

This block gave her the creeps. A sweating, shivering junkie lay in rags on the sidewalk jonesing for skag. Maybe he wasn't a junkie. Maybe he had a disease, she decided. He looked on the verge of death. He couldn't have been more than thirty years old. He was wearing a grey hoodie and blue jeans. He vomited on himself.

She looked away from him. She didn't plan on staying here long.

She parked at a meter a safe distance from the junkie. She didn't want to go anywhere near him. Whatever he had might be contagious.

She got out of her Mini and walked toward the motel.

She wondered if this was where Val had taken Jason for a trick. How could he stand going here? She couldn't believe he was cheating on her to shack up with a streetwalker in a dive like this.

With foreboding she climbed the short flight of cement steps to the entrance. She didn't want to go inside, but she had to get the tramp to stop seeing Jason. She had to confront Val. She could feel her heartbeat ramping up.

She opened the plate-glass door. The sweet pungent odor of marijuana wafted down the foyer toward her.

His brown hair in a man bun, a thirtysomething guy with phlegmy blue eyes was sitting behind the front desk at the opposite end of the lobby, flipping through a glossy skin magazine.

"Hello," said Phoebe. "I'm looking for Val. A friend told me she's staying here."

He looked up from his magazine, showing little interest in her.

"I dunno," he said.

"Can you check your ledger? I need to talk to her. It's very important."

"It's not important to me," he said, looking bored.

Phoebe huffed in frustration. She felt like calling him on the carpet. She decided it wouldn't get her anywhere. He wasn't under any obligation to give her Val's room number. She restrained her anger.

"Please," she implored him.

He scratched his neck and flicked something off it.

She felt like running out of this decrepit hell hole and speeding away in her Mini.

"How much is it worth to you?" he said, sizing her up, figuring she had money since she could afford nice clothes.

She reached into her purse and withdrew her wallet. She held up a twenty.

"Not much, I guess," he said.

She held up another twenty.

"I'll tell you for a hundred," he said.

"For one room number?" she said, indignant.

He picked his nose.

"I guess you don't want to see her that bad," he said, and returned to flipping through his skin magazine.

"This is urgent. Don't you understand?"

"Then pony up," he said, not looking up from his sweat rag. "This may be a free country, but nothing's free in it."

That was all she needed—a dime-store philosopher.

Irritated, she fished out a Ben Franklin from her wallet and handed it to him.

"That's more like it," he said, glomming onto the bill. "Val, you said. Do you know her last name?"

"No."

He consulted the ledger. "Here she is. V. Lewton. That must be her. She's in room 203."

"Val Lewton? Are you kidding me?"

"That's what it says. It's probably not her real name. People that stay here don't use their real names. Do you understand? We don't mind as long as they pony up." He looked baffled. "Who's Val Lewton, anyway? Is she a VIP or something? Don't tell me she's an influencer on Instagram."

"*He* was a horror movie producer in the forties."

"Never heard of him."

He returned to pawing his girlie rag.

Phoebe decided not to take the rickety elevator when its door slid open and revealed obscene graffiti scribbled with a black Magic Marker on the car's walls. The odor of vomit greeted her.

Wincing, she opened the steel fire door to the stairwell and climbed the stairs to the second floor. The stairwell reeked of Lysol that masked the stench of stale urine emanating from the area of the standpipe. She reached the landing and strode onto the carpet, which gave off a musty odor. The floorboards beneath the carpet creaked under her footfalls.

She could hear a woman yelling in a nearby room. She halted in front of room 203, preparing to knock on the door when she realized the yelling was coming from the other side of the shut door.

Phoebe refrained from knocking, her fist poised a few inches from the door. Her pulse raced as she listened to the ruckus inside the room.

Somebody was running around in it hurling things and hollering incoherently. A bottle or glass slammed into a wall and shattered. Shards tinkled on the floor.

What was the woman doing in there? Phoebe wondered, afraid to open the door and find out. Was it Val?

The woman screamed like a berserk animal and continued scampering around the room and throwing things. The woman came to a stop, screamed again, and hurled a chair across the room. The chair crashed to the floor. The woman stamped her feet up and down several times, venting her frustration or whatever was driving her psychotic episode.

Terrified, Phoebe stood rooted to the spot. She didn't want Val to know she was standing outside her door. Val was rampaging in a murderous rage. In her maniacal state she was capable of doing anything.

Was the woman on drugs? Phoebe wondered, her eyes wide with fright. What could Jason see in such a psycho?

Phoebe had come here to confront Val. She hadn't come here to be murdered by her. She had never heard such dreadful sounds coming from a human being. Her legs stiff from nervous tension, she shifted on her feet and heard the floor creak beneath her. She held her breath. She hoped Val hadn't heard the wheezing floorboards.

The deranged woman continued racing around the room yelling gibberish and hurling objects in her wrath. Phoebe wondered what language Val was speaking. It didn't sound human.

Something made of glass smashed against the door, shattered, and fell in pieces on the floor.

Phoebe started, her heart in her mouth.

She heard what sounded like another voice in the room. The voice was screaming. It sounded like a male voice. Was somebody else in Val's room with her?

A sixtyish goateed hunchbacked man wearing a black beret shambled down the hallway toward her, thudding his cane against the carpet. He stopped near her, tilted his head sideways, and glanced at her.

A heavy object crashed against a wall in Val's room and thumped against the floor.

"Did you hear that?" she mouthed to the geezer, her eyes popping.

He didn't respond. Face expressionless, he trudged past her down the hall.

Val continued pelting around her room screaming gibberish, upsetting furniture, and pounding the walls with her fist. She commenced gargling—at least that was what it sounded like to Phoebe.

Phoebe couldn't take it any longer. What if Val opened her door? Whacked out on drugs, Val might try to murder her. Certainly, Val was in no mood to be warned away from Jason—or bought off, for that matter.

Phoebe had to get out of there.

She would have to come back another time—when Val was sober.

Another object crashed against Val's door.

Phoebe all but jumped out of her shoes.

Fearing for her life she fled down the stairs.

22

Chapter 7

Unnerved, Phoebe drove back to her house.

She was still tense when she entered her living room.

Jason entered wearing jeans and a black blazer. "I thought I heard someone at the door." He glanced at the clock on the mantelpiece over the fireplace. "Where were you?"

"I went out for a drive to relax."

"You don't look relaxed."

"Road rage, I guess. Someone cut me off. People drive crazy around here."

"Are you sure that's all it is?" he said, squinting at her with suspicion.

"Of course, that's all. What are you doing here? Why aren't you at work?"

"I had to come back to collect files I brought home."

He ought to go to Val now, she decided. One look at Val in the shape she was in and he would dump her on a dime.

"Oh," she said.

"You look wired. Maybe you need a drink to calm down."

"I'll be all right."

"You made enough noise when you entered."

"I didn't mean to. I was trying to be quiet."

He was the one who should be apologizing, not her, she decided. He was the one doing the cheating. She was mad at herself for apologizing. *He* didn't apologize to her. Why should *she* apologize to him? Cheating on someone was much worse than making noise when returning home.

"Are you sure nothing's wrong?" he said.

"Of course, I'm sure. Is there something you want to get off your chest?"

"Not at all," he said, ducked into his office, and returned, briefcase in hand.

He yawned.

"Are you having trouble sleeping?" she said.

"What makes you say that?"

"You look tired. Maybe because of something you did last night," she said, hoping he'd get the message and come clean.

"Something I did? What are you talking about?"

"There are dangerous people out there. You could get yourself killed if you're in the wrong neighborhood at the wrong time."

"How did we get on this subject?" he said, frowning in befuddlement.

"I'm just saying there are drug addicts out there walking the streets and they're capable of doing anything. You don't want to meet up with junkies, do you?"

"Of course not. But as a politician I meet many people from different walks of life. It's my job."

"Keep your distance from them. I don't want anything to happen to you."

"You worry too much. Not everybody is strung out on drugs."

"Hanging around lunatics and drug addicts is asking for trouble."

"Who the hell is hanging around lunatics and drug addicts?"

She was on the verge of telling him to stay away from Val, but she held her tongue. She wanted him to admit of his own volition that he was cheating on her without her having to tell him she knew about it. She wanted to give him every opportunity to confess.

"I'm not gonna hide in my room for the rest of my life, if that's what you want," he said. "I've got a job to do, and I'm gonna do it. Of course, there are crazies out there. That's the way of the world. You can't let it get to you."

"Keep them at arm's length is all I'm saying."

"That goes without saying."

"Don't go looking for them."

He stared at her. "Why would I?"

"You could get a disease from them."

"Anybody can get a disease anywhere. You're turning into Chicken Little with all your worrying."

"You understand my concern. If you get some disease, you could give it to me."

"Nobody's giving anyone any diseases. OK? I'm going back to work," he said, leaving the room.

You're cheating on me with a hooker who's a junkie and a psycho, she wanted to call after him, but didn't.

He wasn't going to confess on his own, she decided. She would have to get to Val somehow and get her to leave Jason alone. But how could she get to a junkie who freaks out like a wild animal? Val couldn't act like a wild animal all the time. She had to calm down at some point. She had to act normal when she trolled the streets on the prowl for johns.

The problem was Phoebe didn't know if she could reason with a schizophrenic shrew. She doubted she could scare Val off. A woman with such volcanic rage boiling inside her couldn't be bought off.

Maybe Phoebe could get the cops to bust Val. Phoebe knew Jason wouldn't patronize Val in the joint. But Val would get out quickly. Soliciting for prostitution didn't carry a long term in the joint, especially if you had a good lawyer. It wasn't even a felony in California. It was a misdemeanor.

Phoebe figured the best way to deal with Val was to get her to leave town—permanently. But how? wondered Phoebe, scratching her chin.

Chapter 8

Phoebe had a late lunch that afternoon with her father, a reporter at the local newspaper the *Costaguana Courier*. They ate burgers at an Irish pub.

Pushing fifty, Sam Spillane wore jeans and a rumpled powder blue blazer. Sporting a pork pie hat he had a lived-in face with drooping jowls. He took a pull on his Stella and smacked his lips.

"You said you had a story that would make a good article," he said.

"Are you familiar with Cimarron Street?" said Phoebe.

"The Strip. Of course. Where the nightclubs are. What about it?"

"It's not just nightclubs there. There are hookers and junkies shooting up in the alleys."

Sam shrugged.

"Tell me something I don't know," he said with a world-weary voice.

"It's illegal. Why don't the cops raid the area?"

"They turn a blind eye to it. They figure hooking is a victimless crime, so they don't hassle the whores."

"Dealing drugs isn't a victimless crime."

"The cops are OK with it as long as there isn't any violence."

"Getting kids hooked on junk is OK?"

"What can I say? I'm not a cop."

"You can put pressure on them with your pen. The pen is mightier than the sword, and all that. They need to clean up that part of town."

"That's only gonna happen when the people in power want the hookers and the drugs to disappear. I'll let you in on a little secret. A lot of them are frequent patrons of Cimarron Street activities."

Phoebe felt her ears turn red. Did everybody but her know that Jason patronized a hooker on the Strip?

"There are mentally ill people there," she said. "They could hurt someone when they're high on dope."

"The cops won't do anything till the killing starts. I know you're not a prude. That's just the way things are."

"Of course, I'm not a prude." Phoebe paused and leaned across the table toward Sam. "I was there yesterday. There's a hooker there named Val who is violent. They need to get her off the streets."

"Oh, yeah? What did she do?"

"She was screaming incoherently like she was on something and trashed her motel room. She's gonna kill someone, I'm telling you—if she hasn't already."

"Val? Val who?"

"She calls herself Val Lewton."

Sam sniggered. "The horror movie producer? It must be her stage name."

"That's the name she goes by."

"So she trashed her room. That's not much of a story."

"She might have killed someone at the same time. I heard horrible screams coming from her room. Maybe it was her victim."

"If I may be so bold, why were you down on Cimarron Street?"

Phoebe demurred. "Uh—I just happened to be there. It's not really any of your business."

"OK. Look, are you telling me this Val Lewton committed a murder in her motel room?"

"That's what it sounded like."

"You didn't actually see it?"

"No."

"Why tell me? Why not tell the cops?"

"I don't have any proof. I have only strong suspicions. The cops aren't gonna act without proof. You, on the other hand, might want to do a little digging for a newspaper story."

Sam had a faraway look. "*Murder on the Cimarron Strip*." He eyed Phoebe. "It's kind of catchy—if it's true."

"That's where you come in as an investigative reporter. You find the evidence that we can give to the cops."

"Might work. There's an old saying in the newspaper racket— If it bleeds, it leads. That kind of a story could grab me a headline."

He swigged his Stella.

"Then you'll take the story?" said Phoebe, her eyes lighting up.

"Where's her beat?"

"In front of the Lavender Whip. She lives in the pink motel nearby. Room 203."

"I could tell my editor about it. If there's a murder victim involved, I'm sure he'd be interested. But we don't have a corpse, do we?"

"We haven't found it yet, anyway."

"Uh-huh. Then again, it could be a wild-good chase you're sending me on."

"The noises I heard in Val's room yesterday were terrifying. I almost had a heart attack. Val was murdering someone."

"Why?"

"What?"

"Why would she commit murder?"

"I have no idea."

"Why were you there?"

Phoebe sipped her beer. "That's personal."

"My editor is gonna want to know who told me this story."

"I wish to remain anonymous."

"Because of Jason?" he said, knowingly.

"He doesn't want to be connected to anything as shady as this."

"I understand. All of my sources are confidential, especially my own daughter—unless they tell me otherwise."

"Good. Confidentiality is essential."

She had no desire to tell him about Jason's cheating on her. In fact, he was the last person she wanted to tell. She was hoping her father could put Val out of business by shining the bright glare of publicity on her. Publicity was the last thing Val wanted in her sleazy profession.

Sam took a bite of his burger and pulled a face. "Not the best burger I've ever had. It's drowning in mayo."

Chapter 9

Driving her Mini, Phoebe had an idea.

Maybe she could get rid of Val by blackmailing her, by telling her she knew Val had killed someone. But what if Val hadn't murdered someone, even though it sounded like she had while Phoebe was standing outside Val's room?

Then blackmail wouldn't work.

Phoebe couldn't blackmail Val for prostitution either. Val would laugh in her face. Even if Val went to jail, Jason would have her bailed out in no time. He could also have the charges against her dismissed, since he was the mayor. It paid to have lovers in high places.

However, if Val had *murdered* someone, Phoebe's blackmail scheme could work. Even a mayor couldn't get Val bailed out for a murder charge.

If Val had murdered someone, she might try to murder Phoebe, if Phoebe attempted to blackmail her, decided Phoebe, shivering with fear. The sounds she had heard coming from Val's room were godawful. They had sounded more bestial than human. Somebody who could get *that* worked up could commit murder. Phoebe had no doubt of it.

Phoebe could be risking her life by threatening to blackmail Val. She was in no hurry to revisit Val. Still, she had to do something. Her father's investigative reporting might not be enough to scare Val away.

What about her father? Was she endangering his life by sending him to investigate Val? Phoebe hadn't thought of that before.

On the other hand, her father was a professional journalist. He would know how to handle himself on his job without jeopardizing his life.

Those unnerving sounds Val made in her room kept haunting Phoebe. Phoebe couldn't get them out of her mind. She could feel her nerves jangling as she recalled the unworldly shrieks resounding through the room.

She slammed on her brakes. Her head jerked forward. She almost ran a red light.

She took a deep breath, trying to calm down.

If she could somehow get Val's phone number, she wouldn't have to jeopardize her life by visiting Val in person. But how was she going to get Val's number? Jason might have written it down somewhere, she decided. He would be keeping it secret. He wasn't going to leave it lying around the house in plain sight.

Phoebe hammered the Mini steering wheel in frustration. She had to get Val to leave town. Phoebe was obsessed with the idea. The woman was a homewrecker, a drug addict, and a possible murderer. Why was she giving Val the benefit of the doubt?

The more Phoebe thought about it, the more she became convinced Val *had* committed murder inside her room. But how could Val invite tricks to her room with a dead body in it? She would go broke.

Val would have to think up a way to remove the corpse, decided Phoebe. She had to catch Val with the body in her room to make the murder charge stick. If the stiff was found elsewhere, Val couldn't be connected to it. Phoebe was afraid to go to Val's by herself.

Phoebe pulled over to the side of the road and parked at a meter in front of a Ralphs supermarket. She dug her cell phone out of her purse and called Meredith.

Meredith picked up.

"Hi, Meredith. It's me. Do you want to go to a hooker with me?"

Meredith cleared her throat. "Um—I'm not really into hookers, Phoebe."

"Not to hire her, silly. I'm convinced she committed a murder inside her motel room. I want to pay her a visit before she has a chance to move the corpse."

"Jeez. Is this on the level?"

"It happened yesterday. We need to see her ASAP."

"This sounds like a job for the cops, Phoebe. I'm a veterinarian. I—"

"I can't tell the cops yet. This is a sensitive situation. I don't want publicity."

"Isn't there a better way to handle this? What about hiring a PI?"

"There's no time. We need to go to the hooker right away. If she moves the corpse, we won't be able to connect the murder to her."

"Who did she murder?"

"I wish I knew. I haven't seen the body."

"Then how do you know there is one?"

"I heard the murder take place inside the hooker's room while I was standing outside her door yesterday. I'm scared to go there by myself."

"I don't blame you. Why do you want *me* to go with you?"

"You're my best friend. You're the only one I can trust."

"This sounds dangerous."

"That's why I want you to go with me. She won't try anything if two of us go to her room."

"When?" said Meredith, tentatively.

"Now."

"I'm with a patient—"

"Tell her you have an emergency."

"I dunno. What are we supposed to do if we find a body in her room?"

"We blackmail her into leaving town. If she doesn't agree, we'll report the murder to the cops."

"I don't understand why you don't call the cops now," said Meredith, fretting.

"I told you, the publicity. We need to keep the cops out of this. The bad publicity would destroy Jason's career. Our family can't be connected to a murder in any way. Do you understand?"

"There must be a better way of handling this. Blackmail is illegal, if you haven't heard."

"This is sensitive."

Meredith paused. "Is this the woman you suspect Jason is seeing?"

"I don't suspect it. I know it."

"He's cheating on you with a hooker?"

"I know. Can you believe it? Not even a call girl. A trashy streetwalker."

"Tramps turn some men on. Don't ask me why."

"Not only is she a tramp, she's a murderer."

"Yeah. That's too much. How could a killer turn anyone on?"

"Are you with me or against me?"

"I'm with you, of course. But—"

"Where are you?"

"I'm at my office."

"I'll pick you up in fifteen minutes."

"This is crazy."

"Fifteen minutes."

"Phoebe—"

Phoebe ended the call.

She fired the Mini engine and peeled away from the curb.

Chapter 10

Phoebe arrived at Meredith's veterinary hospital twenty minutes later. She parked in front of it and honked her horn to let Meredith know she had arrived.

In her late thirties, dressed in jeans, a white blouse, and sneakers, Meredith Lao strode out of the sliding plate-glass doors of her boutique animal hospital. Sporting fashionable oversized shades she was tall and slender. Born in the gambling mecca of Macau when it belonged to Portugal, she had a Chinese father and an American mother. When the Chinese communist government took over the country, Meredith moved to California and never looked back.

"What's the big rush?" said Meredith, clambering into the Mini shotgun seat.

"We have to get to Val's before she hides the body."

"You're costing me business."

"We're talking about a murder. What's more important? Your business or a murder?"

"Do you really want me to answer that?"

"This is no laughing matter."

"I wasn't joking. I have to make a living. My job is my life."

Phoebe pulled into traffic. "Val is a threat to society. We have to prevent her from murdering again."

"Are you sure?"

"I heard it with my own ears."

"Heard it? You mean, you didn't see it?"

"I couldn't see it. I was outside her room."

"How can you be so sure it was murder?"

"She was hopped up on drugs. I heard screams. Val was yelling gibberish. She was trashing her room, running around, and throwing stuff all over the place. It was horrifying."

"This is a job for the cops, not us."

"That's why I brought you."

"Me? I'm not a cop."

"And," said Phoebe, reaching past Meredith to the glove compartment and withdrawing a pistol, "this."

33

Meredith's eyes widened. "Where did you get a gun?"

"I have it for self-protection."

After showing the pistol to Meredith, Phoebe replaced it inside the glove compartment.

"I hope you have a permit for that thing," said Meredith.

"I do. Being the mayor's wife has its perks."

"Why don't you take Jason with you instead of me? I don't know anything about guns or self-defense."

"He's the last person I can take. If I tell him, he'll know I saw him with Val."

"Maybe that's for the best—confronting him."

Grinding her teeth Phoebe mulled it over. "I'd rather get rid of Val without him knowing about it. I don't want to put additional strain on our marriage."

Meredith adjusted her sunglasses. "It would clear the air if you confronted him."

Phoebe shook her head no. "It would make matters worse."

"Sometimes openness is the best solution."

"Obviously you've never been married."

"This is true. I prefer the company of animals. They don't lie."

Phoebe took her eyes off the road to glance at Meredith. "Being too open can cause problems. I'm trying to save our marriage."

"I don't know why you brought me."

"I'm scared. I don't want to meet Val alone. The woman is capable of extreme violence."

"You should have brought a bodyguard. That's not me."

"She won't try anything if there are two of us at her door."

"You make her sound like a wild animal. Are you sure two people will be enough to keep her in check?"

"Two people and a gun."

Meredith fidgeted. "Something tells me this is a mistake."

"Have you ever been to the Lavender Whip?"

"I'm not into whips."

"It's a nightclub casino. Val lives near there."

"What is she? A sadomasochist? Whips and bondage and all that?" said Meredith, grimacing.

"She sounded like a sadist yesterday. I don't know about the masochist part."

34

A middle-aged man in a black hoodie lurched off the sidewalk into the road. Gasping, Phoebe veered hard to her left to switch lanes to avoid hitting him. The Mini tires burned rubber and shrieked in duress.

Meredith grabbed the dashboard to support herself as the car swerved.

Phoebe straightened out her car after she passed the pedestrian.

"What the hell?" said Meredith.

"One of the homeless," said Phoebe, glancing in the rearview mirror and wincing at the man stumbling behind her. "He must be drunk the way he's staggering around."

"They don't care whether they live or die."

"Or whether *we* live or die."

"Maybe you're driving too fast."

"He walked right in front of me. My speed had nothing to do with it."

Meredith adjusted the seat belt across her chest and shifted in her seat.

Chapter 11

Phoebe parked across the street from the pink stucco motel where Val was staying. For the first time she noticed the name of the motel printed in lilac cursive letters on a neon sign on the flat roof. Sweet Lei. A misnomer in Val's case, Phoebe decided.

"Maybe Val's a dominatrix," said Meredith, unbuckling her seat belt.

"Could be."

"Is Jason into that kinky stuff?"

"Not that I know of. He's got a secret life, so who knows?"

They piled out of the Mini, not before Phoebe flipped open the glove compartment and retrieved the pistol, a SIG Sauer P365—small but it packed a lethal wallop, according to her trainer Gus, a retired cop, at the shooting range where she had taken target practice. She stuffed the SIG into her pocketbook, retrieved quarters from her purse, and fed four of them into the parking meter.

"How long are we gonna be here?" she said.

"I'd just as soon leave right now," said Meredith.

Phoebe fed two more quarters into the meter.

"I don't want to risk a parking ticket," she said. "I don't want anyone to know I was here. A parking ticket would make it a matter of public record."

Meredith adjusted her sunglasses. "A good reason to wear shades like me if you don't want to be recognized. Your problem is the public knows your face because you're the mayor's wife."

Nodding yes, Phoebe withdrew a pair of Ray-Bans from her pocketbook and put them on.

They crossed the street to the shabby motel.

"There's still time to change our minds and beat it," said Meredith, surveying the skeevy area, whose sidewalks, which reeked of stale urine, were littered with trash and used condoms.

"I want to see this through to the end," said Phoebe. "I have no choice. The problem's not gonna go away unless I solve it. Val is the problem."

They entered the motel lobby.

A middle-aged manager with skimpy hair that lay on his head like dry pine needles was working the front desk this time instead of Man Bun, noted Phoebe, thankful she wouldn't be recognized. He was watching the movie *Horror Express* on a small portable color TV near his desk and paid little attention to her and Meredith. Maybe he thought they were hookers like the rest of his tenants.

Enthralled by the actor Telly Savalas chewing scenery on a speeding train on the TV screen, he failed to notice Phoebe and Meredith walk past him, enter the stairwell, and ascend the steps to the second floor.

Palms sweaty, Phoebe approached Val's door. She listened for any sounds behind the door, but heard nothing.

"I guess she's not killing anyone today," whispered Meredith.

"Is that supposed to be funny?" said Phoebe, scowling. "What do we do now?"

Phoebe had to get this over with. She had to confront Val and persuade her to leave town. Her throat dry, Phoebe tapped lightly on the door.

Would a raging maniac greet her? she wondered.

No response.

Phoebe tapped again, straining her ears to hear movement inside the room.

No response.

Phoebe gripped the doorknob and twisted it. To her surprise, it gave.

Meredith widened her eyes. "What are you doing?"

"I have to know what happened in there."

"By breaking and entering?"

"I'm not breaking anything. The door's open."

"Now's the time to get out your gun."

"Not yet."

"She must be in there, or why is the door unlocked?"

"If she's in there, why doesn't she open the door?"

"Maybe she's sleeping. Are you sure this is a good idea?"

"I need to confront her. This can't wait. I'm not gonna let her ruin my marriage."

"It's as much Jason's fault as it is hers, if you ask me."

Meredith had a point, realized Phoebe, but Val was more to blame than Jason in her opinion. Not that Jason was innocent. He wasn't.

"If you get rid of the temptation, there is no temptation," said Phoebe.

"Talking like a fortune cookie isn't the answer."

"Don't overthink this. The answer is action," said Phoebe, and cracked the door.

"You're the one sounding like Confucius."

"If you think too much, you'll do nothing."

"There you go again."

Phoebe hoped she didn't sound as scared as she felt.

Chapter 12

Phoebe heard the door latch slide away from the metal striker plate, which sounded preternaturally loud on account of the silence smothering Val's room.

"If anyone hassles us, we'll say we thought this was our room when we entered," she said.

Dipping her hand into her purse, fixing to whip out her pistol if necessary, she slipped into Val's room. She heard water running on the other side of the room in the kitchen. She darted a glance around the room, seeking Val.

The sound of running water was coming from the kitchen faucet, where tap water was streaming into the aluminum sink. The living room was a mess—couch cushions strewn on the floor, wooden chairs tipped over with broken legs, glass vases shattered on the carpet with their flowers lying helter-skelter nearby. The walls had large dents and cracks in the sheetrock.

The kitchen linoleum floor had a foot-wide crater indenting its center as though someone had jammed a battering ram through it. The warped imitation walnut cupboard doors hung open, exposing tipped-over cereal boxes and disorganized stacks of dishware. Even the door to the oven hung open with its grated shelves hanging out.

"Val?" said Phoebe in a low voice, her nerves tense.

Nobody answered.

"Somebody did a number on this place," said Meredith, taking in the surroundings with wide eyes.

"I told you."

"But I don't see any blood."

"Val could've strangled her victim."

"You're morbid, you know that?"

Phoebe cut her eyes toward the sink. "Or she could have drowned him."

"Him? Val killed a man? Why not a woman? Her john could've been a woman."

"I'm just saying. Look at the mess in this room. Something happened here, and it wasn't a lovefest."

"You can't be sure of that, if she's a dominatrix. They can be pretty rough during their sessions."

Phoebe stared at her. "Holes in the wall? Chairs with broken legs? Sounds more like a gorilla than a dominatrix."

Meredith shrugged. "Some men like to get beat up by women." She looked innocent. "At least, that's what I've read. I don't have any firsthand information."

"They like having their heads bashed through the walls and through the floor? They like being hit with chairs so hard that the chairs break? I don't think so."

"She must have the strength of a gorilla," said Meredith in wonder.

"She could've been on speed or crack. An adrenaline rush shooting through your veins increases strength."

"Now you know why I prefer the company of animals. They don't get off by torturing each other."

Phoebe stroked her chin in thought. "If she's not here, why didn't she lock her door when she left?"

"I have only one question," said Meredith, continuing to scope out the room. "Where's the body?"

"Maybe she was in such a rush to dispose of the body that she forgot to lock the door."

Meredith shook her head. "All you have is speculation. You have no proof a murder was committed."

Phoebe crossed the carpeted room and flung open a closet with a louvered door. She saw clothes draped on hangers, but no sign of a corpse.

"We're trespassing," said Meredith, making a beeline for the front door. "We need to get going."

Setting her jaw with determination, Phoebe strode into the white-painted bedroom to continue her search for the corpse.

The bed wasn't made. The comforter and sheets lay on it in a rumpled mess.

She saw another dent in the drywall the size of a human head.

She flung open the bedroom closet.

More clothes. Some black leather outfits with silver studs. Black whips hanging on one side of the closet.

"I found the S-M stuff," she said.

Meredith entered the bedroom. "See. She didn't kill anyone. It was just S-M you heard when you were here."

40

"You wouldn't say that if you had heard it," said Phoebe, recalling the screams and the rampaging she had heard while she had stood outside Val's door.

"It turns out it's a good thing you didn't tell the cops about this. A trashed motel room proves nothing."

"She must've moved the body somewhere else," said Phoebe, not listening to Meredith.

Meredith blew out her cheeks in exasperation. "You're not paying attention to facts. You're letting your imagination run wild. A dominatrix roughed up her client. That's all that happened."

"A trick wants his head smashed into a wall? Are you kidding me?"

"Well, I'm leaving. There's nothing we can do here."

"Wait a minute," said Phoebe.

She got down on her knees and peeked under the bed. There was nothing there save for a couple of dust kittens.

She stood up, disappointment on her face.

"Satisfied?" said Meredith, and made for the front door.

"We have to find out where she hid the body," said Phoebe, put away her pistol, and caught up to Meredith.

As they entered the hallway, a disheveled wino in his forties with a tanned, heavily creased face and wearing stained jeans grimaced and lurched toward them reaching one of his hands toward them.

Meredith emitted a tiny scream and pelted down the hall to the stairwell. Phoebe bolted after her.

"Why would anyone come here?" said Meredith, rushing down the staircase.

Chapter 13

Sam Spillane paid a visit to Jason's office.

He had told Phoebe he was going to snoop around Val's place and find out what she was up to, but his newspaperman's sixth sense told him the story had something to do with Jason. Why would Phoebe be visiting a hooker's motel room? Maybe Jason was the one who had heard a murder take place at the motel and, to shield his mayoral reputation, Phoebe was pretending she was the one who had heard the murder at the hooker's dive.

Sam knew Phoebe was savvy enough to know it wouldn't look good if the public found out the mayor had been anywhere near a hooker. Sam couldn't picture Phoebe visiting a hooker under any circumstances. She had to be covering for Jason. Which begged the question, what was Jason doing near a hooker's motel room?

Sam was trying to connect the dots to get a clear picture of exactly what was going on.

Jason's secretary, a black woman in her late twenties with a pinched face that wore a no-nonsense expression, peered up at Sam from behind her desk, wearing bifocals attached to a silver-chained lanyard. A potted plastic philodendron stood behind her.

"Yes?" she said.

"I'm Sam Spillane, a journalist for the *Courier*," said Sam. "I'd like to have a word with the mayor."

"The mayor is a busy man."

"I'm investigating a story. I need to talk to him."

The secretary called Jason's office and told him about Sam.

"The mayor will see you now," she said, putting down her handset.

Sam entered Jason's office.

Sitting behind his desk Jason looked surprised.

"The secretary didn't say it was my father-in-law," he said, standing up, smiling, and shaking Sam's hand.

"I'm here on professional business," said Sam.

"It's always good to see members of the fourth estate."

I doubt it, Mr. Mayor.

"Can I ask you a few questions?" said Sam.

"As long as it's understood this conversation is off the record." Sam pouted.

"Sure," he said at last.

"Then fire away."

"We're hearing reports of a possible murder that took place on the Cimarron Strip," said Sam.

"Murder, you say? It sounds like a job for the cops. Why come to me?"

Sam decided to go out on a limb. "My source tells me they saw you on the Cimarron Strip at the time of the murder."

"That's ridiculous."

"How do you explain my source's—"

"Your source is mistaken."

"You don't ever visit the Strip?"

"Why would I? I'm a happily married man. You, of all people, should know that. I couldn't ask for a better wife than Phoebe."

Sam continued his string of lies. "Why would my source say you were there?"

Jason shrugged. "It could've been someone who looks like me." He paused. "Strange that you would come to my office about this instead of going to the cops."

"Like I said, my source said they saw you there."

"That's what happens when you're famous. People you've never met see you all over the place. The price of fame."

"My source says all sorts of crimes are being committed on the Strip, ranging from drug abuse to prostitution. It's a hotbed of vice."

"That's why we have a police force."

"Except they don't ever arrest anyone on the Strip."

"Of course, they do. It just doesn't get much publicity. In fact, it happens so often, our good citizens are blasé about it. They don't care. And the fourth estate never reports it because they know it's not gonna sell copy. It's old hat."

"Are you planning on cleaning up the area?"

"The cops are active there. What more do you want?"

"How about getting the fentanyl and hookers off the Strip?"

"As long as there's a thriving market for that type of thing, it will continue—if not on the Strip, then elsewhere. We're all adults here. Come on, Sam."

"Is that what you tell your constituents?"

"It's what I'm telling you." Jason paused a beat. "Off the record, of course."

Sam had an innate distrust of politicians. From experience he thought they were a pack of power-hungry, self-serving liars. One of the reasons he had become a journalist was to expose politicians who made their living promoting lies.

He was never keen on Phoebe's decision to marry Jason. Sam didn't want to interfere with his daughter's life, though, so he didn't try to block the marriage. He hoped she never found out that politicians spewed lies as easily and as frequently as they breathed. It was a prerequisite of their profession.

Sam knew he could never become a successful politician. He was too honest. He wanted to be a truth-telling journalist, which meant he would never make the big bucks that politicians made. Honesty may have been the best policy, but it wasn't the most profitable one.

Even though they espoused lies in order to get elected, many politicians had successful marriages, Sam knew, which was why he didn't interfere with Phoebe's decision to accept Jason's marriage proposal. Sam wanted her to be happy. This world was so full of misery you needed a little happiness in your life.

Phoebe seemed happy in her marriage to Jason, decided Sam. Then why had Phoebe gone to the Cimarron Strip?

"So you don't know anything about the murder on the Cimarron Strip?" said Sam.

"Murder? What murder? Who got murdered?"

"That's what I'm trying to find out."

"How do you know there was a murder?"

"My source told me."

"Then tell your source to tell the police. Why would you think telling *me* would accomplish anything in regard to this murder?"

Sam wasn't about to tell him Phoebe was his source.

"Are you in favor of legalizing both prostitution and drug taking in public?" he said.

"Men want hookers. Why do you think there are so many of them?

"Is that a yes? Can I quote you for the paper?"

Jason bridled. "This whole conversation is off the record as we agreed at the start."

"Doesn't the public have the right to know your opinion on such matters?"

"I wasn't born yesterday. Don't you think I know what you're gonna do?"

"What is that?"

"You're gonna edit this interview so I come out of it looking like a pimp, or worse." Jason returned to his desk and sat down, staring at the blotter. "If you don't mind, I'm a busy man and must ask you to leave. If you want an interview with me for your paper, arrange it with my secretary." He looked up at Sam. "I agreed to talk to you now only as a favor to your daughter."

Sam couldn't tell if Jason knew more about the murder than he was letting on. The trouble with politicians was that they were consummate liars, Sam knew. It was how they could inveigle so many voters into electing them.

"If you hear anything about that murder, give me a buzz," said Sam, and left the office.

Chapter 14

Phoebe sat in the driver's seat of her Mini parked on Cimarron Street with Meredith in the shotgun seat.

"No point in wasting more time here," said Meredith.

Phoebe was on the point of keying the Mini's ignition, when she saw a woman lurch out of the entrance to the alley in front of them. Her blonde hair bedraggled, the slovenly woman staggered away from Phoebe.

"Another homeless bum," said Meredith. "How sad."

Phoebe widened her eyes. "That looks like Val."

"*That* woman? A hooker? How in the world can she get clients looking like a slob?"

"She didn't look like that when I first saw her."

"Maybe she's stewed to the gills."

Phoebe sprang out of her car. She sprinted to the alley and, glancing into it, saw a body lying next to a green metal Dumpster in the dim light. She stopped in her tracks.

"Where are you going?" said Meredith, trotting up beside her.

"Look," said Phoebe, nodding toward the motionless body.

"Just a drunk sleeping it off. What's the big deal?"

"What's that red fluid on him?"

"Probably wine."

"And what's that stuff on his stomach?"

Disregarding Meredith, Phoebe entered the alley and approached the man. The alley smelled of oranges and rotting garbage. He looked to be in his forties. There was something wrong with the man's throat.

Phoebe walked closer.

His throat was torn apart. The red fluid on his shirt front was blood, which was coagulating. Phoebe winced at the sight. Beneath his chest, his stomach was torn open with his intestines hanging out in bloody coils.

"Jesus," said Meredith, behind her, putting her hand to her mouth in awe. "Some animal tore out his carotid artery."

"An animal named Val."

"What?" said Meredith in disbelief.

46

"This must be the guy Val killed. She took the body out of her room and dumped it here."

Meredith stepped closer to the corpse to get a better look at the mauled throat.

She grimaced. "It looks like bite marks in his throat. An animal must've done this. Maybe a coyote."

"Coyote? Coyotes don't kill humans."

"They've been known to kill babies."

"This guy's an adult."

"But he's drunk. The coyote came up to him, saw he was helpless, and tore out the guy's throat. Then it started eating the guy's stomach."

"That's not what happened. Val murdered him in her room and dumped his body here."

"She tore out his throat with her teeth?" said Meredith, incredulous.

"She was loaded on drugs. They turned her into a wild animal."

"Listen to yourself. Do you really believe that?"

"You would agree with me if you had heard all the screams and horrifying sounds she was making when I stood outside her door last night."

"I can't believe a human being did this. You're talking cannibalism. Look. Some of the intestines were eaten. See how they're frayed at the edges. Those are teeth marks. It must've been a coyote."

Phoebe shook her head no. "It was Val."

"You really think this guy was her john?"

"Why not?"

A rat peeked at them from behind a garbage can, twitching its whiskers.

Phoebe scarfed up an empty soup can from the pavement and threw it at the animal in disgust. The rat squealed and scurried away. The tin can clattered on the asphalt.

"We better call the cops," said Meredith, rooting through her purse for her cell phone.

"No," said Phoebe, staying Meredith's hand.

"What are you doing?"

"I can't afford to be connected to this. It would ruin Jason's career."

"Finding a dead body in an alley?"

"But *I'm* the one who found it, and look where we are—the Cimarron Strip, a red-light district infamous for its hookers and junkies. People are gonna ask all sorts of questions we don't want to answer if we're found here—like what were we doing here? And I'm the mayor's wife, for Chrissake."

"We'll call it in anonymously."

"Then don't use your cell phone. The cops can trace cell phones."

With a reluctant sigh, Meredith stopped searching for her cell phone and snapped her purse shut.

"I hope you know what you're doing," she said.

"We need to find Val."

Chapter 15

Phoebe darted out of the alley and looked down the sidewalk in search of Val. She had disappeared.

"Where is she?" said Meredith, emerging from the alley.

"I should have followed her instead of entering the alley. But I saw that body. I had to take a look."

"Forget it. Let's get out of here and call the cops."

Phoebe shot her a glance of disapproval.

"Anonymously, of course," said Meredith. "From a payphone. Satisfied?"

"I can't have any involvement with this. Jason's career. Bad PR with me finding a murder victim in this skeevy part of town will—will—he'll lose his job. It's a scandal voters won't tolerate. They might even recall him."

"Maybe that would be for the best."

"What? What are you talking about?"

"It would teach him a lesson for cheating on you."

"I'm trying to save our marriage, not destroy it. It's not his fault. It's Val's fault. She seduced him."

"I dunno, Phoebe. It's hard to believe. She looked like a junkie bag lady when she staggered out of the alley. How could that skank seduce anyone?"

"She must be jonesing. When junkies don't get their fix, they look like hell. She didn't look that bad when Jason picked her up last night. She was wearing her hooker threads and strutting around looking hot."

"I'd have to see it to believe it."

"Maybe these S-M types have split personalities."

"More like multiple personalities in her case. She's a bombshell, a dominatrix, a junkie, and a bag lady, according to you."

"And a murderous cannibal. Don't forget that one."

"The only thing is, you can't prove any of this. She could have found that murder victim in this alley like we did. We were also in the alley. That doesn't mean we had anything to do with the murder. Which reminds me, we need to get far away from here ASAP and call the cops."

"I want to find Val," said Phoebe, scoping out the neighborhood, chockablock with strip joints and massage parlors.

"She could be anywhere. There are a lot of alleys around here. God knows what we might find in this part of town. We're better off leaving. Ignorance is bliss."

"I've got to tell her to stay away from Jason," said Phoebe, gnashing her teeth. "I have to deal with her. I can't keep putting it off."

A low-slung fluorescent orange Lamborghini Countach with knife-edge lines pulled over to the curb beside them. The passenger's-side window powered down.

Sporting sharp-angled Oakley shades the middle-aged driver leaned toward them, grinning with even teeth and a Burt Reynolds moustache.

"I'm looking for a date," he said as his car radio blasted Axl Rose of Guns 'n' Roses belting out "Welcome to the Jungle."

"Good luck," said Meredith.

"I have five grand that says I just hit the jackpot with you two foxes."

"Beat it, asshole."

"You don't understand. I want you two to beat *me* off. Didn't you hear me? I said I have five grand."

"Which part of *asshole* don't you understand?"

"I love it when foxes talk dirty to me."

"Go pound dirt."

"I want you two to pound me."

"Get lost. Only losers pay for it."

"Everyone pays for it, one way or the other," he said, widening his grin.

"Go waste somebody else's time."

"You drive a hard bargain. All right, *ten* grand for both of you at the same time."

"Are you still here?"

"I got nose candy and Mollies," he said, turning down the rock music a bit the better to be heard, "to go along with the ten K."

This was all she needed, decided Phoebe. To get picked up on the Cimarron Strip as a two-bit streetwalker. She hoped the jerk at the wheel didn't recognize her. She could see it now. It would be all over the papers. Front-page news. *Mayor's Wife Caught Hooking*. Jason's career shot down in flames. As well as their marriage.

Her day was turning into her worst nightmare. She had to convince this scumbag to peel off.

A couple of hookers in glossy satin hot pants and stiletto heels spotted the Lambo and commenced waving at it, smiling flirtatiously.

"It looks like I'm popular in these parts," said the driver, acknowledging them with a genial wave then turning back to Phoebe and Meredith. "The clock's ticking, ladies. You got competition. Mighty fine competition, I must admit," he said, glancing at the two hookers in stilettos, smacking his lips.

He stroked his thick black mustache.

Phoebe couldn't take it anymore.

Stepping in front of Meredith, she approached the Lambo's open window. She stooped, out of view of the hookers on the other side of the street, whipped her pistol out of her purse, and trained the muzzle on the driver.

"And I got a SIG P365," she said under her breath, "with a nine millimeter slug with your name on it."

"Jesus," said the driver, jacking his eyebrows above his Oakleys, sweat popping out of his low forehead.

The Lambo tore away from the curb, burning rubber, filling the air with an acrid stench.

Phoebe thrust her SIG into her purse before the hookers could spot it.

"Wow," said Meredith, who couldn't see what Phoebe had done nor hear her thanks to Guns 'n' Roses. "What did you say to him?"

"Never mind."

Sneering and thrusting out their hips, the two hookers gave Phoebe the finger as their prospective customer rocketed away with squealing tires.

Chapter 16

"It's time to leave, Bea," said Meredith.

Phoebe was inclined to agree. This was the first time she had pointed a gun at anyone, and she didn't like the feeling. Why hadn't the douchebag in the Lambo bugged out before she was forced to resort to pulling out her piece?

"Not yet," said Phoebe.

"Do you want another john to try to pick us up?" said Meredith, becoming ticked off.

"I have to find Val," she said, unable to banish Val from her thoughts. "What if she murders Jason?"

"He's not here. She can't murder him now. Let's return to the car."

Phoebe heard the whump-whump of a helicopter hovering overhead. She looked up and saw a black helo flying ominously low under a puffy white cloud.

"What if that's the press?" she said with concern.

"Then we don't want them to see us here."

"Don't they have to identify themselves? I don't see any ID on the helo."

"What makes you think they have to ID themselves?"

"I thought they did. Otherwise, cops might shoot at them."

"Damned if I know. You know the law better than me. I'm a veterinarian. Remember?"

"There must be a story breaking here. But what is it?"

"I don't want to find out."

"Right. I don't want to be ID'd here."

"Let's go back to the car," said Meredith, snagging Phoebe's arm and pulling her toward the parked Mini.

Deciding Meredith was right, Phoebe relented and headed back to the Mini, looking up fitfully at the chopper, grimacing thanks to the racket it was churning up.

"Why would the press be here?" she said.

"Dunno. Maybe it's not the press. It could be cops. Don't they have black helos?"

"We can't let the cops see us here either. They're almost as bad as the press."

Reaching the Mini, Phoebe and Meredith piled into it.

"Why would the cops be here?" said Phoebe in the driver's seat.

"Maybe somebody reported the coyote attack to them. Who cares? Let's get moving."

"I'm not leaving till I talk to Val."

"She could be anywhere by now. She could've driven to the other end of town."

"In the shape she was in? I don't think so. She could barely walk. She would crash into a fire hydrant in nothing flat. She's probably shooting up nearby," said Phoebe, scanning the neighborhood for any sign of Val.

A middle-aged vagrant in grimy trousers and a tattered button-down shirt streaked with vomit and with blood on its front lurched out of an alley into the middle of the road and tried to cross it, his unsteady feet shod in ragged sneakers.

"I can't believe how many homeless people there are in this area," said Meredith, watching him with equal parts pity and disgust.

"As long as they're not violent," said Phoebe.

A shot rang out. The vagrant's head exploded.

He sprawled on the tarmac.

"What?" gasped Phoebe.

Chapter 17

Staring with horror at the motionless bum, Phoebe gaped, trying to take in what she had just seen.

She looked up at the helo and could have sworn she saw a rifle barrel withdraw into the interior of the cockpit.

"I can't believe this," said Meredith, frozen in her seat in shock.

"That's not the press up there."

"Then who? Cops? Why would cops shoot a vagrant?"

"Because he was jaywalking?"

Meredith gave her a look and took a deep breath. "Let's not jump to conclusions."

"Somebody in that helo shot a bum in cold blood."

"Maybe it's not what it appears to be. Maybe the guy they shot was an escaped murderer."

"Then why didn't they give him a warning? They didn't even identify themselves as cops."

"I don't know the law," said Meredith. "All I'm saying is, we need to calm down before we go off half-cocked and conclude we just saw a defenseless bum murdered by cops."

"If they're not cops, who are they?"

"We should probably get out of here before they give us a hard time."

"Why would they do that?"

"Because we're witnesses."

"That's true. Maybe they'll shoot *us* too," said Phoebe, cringing at the thought.

"I wouldn't go that far. Cops don't go around shooting witnesses to their actions."

"They're not supposed to gun down bums either."

"He must've committed a crime that we didn't see," said Meredith, thinking about it.

"How can you be sure they know we're here? They only know our car's parked here. They don't know anyone is in it."

"Possible," said Meredith, stroking her cheek. "But they could have seen us walking outside."

"If we drive away now, they'll know we witnessed the killing. Otherwise, they might not know."

"So what are they gonna do if they see us drive away?"

"Who knows? Maybe they'll shoot us like they shot the bum."

"What?" said Meredith, gawking in astonishment. "We're not criminals."

"We don't even know for sure that those guys in the chopper are cops."

"Who else would go around shooting at people from a helicopter?"

Phoebe rubbed her forehead in distress. "We need to find out what's going on."

"None of this makes sense," said Meredith, frustrated.

The whumping of the helicopter hovering above them was getting on Phoebe's nerves. Her Mini was juddering under the draft generated by the chopper's rotating blades.

"Why don't they leave?" she said.

"Where are the patrol cars? Shouldn't they be arriving to take away the body?"

Phoebe shook her head, unable to get her mind wrapped around the situation.

She withdrew her cell phone from her purse.

"Who are you calling?" said Meredith.

"Maybe Jason knows what's going on. After all, he *is* the mayor."

"I'm gonna call the cops," said Meredith, producing her cell phone. "This has got to be reported. Shooting people from helicopters is not acceptable—even if the targets are criminals."

Chapter 18

Phoebe speed-dialed Jason's number.

Nothing happened.

"My call's not going through," she said, puzzled.

"Maybe your battery's dead," said Meredith.

"It doesn't say it is."

Meredith punched out 9-1-1. "That's funny."

"What?"

"The call's not going through."

"This is getting sinister," said Phoebe, grinding her teeth and surveying the area.

Meredith shrugged. "The cell service must be out in this area. It happens."

"Why's it happening after somebody gets shot? Like maybe the cops don't want anyone to report the shooting? Huh?"

"Oh, sure, it's a conspiracy," said Meredith, pulling a face.

"What's *your* explanation?"

"A glitch in cell phone service."

"We just saw a man murdered in broad daylight for Chrissake. Business as usual? I don't think so." Phoebe paused a beat. "And what about Val tearing out that guy's throat in the alley? Did you forget about that?"

"An animal did that."

"You're a veterinarian. What kind of animal tears out human throats?"

"A coyote could have found the man unconscious and started eating his throat and killed him. Then it ate his stomach."

"I never heard of such a thing."

"It happens. Not often, thank goodness. But it happens. The state of California is swarming with coyotes."

"I'm convinced that's the trick Val killed in her apartment and dragged there to hide."

"Let's let the ME for the cops determine the cause of death. That's his job."

"My job is to get Val to leave town to get her away from Jason."

Hearing the rackety chopper Phoebe looked up through the windshield. "Why are they still here?"

"I got a better question. How long are we supposed to sit here and wait?"

"Until they leave."

Meredith heaved an exasperated sigh. "That could take hours."

"It shouldn't take long. The chopper will run out of fuel eventually."

Meredith eyed Phoebe. "Maybe you're being paranoid on this. You think everybody wants to know what you're doing. Maybe they could care less you're the mayor's wife."

"I'm not worried about the ordinary citizen. It's the media that would chew me up alive if they found out I was here."

"I'm glad I'm not a celebrity like you. Always worried about what people think of you."

"Politics is jungle warfare. Somebody's ready to pounce on you the moment they get a chance every second of every day."

"Which is why I prefer the company of animals." Meredith paused for a moment. "You of all people should understand that."

"Are you insinuating something about my marriage?"

"How can you be sure?"

"Sure of what?"

"That he's cheating—"

"I could smell her on him. Her cheap perfume. Her hormones. And . . ."

"And what?"

"I saw him pick her up on the street here."

"Take it from me, you're better off with animals as friends," said Meredith, her expression morose. "They don't betray you."

"Look," said Phoebe, locking her gaze on the opposite side of the street.

"At what?"

"That's what I mean. Where is everybody? I don't see anyone anywhere."

"Yeah," said Meredith, taking stock of the deserted neighborhood. "Is everybody hiding from the chopper?"

"And the traffic. Where are all the cars?"

"Search me."

Phoebe scanned the sidewalk across the street. "I don't even see those two hookers who were working the other side of the street."

"If they think the chopper has cops in it, they're long gone."

Phoebe screwed up her face. "That doesn't explain where everybody else is. Are they all afraid of cops?"

"All the more reason to get out of here, Bea. Maybe the residents here know something we don't."

The ruckus above them became louder. Phoebe looked up at the sky. Another black helo flew into view and hovered near the first one.

Phoebe shivered with apprehension. It wasn't a rogue helicopter working on its own. It had help. They had to be cops, she decided.

Chapter 19

Sitting at his desk in his downtown office, Jason wondered if Phoebe knew he was seeing a hooker.

Phoebe was acting strange of late. But how could she have found out? he wondered. Why would she suspect him?

He couldn't let her find out. He could not afford a messy divorce. It would tarnish his carefully crafted image as a man who championed family values. The people would turn against him and throw him out of office.

They would never understand he needed another outlet for his carnal desires. They would never forgive him for it if they found out. He would not let them find out—no matter what the price. His career meant everything to him. He would not let her destroy it.

However, he couldn't be sure if Phoebe knew he was cheating on her. He only knew she was acting strange. Picking fights with him for no reason. It wasn't like her. How could she have found out, though?

He was careful to the point of obsession whenever he went to see Val. He made sure there were no witnesses when he picked her up. The more he thought about it, the more certain he became that Phoebe couldn't know about Val.

Maybe he was imagining her acting strange. Was a guilty conscience working on him, making him see things that weren't there? He didn't feel guilt for going to a hooker. Why should he feel guilt? His dates with Val were about sexual satisfaction. They had nothing to do with love. He didn't love Phoebe any the less because of his sessions with Val. Couldn't Phoebe understand that? It was carnal pleasure. Sex. Nothing more.

He doubted he could explain it to Phoebe. She wouldn't understand. He had to hope she hadn't found out about Val and would never find out.

Was it a mistake to see Val? he wondered. Probably. But he would continue to see her. And to be discreet about it. He had made mistakes before, and he would no doubt continue to make them. That was life. If you couldn't deal with making mistakes, you wouldn't last long. The only way you could avoid making mistakes was by doing nothing—and then you weren't even alive.

Anyway, maybe it wasn't a mistake to see Val. Maybe it was part and parcel of his personality. Maybe he needed it. If you needed something, was it a mistake to do it?

If seeing Val ended his career or ended his marriage, it was definitely a mistake. Even so, he needed to continue to see Val. Denying the need would deny his personality.

Did that mean he was doomed?

Only if he got caught.

He wasn't going to allow himself to get caught. Getting caught was a mistake he couldn't afford.

He was the mayor of Costaguana, and, like the city—like any city—he had a seamy side. Everyone had. But not everyone acted it out like he did. His actions were what separated him from the ragtag and bobtail—and left him open to a fatal error. He dared to do what others only dreamed about. It was how he had become mayor. You needed to have balls to run for public office. The same balls you needed to screw a hooker.

If seeing Val torpedoed his career and his marriage, so be it.

The urge to see her kept gnawing at him. The only way to satisfy it was to go to her.

It wasn't like he could change himself. He was a risk taker. It was his nature. Somebody who played it safe would never run for mayor.

The phone on his desk rang its shrill note, jerking him out of his thoughts.

Chapter 20

"There's a man here to see you," said his secretary Yvette over the line.

"What man?" Jason checked his desk calendar. "I don't have any appointments at this time."

"He says his name is John Jones."

"I don't know any John Jones. Tell him I'm busy."

"He says it's urgent."

"I'm still busy."

"If you don't see me, I'm going to the newspapers," said a man's gruff voice.

The secretary returned to the phone. "Sorry, Mr. Mayor. He grabbed the phone out of my hand. Should I call security?"

Jason decided he better see the guy. "I'll give him one minute of my valuable time."

The office door burst open before Jason finished his sentence. He cradled the handset and adjusted his necktie.

Clad in jeans and a Windbreaker, a thirtyish guy over six feet tall with big bones strutted into the room. He had long thick brown hair, which he wore brushed back. His face had a manic, protean expression, which could shift from happy to angry in seconds. Now it looked happy.

Maybe the guy was on drugs, decided Jason, planning to give him the bum's rush in short order.

The guy closed the door behind him, grinning.

"I'm sure you don't want her to hear what I have to say," he said.

"The clock's ticking," said Jason, glancing at his wristwatch. "Am I supposed to know you?"

"I doubt it."

"What's your name?" demanded Jason, trying to put Jones on the defensive. "What do you do for a living?"

"John Jones. I drive for Uber—if that makes any difference. Don't you pooh-bahs grant meetings to guys who work for Uber? Are you too good for us?"

61

"Nonsense. I grant meetings to all of my constituents. I represent everybody equally."

"If you say so," said Jones, not convinced.

"OK, Mr. Jones. What's this about? Out with it," said Jason, snapping his fingers.

"No problem. But I don't like your tone. I'm not one of your flunkies."

"You're wasting my time." Jason scoffed up the handset. "I'm calling security."

Jones laughed. "You don't want to do that."

"Then start talking."

Jones jacked his bushy eyebrows with indifference. "Let's cut to the chase. I saw you propositioning a hooker last night, and I'm thinking about telling the papers."

"You're out of your mind," said Jason, cradling the handset, his pulse racing. "I was working last night."

"You were working all right. Working your schlong."

"You came all the way here to tell me bullshit?" said Jason, slapping his hands on his desktop.

"You and I both know it's true. Time to pony up."

Jason snatched up the handset again. "I'm calling security."

"Fine. I'll tell them you were at the Lavender Whip playing hide the salami with a hooker."

Jason lowered the handset slowly, trying to look composed.

"You came here to make false accusations against me?" he said.

Leaning toward Jason, Jones lowered his voice. "I came here to get fifty thousand bucks from you."

A shakedown, decided Jason, trying to put the kibosh on the anger smoldering inside him. The Uber punk thought he had a winning hand. And maybe he had—unfortunately. Jason couldn't afford to be exposed as a john.

"Do you have any proof of this slanderous lie?" he said. "If the papers publish it, I'll sue them for libel."

"I saw you. I'm an eyewitness."

"Nobody will believe you."

Jones grinned. "What if I told you I took photos?"

He held up his cell phone for Jason to see and prepared to place his right thumb on the print reader on the screen.

62

Jason considered himself cool under pressure. On this occasion he was barely maintaining his cool, feeling the pressure building. He ground his teeth, hoping Jones couldn't see his mouth moving, couldn't see the tension.

"You really think you can get away with blackmailing me?" he said.

"Uh-huh."

Jones's grinning mouth curved into a sneer.

What about Phoebe? wondered Jason. If she heard about this from the papers, it would destroy his marriage as well as his career. He couldn't let either happen.

"You think you can scare me into paying you?" he said.

"Are you gonna call security? I'd be glad to tell them about your hooker habit and show them my photos of you."

Jason released his grasp on the handset.

"Well?" said Jones.

"Well what?"

"Are you gonna pay me not to talk?"

"I don't have that kind of money in my office."

"Of course not. I'm not in a rush. I can give you a couple of hours to get the cash."

"I need another day at least."

"My lips are dying to blab to the papers. I can't hold them back for longer than two hours."

"You're not giving me enough time to get the money together. That's a large sum of cash."

"I'm sure the bank will give it to you. You're the mayor. Nobody wants to piss off the mayor."

"Except you."

"I'm conducting a business agreement with you. Do you want to do business with me or not?"

"I need until tomorrow."

Jones shook his head no.

"Then it's time to go to the papers," he said, slewing around to face the door.

"Wait a minute. I'll see what I can do. But I'm not making any promises. I don't have that amount of cash in my checking account. I'll have to sell stock holdings."

"Just get it in two hours."

"It doesn't work that way. My broker's in New York. It takes a day or two to sell stock—"

"You don't have a day or two," cut in Jones, his expression angry. "Am I getting through to you?"

Jason felt sweat beading above his upper lip. He hoped Jones couldn't see it. Jones would love to know he was ginning up anguish in Jason. Jason didn't want to give him the satisfaction of seeing nervous sweat.

Jones snagged the doorknob, flung open the door, and stalked out of the office.

Jason briefly considered reporting Jones's blackmail attempt to the cops. But what if the guy *did* have photos of Jason with Val? If he did, why didn't he show them to Jason? Jones had only held up his cell phone. Which didn't mean it had pictures of him with Val on it. It could be a bluff. But he couldn't take that chance.

Jason had to figure the photos of him with Val existed. If only there was some way he could destroy those photos before Jones had a chance to show them to anyone. Still, Jones could blab to the papers. But without evidence, there was a good chance no one would believe him.

If there were any photos, they would be on Jones's cell phone, decided Jason. Jones wouldn't be lugging a camera around with him while he was working at Uber, but he would have a cell phone handy to receive assignments for his job. And he had held up his cell phone when he had mentioned the photos. The photos had to be on Jones's cell phone.

Jason knew what he had to do. Jones had left him no other choice.

Chapter 21

"Those choppers are spelling each other," said Phoebe, at the wheel of her parked Mini, narrowing her eyes with worry.

"The question is, why?" said Meredith in the shotgun seat.

"They must be surveilling this street."

"Again, why? And don't tell me they're spying on us."

"How could they be spying on us? They don't know we're here." Phoebe paused. "Or do they?"

"It doesn't have anything to do with us. We just happened to be in the wrong place at the wrong time. It's time we leave. I don't know about you, but I'm not gonna sit here for the rest of the night," said Meredith, reaching for her door handle. "I'm walking out of here if you're not starting the car right now."

"Wait," said Phoebe, snagging Meredith's left hand. "We can't let them know we're here. If we do, they'll know we witnessed the shooting."

"They're cops. They can shoot a criminal if he's trying to escape. What's the big deal? Why would they care if we saw it?"

"Maybe they're not cops. And maybe that guy they shot wasn't a criminal."

"Who else but cops would go flying around in choppers shooting at people?"

"If they're cops, why didn't they identify themselves before they opened fire?" demanded Phoebe, fixing her gaze on Meredith.

"Who knows? Maybe they didn't have time. Don't make this into a big conspiracy."

Phoebe thought about it. "Could this have anything to do with Val?"

"How could it?" said Meredith, bewildered.

"Val murdered her john and left him in the alley."

"You're speculating. The evidence points to a coyote killing that guy by ripping out his carotid artery."

Phoebe scowled. "Val did it. I heard her killing him yesterday."

"Even if it's true Val killed her john, how does that have anything to do with the guy we saw shot by the crew in the chopper?"

"Just coincidence we're in a neighborhood with two murder victims in it at the same time?"

"I don't see any way to connect the two. Let's get out of here before we go nuts thinking about it." Meredith shifted in her seat restlessly. "The circulation in my legs is cut off."

"We can't risk going outside with that chopper over us," said Phoebe, looking up through the tinted upper part of the Mini's windshield at the hovering aircraft.

"Then let's drive away."

"Then they'll know we witnessed their killing the guy in the street. Haven't you been listening to me?"

"So what?"

"They'll come after us."

"We have to do something. We can't just sit here and do nothing for the rest of the night."

"Maybe the chopper will leave."

"And another one will take its place, according to you."

"No matter what we do, it will be wrong."

"That's no way to think. We have to do something."

"Not yet."

"What's wrong with you?"

"I don't have a history of making good decisions," said Phoebe, feeling depressed recalling the many mistakes she had made in her life.

"So doing nothing is your answer?"

"We have to be careful. We have to know what's going on."

"How are we going to know that?"

Phoebe looked lost.

"Phoebe, there's no bathroom in here. Understand?"

Chapter 22

Dusk fell, throwing the Strip into darkness.

Phoebe produced her cell phone and tried calling Jason. She shook her head in dismay.

"What the hell happened to the cell service here?" she said.

"It's like we're in the center of a black hole," said Meredith, surveying the dark, deserted neighborhood, silent save for the nerve-racking churning of the helo.

"I don't understand why that chopper doesn't leave. It's driving me nuts."

"Maybe there are more criminals in this area they're looking for."

As if on cue, a spotlight from the helo flashed on, casting its beam on the body of the shooting victim crumpled in the middle of the street. The beam swung along the empty sidewalks.

"What rotten luck," said Phoebe. "We're in the middle of a crime scene."

"We did nothing wrong. Let's drive away."

"Can they see us in here with that spotlight?"

"Beats me."

"Don't move. Sit perfectly still."

"They must be cops. Why else would they have a spotlight? They can't arrest us for driving away."

"They could shoot us like they shot that guy in the street."

The wash of the spotlight passed over the Mini.

Phoebe let out a sigh of relief. "I guess they didn't see us in the car."

"I'm gonna scream if you don't drive us out of here," said Meredith, at her wit's end.

She reached for the key in the ignition.

Phoebe saw what she was doing and snatched Meredith's wrist.

"I never should have agreed to come with you," said Meredith, withdrawing her hand in frustration.

"They'll hear the engine start and know we're here."

Gnashing her teeth Meredith slammed her open hand into the Mini's headliner, venting her anger.

67

"Don't make any noise," said Phoebe. "They'll hear us."

"Where is everybody? This is a red-light district. It should be jumping with hookers strutting their stuff."

Phoebe was lost in thought. "If your life is doomed, do you continue to live it?"

"What? Don't get bummed out on me, Bea."

"Why is this happening to us?"

"Why ask why? Turn on the ignition and put the pedal to the metal."

A thirtyish peroxide blonde staggered out of an alley, her low-cut blouse half-unbuttoned. She smoothed her rumpled tiger-patterned microskirt as she stood unsteadily on black stiletto heels. Swaying, she lurched into the street. Blood trickled from the corner of her mouth and from her ear canals.

The chopper's spotlight picked her up, highlighting her figure. Squinting in the bright light, she looked confused, wondering where the light was coming from.

An AR-15 protruded from the chopper cockpit and strafed the woman. A bullet tore into her skull and flung her parietal bone into the street, where it skidded to a halt. The woman collapsed on the tarmac, her naked legs jackknifed beneath her.

"Jesus," said Phoebe in horror. "Did you see that?"

Meredith screamed and gawked at the inert woman, holding her hand over her mouth.

"Do you still think it's safe to let them know we're here?" said Phoebe.

"Did they hear me?"

"Maybe not, thanks to the gunfire."

The spotlight beam whipped back and forth across the street. Perhaps searching for the person who had screamed, decided Phoebe.

"Don't move a muscle," she said, petrified with terror, her face drained of color.

She couldn't move if she wanted to.

"You make it sound like we're guilty criminals who have something to hide," said Meredith, barely moving her lips like a ventriloquist as she sat put.

"Let me remind you, we witnessed two murders."

"Let's take our chances and drive away. Anything's better than sitting here crippled with fear."

"You're moving too much," said Phoebe, glimpsing Meredith shifting in her seat.

"They'll never shoot at us if we leave the vehicle and show ourselves."

"Haven't you been listening?" said Phoebe, miffed.

"Don't you understand? When they see it's you, the mayor's wife, they'll never shoot you."

Phoebe mulled it over. "You might have a point. But if they ID me here in the red-light district, the bad optics will sink Jason's career."

"I refuse to sit here like a mannequin all night," said Meredith, on the verge of tears. "And my bladder, Phoebe. I can't hold it much longer."

"They're shooting everyone who moves on the street. The more I think about it, the more I doubt they care I'm the mayor's wife," said Phoebe, taking in the two dead bodies lying in the middle of the street.

Chapter 23

Jason met a man in Ben's Steakhouse, a favorite haunt of his. It was an upscale restaurant, dimly lit for people in the limelight who didn't want to be seen or annoyed by strangers.

Jason and the man were sitting across from each other at a secluded mahogany table. Pushing forty, wearing a conservative business suit, the bald man wore wire-rim glasses with round lenses. With his average build he didn't look threatening. From his appearance he could have been a clerk like a CPA. You couldn't tell when he was sitting, but he had bow legs.

His name was Declan Hardy. He unfolded his white cloth napkin and placed it on his lap.

"Glad you could make it," said Jason, and took a pull on his Stella.

"When you need something fixed, I'm your man."

"I got a problem," said Jason, gazing at his fixer.

"What is the name of your problem?" said Hardy, reaching for a sourdough roll on a plate in the center of the table.

"He calls himself John Jones."

Hardy took a bite of his roll.

After he finished chewing he said, "How is he your problem?"

The raised voices of patrons in the steakhouse prevented anyone from hearing Jason's conversation.

"He has a photo that needs to be disposed of," said Jason.

"A glossy photo?"

Jason shook his head no. "A photo on his cell phone."

"You want me to dispose of the cell phone."

"The problem must be disposed of."

Hardy's gaze lingered on Jason's face. "You're talking about the removal of more than the phone. Correct?"

"He knows things that I don't want made public."

"The removal of the phone won't be enough?"

"He can still talk to the media without his phone. I don't know if anyone would believe him without the corroborating evidence of the photo. I do know his blabbing to the media would result in bad PR for me."

"He said he's going to the media?"

"Yeah."

"You can't weather the bad PR?" said Hardy, and took another bite of his roll, evincing pleasure with its taste.

"Maybe it would blow over—if he didn't have proof. But this is an election year. The mud might stick long enough to me to have a negative impact on the outcome of the election." Jason took another pull on his beer. "I can't risk that."

"Complete removal of the problem will cost you."

"I understand. You know I'm good for it."

"I wouldn't take another job from you, otherwise." Hardy smiled briefly. "You don't get to be mayor without a significant bankroll."

"Politics is not an easy profession, my friend."

"Neither is the job of fixer, I'm afraid. I expose myself to great risk, namely being caught committing a criminal act."

"I understand. You will be paid your usual removal fee."

"Complete removal."

"Of course."

"I'm looking forward to the New York Strip steak they serve here."

"For me it's their massive rib eye that hits the spot."

"I wish they had popovers here like they have at Delmonico's in Vegas."

Jason knocked back his beer. "It goes without saying I'll need proof of Jones's removal."

"A body part?" said Hardy, not surprised at the request.

"His thumb would do nicely. His right thumb. As mayor, I have access to fingerprints in the DMV's database and I will be able to ID his print."

"I think a million dollars should cover it."

"Why so expensive?" said Jason, stunned. "You charged only $400,000 for your last job."

"I didn't have to remove a body last time. Just evidence that incriminated you."

"Keep your voice down if you don't mind," said Jason, leaning over the tabletop toward Hardy and lowering his voice.

"There's too much noise in here for anyone to overhear us," said Hardy, closing his eyes and looking smug, displeased with Jason's glare.

Jason composed himself and leaned back in his seat.

"I have a lot to lose if this Jones character has his way," he said.

"You could pay him—he *does* want money, doesn't he to keep his mouth shut?"

"He would keep coming back for more. We both know how that works. If you ever cave into a blackmailer's demands, there'll be no end to them."

"Which is why you're getting off cheap by paying me a million bucks."

Jason shot him a skeptical look.

Hardy picked up another sourdough roll and examined it. "These are quite good, you know." He took a bite of it. "Not as good as Delmonico's popovers, but good nonetheless."

"A million dollars is never cheap."

"Everything is relative," said Hardy, enjoying the taste of his roll.

Jason didn't know any other fixers. They were hard to come by. You had to consider yourself lucky if you could find one on the dark web, he knew. Which meant they could dictate outrageous terms, such as million-buck fees. He didn't have time to search for another fixer. Jones had to be taken care of on the double. He was like a ticking time bomb getting ready to explode and to demolish Jason's career, a bomb that needed to be defused—permanently.

What Jason liked about Hardy was his ability to keep his lips sealed. Jason had used him before and knew this to be true. The guy wouldn't spill the beans about the fix—even if the amount of his demanded fee was preposterous. And Jason knew another thing. Hardy got results. If he said he would take care of the problem, he *would* take care of it.

Jason also knew Hardy had the perfect cover for his job. To look at him one would never suspect he was a paid assassin. He looked like a meek bookkeeper who pushed a pencil for a living, not a ruthless hit man who squeezed a trigger. It explained why Hardy had never been caught. It didn't hurt that he was good at cleaning up after his hits.

"Nothing must go wrong with your assignment," said Jason.

"I'm a professional," said Hardy. "Nothing *will* go wrong."

"We have a deal."

"Excellent."

"I have to use the head. If you'll excuse me . . ."

Hardy nodded.

In the hall that led to the men's room Jason produced his cell phone and called Phoebe. He had tried to reach her earlier and failed. He had no idea where she was. It wasn't like her to neglect to tell him where she was going. He speed-dialed her mobile number.

The call went to voicemail.

"Phoebe, where are you?" he said into his phone. "Call me when you get the chance."

She would call him back soon, he figured. No problem.

He shrugged it off, pocketed his cell, and used the head.

Chapter 24

"What are you scared of, Meredith?" said Phoebe, sitting in the Mini Cooper driver's seat, staring out the windshield.

"Sitting here in your car for the rest of the night," said Meredith.

"I'm serious."

"So am I."

"Come on. Be honest. We may be here for a while."

"Not me. I'm getting ready to bug out."

Meredith glanced up into the sky at the hovering black chopper illuminated by its running lights. She didn't move, worried she might attract the flight crew's attention.

Phoebe heaved a sigh. "This is serious. I want to know what scares you."

"What's the point?"

"It'll get our minds off the chopper."

"Fine. OK." Meredith chewed it over. "I guess I'm scared of trusting someone."

"Why?"

"Because I always get burned when I do. Which is why I prefer the company of pets."

"Somebody must have hurt you bad."

"The ones you trust are the only ones who can hurt you. The others, you expect the worst from them, so you're never gonna waste your time trusting them."

"It's difficult to find someone you can trust."

"To me it's scary when I think I can trust someone. Because deep down I know I'm probably gonna be wrong and end up trusting the wrong person."

"Sooner or later you have to trust someone."

"That's what I'm afraid of." Meredith paused a beat. "Now it's your turn. What are you afraid of?"

Phoebe didn't take long to answer.

"Of making the wrong decision and failing," she said.

"Failing? Failing what?"

"Anything. Everything."

"If you're human, you're gonna make the wrong decision eventually."

"For me it's every decision. I always make the wrong one."

"How can you do anything if you're afraid of failing?"

Phoebe knew Meredith was right. Yet Phoebe couldn't do anything about it. She couldn't change being afraid of making another wrong decision and failing.

"There's another thing I'm afraid of," said Meredith.

"What's that?"

"Peeing my pants."

Phoebe groaned.

"No kidding," said Meredith. "My bladder's gonna burst. I'm gonna make a run for it whether you go with me or not."

"What's worse? Peeing your pants, or getting shot?"

"There's no guarantee they're gonna shoot me."

"They shot those other two people."

"I'll take my chances. I'm done arguing with you. I have to get out of here."

Phoebe grabbed Meredith's arm. "You said you're afraid of trusting people. How can you possibly trust those guys with guns in the chopper? You saw what they did."

"I *don't* trust them. I'm not going out to greet them. I'm running for cover. It's dark outside. I bet I can make it into a building before they see me."

"The spotlight will pick you up."

"I'll run when it's not aimed at our car." Meredith pulled her arm out of Phoebe's grasp. "Why don't you come with me?"

Perplexed, Phoebe rubbed her forehead and closed her eyes, pondering what to do.

"I don't want to make another wrong decision," she said.

"Don't you see? You're making a wrong decision by choosing not to do anything."

"What?" said Phoebe, looking at Meredith in confusion.

"By making a decision to do nothing, you *are* making a decision. The wrong one, in this case. You can't go through life without making a decision. No matter what we do or don't do, we're always making decisions—even when we decide to do nothing."

Phoebe shook her head in bewilderment, trying to get her head around Meredith's words.

"You're twisting my words," said Phoebe, peeved.

"You know I'm right." Meredith glanced out her window. "Let's make a run for it. To that building. It looks like a hotel."

Chapter 25

Phoebe took in the nondescript two-story, faded, white-painted clapboard building with a flat, red-tiled roof that Meredith had indicated. A short flight of concrete steps led to the plate-glass entrance.

The building nestled in the shadows as if it didn't want to be recognized. A broken rectangular neon sign consisting of round, feeble turquoise lights that lined its perimeter blinked at regular intervals. Beneath the top row of turquoise lights was a washed-out picture of a six-foot-tall apricot and pink conch shell. Below the picture, in cerise cursive script the sign said Welcome to the Shell. The broken *S* was faded and hard to see as was the word *the*. The blinking turquoise lights didn't help. Welcome to hell.

The building looked more ominous than welcoming, decided Phoebe. It wasn't far from the Mini. If they got lucky, they might be able to make it to the entrance before getting shot. Meredith was right about remaining in the car being a decision. You couldn't escape making a decision. Choosing to do nothing was in itself a decision.

Her bladder was bursting too, she realized. Maybe that was what the chopper crew was counting on—that the Mini's passengers would have to make a dash from the car to relieve themselves. Or was the homicidal crew ignorant of anybody being in the Mini? Or did they care?

Phoebe didn't want to think about it anymore.

"We both need to run for it at the same time," said Meredith. "Otherwise, they'll be watching the car for the second person after they spot me, and you won't have a chance—if they plan on shooting us, that is."

"They do."

"Shoot first and ask questions later, huh?"

Phoebe nodded yes. "You saw what happened to the other two."

"When I see the spotlight swing to the other side of the street, I'm outa here."

They watched the conical wash of the spotlight glide over the tarmac, not even lingering as it highlighted the two sprawled corpses.

Phoebe knew she would have a farther distance to run to the hotel than Meredith since she was sitting in the driver's seat while Meredith sat in the shotgun seat nearer to the hotel. There was nothing Phoebe could do about it. If they ran in the opposite direction across the street, it would expose them longer to gunfire. The hotel was the building nearest to them, their best chance for escape.

"Get ready," said Meredith, eyes glued to the spotlight's wash, waiting for it to reach the buildings on the other side of the street.

"We have to think about something else and relax," said Phoebe. "What did you have for breakfast today?"

Meredith screwed up her face. "This is life or death. Why are we talking about breakfast?"

"We don't want to make a hasty decision."

"You don't want to make any decision."

"I had a slice of cantaloupe, toast, and oatmeal."

"OK. I'll play along. I had a banana, an English muffin with marmalade, and—uh, let's see—peach yogurt."

"Don't you feel better now?"

"Because I had breakfast?"

"Because you're thinking about something else, something good."

"Damn, you made me miss my escape schedule," said Meredith, slumping in her seat. "The spotlight is coming back in this direction already. Now I have to wait for it to return to the other side of the street again."

"Maybe it's an omen that you shouldn't make a run for it."

"I'm a scientist. I don't believe in omens. We can succeed if we set our minds to it."

"I haven't had much in the way of success in my life," said Phoebe, pouting.

"What do you mean? You're married to the mayor. People look up to you."

"The reason I'm in this predicament is because of Jason meeting Val," said Phoebe, ticked off. "I never would have come here otherwise. Getting married to him might be the worst mistake I ever made."

78

"No use kicking yourself about it. It's water under the bridge."

Phoebe felt helpless. She said nothing.

"We need to deal with the problem at hand," said Meredith.

"You can see why I'm reluctant to make another decision," said Phoebe, her face expressionless.

"Forget it."

"How?"

"I don't know about you, but I'm not giving up. I'm not gonna sit here all night like a caged rat scared to move a muscle."

Meredith watched the tracking spotlight's beam, waiting for it to return to the other side of the street.

"I'm definitely making a run for it this time," she said, widening her eyes with anticipation. She glanced at Phoebe, who sat motionless in a funk. "You need to snap out of it."

"I'm OK."

"You don't look OK."

"Why can't I ever make a right decision?"

"You think too much. We can't let our thoughts imprison us."

"I can barely breathe. I feel like the walls are closing in on me."

"We're getting out of here. We're running to that hotel. That's all you need to think about. Nothing else."

"Life sucks."

"Look alive, Bea. This is serious. Get ready to run for your life."

Phoebe stiffened. "I don't like being told what to do."

"Then you need to make a decision for yourself."

"Even when it's always wrong?"

"So what if it's wrong?" said Meredith, put out. "Everybody makes mistakes."

"A wrong decision here could be fatal."

"I'm done arguing with you," said Meredith, exasperated. She watched the spotlight beam as it swept toward its apogee. "I'm leaving whether you're coming with me or not. I'm not staying trapped in your car all night."

"I—," Phoebe began to say, but she knew Meredith was right.

Chapter 26

Her face working, Meredith flung open the Mini door and bolted out of her seat.

Phoebe watched her. Her bladder was killing her. She felt her pulse racing. Her face broke into a sweat. She jerked her head back toward the spotlight at the opposite side of the street. If she was going to leave, she had to go now.

She unsnapped her seat belt and shoved open her door. The racket of the chopper blades was louder now with the door open. She felt their downdraft blowing against her, tangling her hair. Her legs felt stiff from so much inactivity. Nevertheless, she sprang out of the car.

She almost fell as she straightened out on the tarmac. Her legs hurt. Out of the corner of her eye, she could see the spotlight beam sweeping back toward the Mini. She couldn't turn back now. When the spotlight beam reached the Mini, it would highlight the open passenger's-side door. The chopper crew would know someone had been in the Mini. They might decide to riddle the Mini with slugs to make sure no witnesses were left inside.

She was glad she had worn jeans and sneakers. Running in high heels would never have worked.

Grinding her teeth she sprinted on her sore legs after Meredith, who was making a beeline for the shabby hotel. Pumping her legs Phoebe tore after Meredith, all the while knowing the spotlight beam was headed in her direction and would pick her up any second.

Without warning, the beam caught her in its wash. The chopper crew must have seen her running even without the beam's aid. Now they could see her clearly. She felt trapped in the beam as she dashed after Meredith.

A shot rang out.

Phoebe tensed, her heart in her mouth. She decided she wasn't going to stop, no matter what. She kept churning her legs, gulping for air.

Had she been hit by the bullet? She couldn't tell. Her body was so full of adrenaline she felt nothing. She was impervious to pain.

Even her legs had stopped throbbing. She thrust her way forward, determined to reach the hotel.

Bullets strafed the sidewalk near her feet, kicking up shards of concrete and sparking as they ricocheted.

"Hurry," cried Meredith from the lobby entrance, her face twisted with concern.

Should she have stayed in the car? Phoebe wondered. No, she wasn't going to think about it. She had made her decision. She was going to reach the hotel. Hearing the sound of the bullets striking near her feet unleashed another burst of adrenaline through her body.

She barreled toward Meredith, not knowing whether a bullet had ripped into her flesh, not caring. She cared about one thing— reaching the hotel.

The chopper was closer now, its ungodly roar becoming louder, rattling her chest, blotting out all other sounds.

Beckoning to Phoebe, holding the plate-glass door open, Meredith withdrew from the motel entrance to make room for her to enter the lobby.

Phoebe blew into the entrance, gasping for breath, her lungs bursting.

Meredith swung the door shut. At that moment, the door's plate glass shattered as a burst of bullets tore into it. She backed away from the spray of glass fragments.

Phoebe halted in the lobby, bent over, her hands on her knees, and tried to catch her breath.

"Are you hurt?" said Meredith, watching her.

"I don't think so," Phoebe gasped, winded. "I don't know. I can't feel anything except my lungs bursting."

"I don't see any blood on you."

"I told you they would shoot us," said Phoebe, still breathing hard. "They don't want any witnesses."

"I can't believe cops would do something like this," said Meredith.

"If they are cops."

"Are they gonna send foot soldiers after us?"

"I didn't see any cops patrolling the street."

"Now we know for sure they want us dead," said Meredith, her face ashen.

The thought chilled Phoebe even as she heard Meredith speak the words. The idea that somebody wanted her dead was hard to assimilate. She had come here to save her marriage, and all hell had broken loose.

She heard more gunfire. But the bullets weren't striking what remained of the shattered door. Curious, she ventured circumspectly toward the door and peered out at the dark street.

She saw the AR-15 barrel aiming out the chopper at her car, which was spotlighted. Bullets were boring into the car metal and spiderwebbing the windshield. Bullets perforated the tires, flattening them. Bullets continued raining down on the Mini, turning it into a colander. As a car and a means of escape it was useless.

Phoebe knew that if she had stayed in the Mini, she would be a corpse sitting in the driver's seat. Her throat felt tight. She had made the right decision by running. At least she was still alive, in any case—for the moment. The way things were going, that could change any time now.

She saw the barrel of an RPG-7 stick out of the chopper cockpit aiming at her Mini. She heard a blast. The RPG-7 fired. With a turn, she saw her Mini rock, bounce off the tarmac, and erupt into a ball of flames.

"I guess they want to make sure everyone inside is dead," said Meredith, her eyes wide as she watched the flame-engulfed Mini spew smoke into the sky.

"I can't believe this is happening," said Phoebe, stricken.

"Why not?" said a female voice behind her.

Chapter 27

Wheeling around, Phoebe saw a twentysomething woman wearing black fishnet stockings wrapping her long white muscular legs and a scarlet sateen tube shirt hugging her silicone-enhanced breasts. She stood in the elevator in lavender stilettos, her body preventing its door from closing. Tattoos of roses and canaries embellished her arms.

"Did you see what happened?" said Phoebe.

"It happens all the time here. This is the Strip."

"Do you know where the restroom is?" said Meredith.

"Near the manager's office."

Meredith strode to the manager's office and found the restroom.

Phoebe followed her. With all the excitement she had forgotten about her full bladder.

When they were finished using the restroom, they returned to the lobby.

"Who are you?" Meredith asked the woman, who had exited the elevator and was standing in the lobby.

"Courtney. Who are you?"

"I'm Meredith, and this is Phoebe."

"Are you two looking for a job?"

"What?" said Phoebe, flabbergasted. "Did you see? Cops. The cops just blew up my car, and you stand there and say it happens all the time?"

"It does."

"And nobody complains?" said Phoebe, not believing her ears.

Courtney shrugged. "What good would it do? They're cops. They work for the government. They do whatever they want."

"They murdered two people on the street in cold blood. Did you know that?"

"Uh-huh."

"Is that all you can say?"

"Didn't you hear me? They can do whatever they want."

"Why would they do such a thing?"

"Probably mad 'cause the casino boss didn't pony up their payoff this week. The cops get pissed when they come to collect and don't get their dough."

"There's something called the law," said Meredith. "Gunning down innocent people in the street is illegal."

"Maybe where you live. Not here on the Strip."

"Tell the mayor," said Phoebe, outraged. "This is unconscionable behavior. It needs to be reported."

"Yeah, the mayor."

"What's that supposed to mean?"

"It wouldn't do a bit of good. This is the Strip. We're like a city unto ourselves with no law here. Dodge City. Get the picture?"

Phoebe got an idea. "Do you know Val?"

"What's it to you?"

"I'm looking for Val. I have reason to believe she murdered a man."

"If Val did it, it's murder. If the cops do it, it's OK," said Courtney, warping her lips into a cynical smile.

"Do you know her?"

"I know a lot of girls. A lot of 'em work here."

"Did you see what happened out there?" said Meredith. "The cops tried to kill us."

"Yeah. They don't cotton to strangers in these parts, especially when they're pissed at someone in the hood."

"I want to talk to Val," said Phoebe. "Do you know where I can find her? I saw her in a nearby alley a little while ago."

"Maybe she was trolling for johns."

"We saw her kill a guy in the alley—"

"Phoebe, we didn't actually see that," cut in Meredith.

"She looked like she was spaced out on drugs."

"Drugs, you say?" said Courtney.

"She was all messed up."

"Who isn't on drugs around here?" said Courtney, laughing. "Do you think anyone can stand living here?"

"Why don't you leave?" said Meredith, taken aback by Courtney's laughter.

"And do what? I can't get a job anywhere else. At least, here I can make a decent living without having to slave away at Mickey D's for pennies."

"Aren't you afraid to walk on the streets?"

84

"When the government's here, yeah. That's why I'm staying inside—like everybody else in the hood."

"That explains why the streets are deserted," said Meredith.

"Aren't you concerned they'll come after you here?" Phoebe asked Courtney.

"They usually just shoot the people outside."

"How can you be so matter-of-fact about it?" said Meredith.

"What do you want me to do? Throw a fit?" said Courtney, becoming angry. "Froth at the mouth?"

"Call the cops."

Courtney heaved a sigh. "The cops are already here."

"These must be rogue cops. Call a decent cop."

Courtney laughed scornfully. "A *decent* cop? Where do you find one of them?"

"They can't all be corrupt."

"You obviously don't know many cops."

"I'm no expert, but how can a city exist if the cops are all corrupt."

"I got news for you, honey. They're all bought and paid for in Costaguana."

Chapter 28

Phoebe frowned in bafflement. "Explain something to me. How can you make a living soliciting johns if the cops are shooting everyone outside?"

Courtney strutted over to the vacant front desk and absently flipped through the ledger, whose page for today was blank.

"They don't come in shooting every night," she said. "Only when they're teed off."

"They're killing people in cold blood out there for Chrissake. They blew up my car. How can you be so blasé about it?"

"Welcome to the Strip."

Phoebe shook her head in dismay.

"They saw us flee the car outside," said Meredith. "Do you think they'll come in here to shoot us, Courtney?"

"Good question. They don't like it if they shoot at someone and the person escapes. They don't want survivors reporting them."

"Which begs the question," said Phoebe. "Why don't *you* report them?"

"I mind my own business. That's why I'm still alive and kicking."

"You didn't answer my question," said Meredith. "Will the cops come in here to kill us since they missed us on the street?"

"I'm not the answer man. How should I know?"

Meredith turned to Phoebe. "Do you think we're safe here?"

Phoebe scratched her head in perplexity. "I've never encountered anything like this. What are we supposed to do?"

"This is your fault for bringing me here."

"I'm not the one shooting people in the streets," said Phoebe, resenting Meredith's accusation.

"*You* brought me to this killing ground."

"Val murdered someone. We need to find the evidence and put her behind bars."

"She might spill the beans about her black book in jail," said Meredith, slyly.

"Stop."

"What did I say?" said Meredith, feigning innocence.

86

"If Val agrees to leave town, that's the best of both worlds."

"She didn't look like she wanted to talk to anyone in her condition."

"Did you two come here to work the streets?" said Courtney. "Is that why you're so pissed the cops are shooting everyone outside?"

Folding her arms across her chest, looking haughty, Meredith gave her a look. "I'm a well-respected veterinarian. I don't need another job."

Courtney jacked her eyebrows. "Excuse me, Your Highness, but these days, with inflation you never know how many jobs you need to hold to pay the rent—even if you're royalty. A little moonlighting never hurt anyone." She sized them up. "You both look like you're in pretty good shape."

"I wouldn't work here if you paid me," said Phoebe. "If you haven't noticed, the streets aren't safe."

"So you're a spoiled heiress. Is that about the size of it?"

"If you must know, I was ready to declare bankruptcy when my start-up failed. Satisfied?"

It wasn't a subject Phoebe wanted to dwell on, but Courtney had touched a nerve with that remark accusing her of being a spoiled heiress.

"All the more reason to start a new job trolling for johns," said Courtney with the flicker of a smile.

"I come from a good family. I'd rather kill myself than take a job doing what you do."

"Touchy, aren't you?"

"I'm sorry. I didn't mean to put you down. We all do what we have to to survive."

"Us trailer-trash rednecks are all the same, you mean?"

"I said I'm sorry."

"Can your pity. Don't waste it on me. So I come from the wrong side of the tracks? What are you gonna do about it?"

"This isn't about you. We want Val."

"You think she's better than me?"

"We think she *killed* someone."

"Why do you keep telling me that? I don't care." Courtney changed the subject. "If you two want work, it's nothing to be ashamed of. After all, hooking is the oldest profession. There's nothing wrong with using what nature gave us and a little help from modern science"—she thrust out her silicone-augmented breasts—"in order to make a living. I can fix you two up with some nice clothes to attract the men. I can even give you the name of a plastic surgeon to do a little augmentation in all the right places."

Chapter 29

Phoebe pulled Meredith aside and lowered her voice.

"We need to get Val."

"If you think I'm going outside with that chopper out there, you're crazy," said Meredith.

"We saw her outside," said Phoebe, gazing out the broken plate-glass door into the darkness, where the spotlight beam continued to play across the street seeking pedestrians.

There was no vehicle traffic that she could see. The cops must have had the road blocked, she decided.

"You saw what they did to your car," said Meredith.

"As long as you're here, this being a slow night, do either of you two like girls?" said Courtney, batting her eyes at them, her turquoise eye shadow flickering under the lamplight.

Meredith rolled her eyes. "I wish I was back in my office with my animal patients."

"At least we have something in common. We both like dogs. Do you have any French bulldogs in your office?"

"Not at the moment."

"Why don't you bring one of your dogs the next time you visit?"

"I don't plan on returning."

"You don't like this side of paradise?"

"Don't tell me you've read Fitzgerald," said Meredith in surprise.

"Who?"

"I don't mean to break this up," said Phoebe, "but I think the cops are gonna come after us. We're not safe here. They know we're witnesses to the murders they committed tonight."

"They won't come in here," said Courtney.

"What makes you so sure?"

"It's not the way they operate."

Courtney sat on a vinyl-upholstered sofa next to a rectangular particleboard coffee table. Several plastic bottles of water stood on the tabletop. She took one, unscrewed its plastic cap, and took a swig.

Phoebe felt the pall of depression coming on. She sat on the sofa opposite Courtney and slumped in her seat. Phoebe's sofa had a slit in its vinyl upholstery which scratched her forefinger as she put her hand down. She jerked her hand away as if she had burned it on a stovetop.

"It's funny how making just one mistake in this world can ruin your entire life," she said, her face haggard.

"What kind of mistake?"

"Like trusting the wrong person."

"Ain't it the truth. But life goes on even when it's ruined."

"That's the problem."

"Baby, you got the blues. I've trusted the wrong person—I figure you're talking about a man—and I'm still here. My first boyfriend was a world-class douchebag. Talk about wrecking a life. The guy was a one-man wrecking crew. He couldn't open his mouth without lying. He conned and scammed me. I get sick just thinking about him."

"Do you still see him?"

"No way. I don't let that slimy guy anywhere near me. I'm never gonna say another word to him. My advice to you is forget him and move on. You gotta roll with the punches and get on with your life."

Phoebe wondered if she should divorce Jason. Had it come to that? She still held out hope that she could fix the problem by chasing Val out of town. After all, Val was a murderer as well as a homewrecker. No matter how you looked at it, Val had to go.

Chapter 30

"Do you have a phone we could use?" Meredith asked Courtney.

"The cell phones are out of order," answered Courtney. "It always happens when the cops come in their choppers. We think they're jamming the signals."

"What about a landline?" said Meredith, scoping out the lobby in search of a phone.

She saw one on the front desk and darted toward it. She lifted the silver plastic handset to her ear.

"Don't bother," said Courtney. "The landlines don't work either."

Meredith slammed the handset into the cradle in frustration.

"You might as well sit back and relax till this is over," said Courtney.

"How long will that be?"

"It could go on all night. It's hard to sleep when the choppers are in the sky making so much noise."

"I don't know how you can live like this."

"You can get used to anything," said Courtney in a weary voice. "It's not like we have a choice."

"I can't believe the mayor allows this to happen," said Phoebe.

"You good friends with him?" said Courtney. "Is he as incorruptible as everyone says?"

Phoebe didn't want to let on that she was married to Jason. She was here incognito and wanted to stay that way. She kept her lips sealed. Courtney must not read the papers, or she would have seen Phoebe's photo in it. She must not watch the local news on TV either.

"If he knew this was going on, he'd put a stop to it, I'm sure," said Phoebe.

"Settle down and have a water," said Courtney, gesturing to the constellation of water bottles on the coffee table. "It could be a long night."

Phoebe took a water bottle, opened it, and took a pull.

"I'm worried about those cops coming in here," said Meredith, pacing near the coffee table.

"Sit down and relax," said Courtney. "I wish I had a beer. But there's no way we can get across the street to the Lavender Whip without getting shot. They must be living it up like there's no tomorrow over there."

"How can you be sure the cops won't come in here?"

"They kill only the people outside."

"They saw us outside, shot at us, and missed. They'll come in here any minute to finish us off."

Courtney shrugged. "Maybe. After all, they did see you outside."

Meredith pulled a face. "Thanks. I feel a whole lot more relaxed."

"What if they're not cops?" said Phoebe. "What if they're some other group? If they were cops, they would ID themselves before shooting."

"They don't follow cop protocol on the Strip," said Courtney. "They act like they rule the roost in these parts."

"Do you have a car we could use to get out of here?"

"This is a hotel, not a motel. There's no garage."

Meredith approached the broken door, stood among glass shards strewn on the floor, and listened. "The chopper hasn't left."

"Sit down and wait. Worrying doesn't help. Waiting is not inactivity. It's a strategy."

Meredith did a double take. "Confucius?"

"Huh?"

"They could come barreling into the lobby any second," said Meredith, raising her voice with apprehension.

Courtney waved her off. "Take your sneaks off, pull up a chair, sit back, and relax."

"Why should you worry? You're not the one they saw witness their crimes out there."

Courtney kicked off her stilettos, sprawled on the sofa, lifted her legs, and, sighing with satisfaction, stretched them on the coffee table.

Not eager to sniff Courtney's feet, Phoebe pulled away from the table.

Phoebe started when she heard a bullhorn boom outside.

"Attention, attention. No one is allowed to leave this area," said the electronically amplified male voice. "Do *not* leave your dwellings."

"That's a new one," said Courtney, puzzled. "They don't usually say anything."

Meredith peeked out the shattered door into the sky. "The voice is coming from the chopper."

"Why don't they identify themselves?" said Phoebe.

"We need to get out of here," said Meredith, angling toward her.

"We'll leave after we find Val."

"The hell with Val. Our lives are in danger."

Phoebe produced her cell phone and tried to call Jason. The call didn't go through.

"It's hopeless," she said, putting away her phone.

A burst from an AR-15 cracked the silence.

Chapter 31

Her eyes wide, Phoebe bolted off her sofa and raced to the front door, where Meredith was already standing staring out at the bullet-raked street. Phoebe peeked over her shoulder at the chopper spotlight beam lighting the road.

Highlighted by the beam, a fortysomething man wearing a navy blue wool watch cap, a Rams racing jacket, and jeans was staggering toward the opposite side of the street in Adidas.

Phoebe couldn't tell if he had been wounded by the gunfire. She couldn't see blood dripping from his body.

The AR-15 protruding from the chopper cockpit opened fire again. The bullets stitched a line that carved a path across the tarmac to the staggering man, who jerked and spasmed. He came to a halt. His head blew apart in his watch cap as bullets struck his skull. He crumpled on rubber knees to the tarmac and sprawled motionless.

"When are they gonna stop this madness?" said Meredith, appalled at yet another murder.

The chopper descended.

Phoebe could feel the downdraft of its rotor blades whoosh through the broken entrance door and through her hair.

"Are they landing?" she said.

"Maybe they're trying to get a closer look to make sure the guy's dead."

"What did he do to deserve being shot?" said Phoebe, latching onto Meredith's upper arm with fingers digging into her flesh like eagle talons.

"Ow," said Meredith. "My arm's going numb."

"Oh," said Phoebe, feeling sorry and relaxing her grip.

"He could be a crook for all we know. We can't jump to conclusions."

"It doesn't look like he's armed. I don't see a gun near him. Why did the cops kill him?"

Bewildered, Meredith shook her head. "Maybe they're not cops." She gazed up at the chopper cockpit's tinted windows. "I can't see who's in the chopper."

"They say justice is blind," said Courtney from her sofa seat. "Ain't it the truth? If she could see, there wouldn't be all these criminals walking the streets and flying around in helicopters."

"How can you sit there so calm?" said Meredith, craning around to look at Courtney. "There are people getting shot in the street."

"The cops can do whatever they want."

"We don't know they're cops."

"Who else would it be?"

"That's what we're trying to figure out."

"How do we get them to stop?" Phoebe asked Meredith. Meredith shook her head in confusion.

"Mind your own business is what I always say," said Courtney. "You'll live longer that way, especially on the Strip."

"How am I supposed to find Val with those murderers in the chopper killing everyone?" said Phoebe, ignoring Courtney.

"Let's try to find her another day," said Meredith.

"She's a psychotic murderer. We need to run her out of town chop-chop," said Phoebe, pounding her fist twice against her open palm.

"The psychos in the chopper have other ideas." Meredith paused a beat. "How do you expect to run Val out of town anyway? Have you thought about that?"

"I'll tell her I saw her murder someone and I'm gonna tell the cops. She'll flee like a bat out of hell."

"We're still not sure she actually *did* murder someone."

"What do you mean? We saw her standing over a butchered corpse in the alley."

"We didn't see her kill the guy."

Phoebe wrung her hands in frustration. "If that doesn't work, I'll pay her to leave."

"Why do you want her to leave so bad?" chimed in Courtney, her curiosity piqued.

"I thought you believed in minding your own business."

"I know Val. I don't want something to happen to her."

"Do you know she's a murderer?"

"No way. Not Val."

"She has a horrible temper. Maybe she's on drugs. She acts like a wild animal sometimes. Anyway, she killed a man in her room in a blind rage and hid his body in an alley. She ripped out his throat and his intestines."

"I still say an animal did it," said Meredith. "Those were teeth marks in the victim's throat."

"*Her* teeth. You should've heard what she was doing to that guy when I was standing outside her door yesterday. Your hair would've stood on end. I get goose bumps just thinking about it. She had to be high on drugs. Something like crack or crystal meth. Maybe she was on an acid trip that went bad."

"The point is you didn't *see* anything. You didn't *see* her commit murder."

"I heard it. I heard the gut-wrenching screams of somebody getting killed."

"No court in the country would convict her on your testimony."

"Ah, what do you know?" said Phoebe, waving her off.

Meredith glanced out the broken front door. "That whole chopper crew is on drugs if you ask me."

"It's too noisy," said Phoebe, covering her ears with her hands. "It's grating on my nerves. Like a gardener using a gas-powered leaf blower."

Meredith winced. "Ugh."

"You're standing too close to the door," said Courtney from her sofa. "It's not so loud over here."

An ungodly scream rent the air.

Chapter 32

Even with her ears covered, Phoebe started at the shriek. It was coming from outside, she decided. She peered out the door into the street.

A burly fiftyish man wearing a waxed trucker jacket the color of shellacked wood was throttling a young brunette in a grey sweatsuit. She broke free and, screaming, ran across the street, her long hair blowing behind her. The enraged man charged after her, his large hands outstretched. He caught up to her, snagged her hair, and yanked her head toward him, stopping her in her tracks. He opened his mouth and sank his teeth into her throat.

She screamed in agony as blood jetted from her torn carotid artery. She craned around and tried to gouge his eyes out. Her long enameled nails raked his cheeks, spilling blood. Infuriated, he bit her throat again and ripped out a chunk of flesh, which he chewed with relish.

Watching the spectacle with fear-wide eyes, Phoebe felt sick. Her knees wobbled. She thought she might collapse.

The chopper hovered toward the melee, picking it out with the spotlight beam.

The shooter in the chopper leveled his AR-15 at the two combatants and fired a burst. A barrage of bullets cut them down.

The man was still alive. He crawled onto the fallen woman and commenced chewing on her cheek, ripping her flesh out and consuming it. The shooter let loose another burst and blew the man's head apart. The man shuddered and sprawled motionless on the dead woman.

"What was that all about?" said Meredith, her face wan, turning her gaze away from the corpses toward Phoebe.

"At least it makes some kind of sense," said Phoebe, gathering herself.

"What?" said Meredith, unsure she had heard Phoebe correctly.

"That guy was assaulting the woman. The cops shot him."

"But they also shot the woman. Why shoot her?"

"It must've been a mistake. One of their bullets went wild and hit her."

"I think they wanted to kill both of them."

"That doesn't make sense."

"Did you see how he attacked her? He took a bite out of her throat," said Meredith, shivering. "Maybe he's the one that killed the guy in the alley where we saw Val."

"Val killed that guy in her room then dragged the corpse to the alley."

Meredith shook her head. "You won't let that go. Think about it without coloring your thoughts with Val. The corpse in the alley had his throat ripped out. And the guy in the trucker jacket did the same thing to that poor girl out there."

Phoebe refused to budge from her position. "Val is a murderer."

"Can't you look at it objectively for a second?"

"I heard her kill him yesterday."

"Did they shoot a hostess?" said Courtney, still sitting at the coffee table looking calm.

She took a package of Marlboros out of her purse, tapped out a cigarette, and, flicking open a lighter, lit up.

"I don't know about any hostess," said Phoebe.

"That's what we call hookers in these parts."

"She's dressed in sweats. Do you people dress in sweats to attract clients?"

"Everybody does their own thing. Whatever works."

Courtney inhaled a draft from her cigarette and exhaled a cone of grey smoke.

"People are getting gunned down in the street and you sit there enjoying a smoke," said Meredith.

"It's not the first time this has happened. The cops do whatever they want."

"Do you mind not smoking?" said Meredith with a scowl. "If you don't care about your own health, at least respect the health of others."

"I *do* mind," said Courtney, and made a show of blowing out more tobacco smoke.

"Everybody must be on drugs here," said Phoebe, trying to understand what was going on. "Ripping out someone's carotid isn't a normal way to commit murder. That guy must've been high."

The shooter in the chopper fired another burst at the two bodies lying in a heap on the street, making sure they were dead. The bodies twitched as the bullets struck them.

"The hostesses usually keep off the streets when the cops show up," said Courtney. "They know better than to be outside with cops here."

"Don't you understand?" said Phoebe. "That man assaulted her."

"Hazards of the trade," said Courtney, blowing out smoke pensively.

"You must be on downers to be this calm."

"Life is hard and then you die."

"What's that supposed to mean?"

"It means you gotta be on something to go on living in this neighborhood. This ain't 90210, you know. Every day's a struggle here. Every day could be your last."

"Then you should be working your tail off so you can move out of here."

Courtney rose to her feet, defiant. "Where do you come off, all high and mighty, telling me what to do?"

Perplexed, Phoebe rubbed her face. "I'm not telling you what to do. But we're in trouble here. We have to do *something* to save our lives."

"What's the big deal? It's just another day in paradise."

Courtney plumped down on the sofa.

"Arguing among ourselves isn't gonna solve anything," said Meredith.

"I need another drink," said Courtney. "I should've brought a bottle of Sancerre down from my room. You two are getting on my nerves, having cows."

"You're divorced from reality," said Phoebe.

Courtney laughed. "Maybe that's it. Maybe we're in an alternate reality. Nah. Give me a break. It's business as usual here. You two live sheltered lives."

"There's nothing sheltered about my life," said Meredith. "I see sick pets every day and try to cure them."

Courtney nodded yes. "I guess that's a bummer. I don't like seeing sick pets. I don't even like seeing sick strays."

"Can you call Val and get her to come here?" said Phoebe.

"My phone doesn't work," said Courtney, yawning.

True, decided Phoebe. None of the phones were working.

Meredith gazed out the door watching the chopper descend. "If that chopper lands and the cops come out, we're in deep shit."

"They'll only land if they want to party," said Courtney. "You two better be ready to party when that time comes."

Appalled at Courtney's suggestion, Phoebe wondered how her life had taken such a dramatic turn for the worse in such a short time. She had had it made as the mayor's wife, and now the wheels were falling off. Oh brother, were they falling off.

"We're not members of your profession," she said.

"The cops aren't gonna like that. After they shoot someone, they get horny."

"I can't believe we're even having this discussion," said Meredith.

She kept looking at the helicopter. The downdraft from its rotor blades kicked up dust on the street as the chopper neared the ground.

Phoebe approached her and watched the chopper, her nerves tightening. "Do they want to get a better look at the corpses?"

Maybe it was wishful thinking on her part, decided Phoebe. It would be much worse if they were getting ready to land and enter the lobby. She had no desire to meet up with the homicidal crew.

The chopper hovered some ten feet off the tarmac over the two new corpses for thirty seconds then ascended.

Without realizing it, Phoebe heaved a sigh of relief.

She strode to the door and watched the chopper ascend.

"I hope they're leaving," she said.

The helo leveled off. It continued hovering over the street and swept its spotlight beam back and forth.

Distraught, she slouched her shoulders.

"They're not done yet," said Meredith, her face glum.

"It's all good," said Courtney.

Phoebe couldn't tell where Courtney was coming from. Was Courtney joking or was she serious? How could she be serious?

Chapter 33

Declan Hardy followed John Jones into an Irish pub. Hardy wondered if John Jones was the guy's real name. It sounded like an alias.

Jones sat on a leather stool at the bar.

Twenty feet away, at a banquette with forest green leather upholstery fastened with brass studs, Hardy sat and watched him.

He produced his cell phone and called Jason. Jones was too far away to hear them, Hardy knew.

"Do you care how Jones disappears?" said Hardy into the transmitter, keeping watch of Jones, who was ordering a Guinness.

"What?" said Jason. "What are you talking about?"

"Do you want it to look like an accident, or does it matter?"

There was a pause on the line.

"Uh—let's see," said Jason. "He might have been seen entering my office. My secretary saw him for sure. Uh—best to make it look like an accident."

"No problem. Can you tell me anything about him?"

"He said he drives an Uber. That's all I know."

"I did a little digging on the Internet." Hardy laughed. "His name *really* is John Jones. Can you believe it?"

"Is this important?"

Hardy became serious. "I found out he has a wife and an eleven-year-old daughter—"

"The less I know about him the better," cut in Jason, nettled. "It's your job, not mine. I don't want to know anything about it."

Jason hung up with a loud click.

Hardy pulled his phone away from his ear with a slight wince. He ordered a Coors draft from the waiter and chewed over methods of disposing of Jones. Coming up with an idea, he approached the bar, his glass of Coors in hand. He claimed the vacant seat next to Jones.

Jones paid him little attention, talking to his wife on his cell phone.

It was a peculiarity Hardy had. He liked to get close to a person before he killed them—sort of like Alfred Hitchcock making a point of appearing in all of his movies. It served no purpose, but it was a way of saying this is my work.

Hardy returned to his table with his beer and waited for Jones to leave. Hardy liked to see his victims squirm. It would be a pleasure to watch Jones when it was his turn to face the consequences of his blackmail scheme. Not that he had anything against Jones. He just didn't like evil people getting away with it. Besides, there were too many people on the planet, and every one of them was causing global warming with their methane farts. Hardy was culling the herd. And truth be told, most everyone was evil.

Jones left the bar twenty minutes later.

Hardy slipped on a pair of leather driving gloves and followed him out into the parking lot, where Jones got into his reupholstered black Toyota that had a dented front fender. Jones was having trouble making ends meet, decided Hardy. No wonder the guy had turned to blackmail.

Hardy stepped up to the driver's-side Toyota window before Jones had time to key the ignition. Hardy saw tufts of blond dog fur on the black and red nylon upholstery on the shotgun seat. In his hand Hardy gripped a .380 ACP Ruger LCP compact handgun.

"Don't move," he said.

"I don't have any money."

"Give me your car key."

"Don't jack my car, man. It's how I make a living. You're taking food out of my mouth."

Hardy pressed the Ruger's muzzle against Jones's temple. "The key."

Jones gave Hardy his car key fob.

Hardy scoped out the parking lot. He didn't see anyone. Keeping the Ruger trained on Jones, he walked to the other side of the Toyota and tried the door. It was locked. He used the fob to unlock the door, scooched onto the seat, and shut the door behind him.

"I told you I don't have any money," said Jones, fear in his eyes as Hardy continued to aim the Ruger at him.

"I don't want your money."

Hardy pulled a folded sheet of stationery out of his Windbreaker pocket.

"What's that?" said Jones, eying the paper.

"It's your suicide note."

Jones widened his eyes. "This is insane. I'm not killing myself."

"I believe you're about to change your mind."

"I would never do such a thing. It's against my religion. I'm a Roman Catholic."

"I know you have a little daughter named Debbie."

"How do you know that? I've never seen you before," said Jones, raising his bushy eyebrows in bewilderment.

"It's easy to find out about people nowadays ever since the Internet. You have pictures of her and your wife on your Facebook page. She's a cute little girl with chestnut pigtails."

"Get out of my car this minute. Your sick joke is over."

"I'll leave after you kill yourself."

"Not gonna happen."

Hardy handed Jones the note. "Read it out loud."

"I am a failure in life," said Jones, reading the typed missive. "I owe two hundred thousand dollars to credit companies. I can't take it anymore." He looked up at Hardy. "How do you know?"

"You can find out anything on the Internet if you know how."

"This note means nothing. I'm not killing myself."

"You're gonna change your mind."

"If you want me dead, you'll have to pull the trigger," said Jones, crossing his arms in defiance.

"If you don't do it, I'll kill Debbie," said Hardy in a low voice.

"You sick bastard," said Jones, slumping in his seat, his face stricken with fear and a sense of hopelessness.

"Sign the note."

"I don't have a pen."

Hardy fished a ballpoint out of his trouser pocket and handed it to him.

"Why are you doing this?" said Jones. "Do I know you?"

"We've never met."

"Then why?" said Jones, contorting his face with puzzlement.

"Not all questions have answers."

"I want to know why you're doing this."

"Just sign the note," said Hardy, wagging the pen in his hand to get Jones's attention.

"I can't believe you would kill a young girl. She's just a child. What's the point?"

"The point is if you don't kill yourself, I will kill her."

Anguished, Jones decided to sign the suicide note. He placed it on the console between him and Hardy, took the pen from Hardy, and scribbled his signature on the bottom of the stationery.

"What do you want me to do with the note?"

"Leave it on the console."

"Now what?"

"Give me back the pen," said Hardy. "And one other thing. Hand over your cell phone."

"Why do you want my cell phone?"

"So you won't warn your daughter that I'm gonna waste her— in case you change your mind about shooting yourself, that is."

Jones withdrew his cell phone from his trouser pocket.

Hardy snatched the phone from Jones's hand and pocketed it.

"How am I supposed to kill myself?" said Jones. "I don't have a gun."

Hardy reached into his Windbreaker pocket and pulled out another Ruger LCP.

"It's cold," said Hardy. "Can't be traced."

He heard a commotion and looked toward the entrance to the bar. A young couple was laughing and making out as they exited the bar wrapped in each other's arms.

Jones reached for the second Ruger.

Hardy jerked it out of Jones's reach. "Not here. Too crowded. Drive."

Chapter 34

"Where to?" said Jones, hands on the wheel at ten past ten.

"Out of the lot and turn right," said Hardy.

Jones merged with the traffic, becoming another link in the necklace of headlights that adorned the boulevard under the sodium vapor streetlamps arching from the sidewalks.

Hardy kept his Ruger trained on Jones's stomach. Sweat beaded on Jones's forehead.

"You haven't got the guts to pull that trigger," said Jones, watching the light up ahead turn green.

"You think?" said Hardy with a half-smile.

"That's why you want me to kill myself, because you can't do it."

Hardy's expression turned stony. "Interesting idea."

"Why else would you want me to shoot myself? It lets you off the hook. You can't bring yourself to pull the trigger."

"You sound pretty sure of yourself."

"It's the only thing that makes sense."

"Chew on this. Maybe I don't want to shoot you myself because I don't want your blood on my clothes. It would incriminate me."

Jones clenched his jaw and ground his teeth.

"You get your kicks killing innocent little kids?" he said.

"I'm not killing anyone if you do what you're told."

"Is this some kind of perverted game you like to play with people? How many other victims have you done this to?"

"Shut up. There up ahead, you see," said Hardy. "Turn right into that dark alley." He stared at Jones. "Don't even think about it."

"About what?"

"Disobeying me," said Hardy, jamming the Ruger's muzzle into Jones's rib cage.

Jones grimaced at the pain. "You won't shoot me."

"I don't want to, but if I have to, I'll shoot you in the head and make it look like you took your own life." Hardy paused a beat. "And then I'll whack out your darling Debbie."

105

"You son of a bitch," Jones hissed.

"It's up to you to save her life. Only you can save her by shooting yourself."

Jones hung a right into the dim-lit, deserted alley, which turned out to be a cul-de-sac with a green and a blue Dumpster at the end of it.

"Kill your lights," said Hardy.

Jones doused the Toyota headlights.

The only light in the alley was from an amber bug lamp in a metal cage mounted over the rear loading dock of the nondescript building on their left.

Hardy and Jones sat motionless in the dusk, breathing the same air in the Toyota.

"Get on with it," said Hardy.

"My blood will get on your clothing if I do it now."

"I'll stand outside if you're embarrassed about shooting yourself. Are you one of those shy guys who pees in a stall instead of a urinal?"

"You'll never get away before the cops come."

"So what? I'm not the one who shot you. They're not gonna bother me."

"What's to prevent me from shooting you when you hand me that gun?"

"If my partner doesn't hear from me"—Hardy rolled up his Windbreaker sleeve and glanced at his wristwatch—"in the next five minutes, he'll take out Debbie."

"I don't get it," said Jones in frustration. "What's the point? What do you get out of this?"

"Why do you care? You're dead, no matter what my reason."

"You must have a reason. You're not even robbing me. It makes no sense."

"I have nothing else to do. Maybe this is how I get my kicks."

"I'm not buying it." Jones thought about it. "Oh, I get it."

"Get what?"

"You took my cell phone," said Jones, and nodded. "The mayor sent you. You're working for him."

"We don't hang in the same circles."

"It's the only explanation that makes sense. I'll cut a deal with you. I'll get rid of the incriminating photos on my cell phone, if you let me go."

"This discussion is over."

"Do you know how hard it is to support a family by working at Uber? It's impossible."

"No wonder you're committing suicide."

"Didn't you hear me?" said Jones, his voice desperate. "I said I'll delete my photos of the mayor with a hooker."

Hardy cocked an eyebrow with interest. "With a hooker?"

"That's what he wants me to delete."

"Interesting."

"Hand me my phone and I'll take care of it."

"This is taking too long. Shoot yourself, or I'll call my partner and tell him to take out Debbie."

Hardy placed the second Ruger next to the suicide note on the console.

Jones glanced at the piece with disgust.

"Give me the car key," said Hardy.

His face sweaty, Jones withdrew the key from the ignition and handed it to Hardy, who pocketed it.

"I'm gonna leave the car," said Hardy. "Shoot yourself in the head after I leave the car."

"Where in the head?"

"What?" said Hardy, pausing as he opened the passenger's-side door to get out.

"I've never done this before. Where do I aim?"

"At your temple. Or shoot yourself through the roof of your mouth." Hardy opened his mouth and demonstrated with his pistol. "Like so."

"What about between the eyes?"

"That's an awkward position for you to pull the trigger. You might miss."

"Then what?"

"What?" said Hardy, not understanding the question.

"What happens if I miss?"

"Don't. There's only one round in your piece. I know what you're thinking. You're planning on missing deliberately. Doing so will jeopardize Debbie's life. I'll call my partner, and he'll take out Debbie. Understand?"

His expression gloomy, Jones nodded.

"What am I supposed to do?" he said, his face twisted with agony.

"Shoot yourself. Isn't it obvious?"

"You're putting me through hell."

"Sucks to be you."

"How could you do this to me?"

"Nothing personal. Just doing my job. I gotta put bread on the table."

"So do I."

"Not anymore."

Hardy closed the car door behind him and stole toward the mouth of the alley, glancing back fitfully at Jones's Toyota.

After Jones fired his Ruger, Hardy would walk away on the sidewalk. A pedestrian returning from a pub crawl.

Hardy gripped his Ruger in his Windbreaker pocket. The guy was taking longer to pull the trigger than Hardy had expected. Granted, not many people wanted to shoot themselves. But Jones sounded like his life was a mess. What was the big deal about ending it? wondered Hardy. Even losers wanted to live another day no matter how bad their lives were. But his daughter. Didn't he care about her?

Chapter 35

Holding the Ruger on his lap, Jones was thinking about what a train wreck his life was. How had he messed it up so bad?

Too many debts. Too many maxed out credit cards. A job that paid minimum wage—on a good day. How was he supposed to raise a family?

His gambling didn't help, he supposed. He bought lottery tickets and played the ponies. So did a lot of people. They didn't end up pointing guns at their heads.

He couldn't see any way out of his predicament. He was sweating like a pig. He had to do what the killer wanted. Why did he call the hit man a killer? The guy wasn't killing anyone. Jones was doing the job for him. He had to do it, or they would kill Debbie. She was just a kid. It wasn't right to have her life cut short at such a young age.

Jones snorted a laugh. It was hopeless. What else could he do but laugh?

He could barely see the killer's silhouette in the rearview mirror. The guy was standing at the alley entrance, his body backlit by the headlights of cars streaming by on the boulevard.

How long would the SOB wait before he called his partner and told him to kill Debbie? wondered Jones.

Jones felt the gun in his hand. To think he would end up like this. He knew he had messed his life up bad, but did he deserve suicide forced on him as a result? There were worse people in the world than him who didn't end up suicided.

Life wasn't fair. How many times had he heard that cliché? It just went to show that the clichés were true.

He could get out of this quandary if he let them kill Debbie instead. How could anyone take the life of a little girl? The killer wasn't human. The guy had to be a sociopath.

Maybe he deserved this miserable end to his life because he had tried to blackmail the good mayor, decided Jones. The *good* mayor. What a laugh. The piece of work had hired a hit man to remove his blackmail problem.

Jones wanted to kick himself. He should have figured the mayor would retaliate against a blackmailer. But he figured the mayor would pay up. It was the simplest way to take care of the problem. Everybody knew the mayor was loaded. And he had the reputation of being incorruptible. Why would such a guy hire a hit man? It would besmirch the mayor's image if anyone found out. Which could mean only one thing. The mayor was desperate.

As was Jones.

Jones blew out his cheeks in despair.

No more driving passengers around town for Uber. No more hoping for a good tip. No more small talk. No more cleaning the Toyota to make it look nice. No more . . .

He looked at the pistol.

He didn't know anything about guns.

The hit man had said there was only one round in it. Jones wondered if he could use the gun to shoot the hit man. The problem was Jones was a lousy shot. He had never fired a gun before. What if he missed the guy? The guy would shoot both him and Debbie. Then Jones would feel responsible for two murders.

Why did he have to see the mayor with a hooker? he wondered in dismay. It would have been fine if he had just ignored them, but no, he had to act like a smartass and take pictures and blackmail the mayor.

Jones got to feeling he was better than everybody else because he was going to score thousands of bucks with his blackmail scheme. Pride goeth before the fall. How many times had he heard that? Maybe he should have listened for once in his life. He wasn't better than anybody else. He was just another schmuck in the neighborhood.

He needed to think clearly now and consider his options objectively.

He doubted he could hit the fixer from here in the dark with a handgun. The guy was too far away and concealed in the shadows.

How could he think clearly with a gun pointed at his head?

Nevertheless, he saw no future for himself. Without the blackmail money from the mayor, Jones saw no way he could ever pay off his debts. He owed too much on his credit cards. Not only that, he owed five thousand dollars to the IRS. He could do the math. He would never be able to pay them off if he stayed at his job at Uber. He did not make enough.

He was in an impossible position. The IRS would put him in jail for tax evasion.

Maybe the mayor's fixer had offered him the only viable solution.

Jones felt the Ruger in his hand. He raised the muzzle to his temple.

He refused to look at his reflection in the rearview mirror. He could never squeeze the trigger if he watched himself in the act. The idea of his head exploding and messing up his car with bone chips, blood, and brains unnerved him. He worked hard to keep his car clean for his customers. They appreciated a clean ride.

His wife Jeanie would have to raise Debbie by herself. He didn't like Jeanie's chances. Maybe she would have to take a job at Uber. But not with his Toyota. The upholstery and dash would be ruined when he was done. Could you ever get bloodstains out of upholstery?

He didn't want to think about it.

The most important thing was to save Debbie.

If he shot himself, he would save Debbie's life. Debbie had her whole life ahead of her.

If he kept on living, he would go on making a mess of his life and his family's lives. He was a Jonah.

The muzzle felt cold on his temple.

Chapter 36

The gunshot that punctuated the whoosh of cars rushing down the boulevard interrupted Hardy's thoughts. Jones's Toyota horn blared as dead weight leaned against it.

Hardy released his grip on his Ruger in his Windbreaker pocket and picked up his gait as he strode down the sidewalk away from Jones's Toyota. Hunching forward and narrowing his eyes into slits, he had to fight the wind that was gusting and blowing grit into his face.

As far as the cops were concerned, Jones had taken his own life. There would be no murder investigation, Hardy knew. The gun was in the guy's hand, and his prints were on the gun. And don't forget the suicide note. Case closed.

The cops might think it strange Jones's car keys were missing, but it wouldn't change their conclusion that Jones had committed suicide. In any case, Hardy wasn't going to return to the Toyota to put the key in the ignition. He didn't want to be seen anywhere near a car with a corpse in it.

He wondered how much Jason's wife would be willing to pay to see the pictures Jones had taken of Jason with a hooker.

It was a shame to put blackmail photos to waste, decided Hardy.

He slowed his gait.

He produced Jones's cell phone and tried to access it. As he had thought, it was password protected. It also had a fingerprint ID button. He would have to go back to Jones's car to get a fingerprint.

Hardy wondered if it was worth the risk. How fast would somebody find the corpse? Wait a minute.

He came to an abrupt halt on the sidewalk.

Maybe there wasn't a corpse. He hadn't actually seen one. He had heard the Toyota horn beep and had assumed Jones's dead body had fallen against it. Why else would the horn sound?

He turned around and thought about going back to the Toyota, the wind blowing against his back now.

Even if Jones wasn't dead, he was neutralized. He couldn't hurt the mayor without his cell phone, which Hardy possessed. Unless Jones had uploaded the photos of Jason onto the cloud. A distinct possibility in this day and age.

He caught sight of a middle-aged woman wearing a metallic green down jacket and a long carmine scarf making for the alley, her curiosity aroused by the wailing horn. She was walking her Beagle, who was straining at his leather leash leading her into the alley.

Too late, Hardy told himself.

If he entered the alley, the lady would see him and she would be able to ID him to the cops. He didn't want anybody to know he had been anywhere near Jones's suicide. He wouldn't last long in his line of work by letting himself be seen at crime scenes.

He wheeled around and headed in the opposite direction, against the wind.

He chided himself for worrying. Jones *had* killed himself. He was a loser. He had nothing to live for. Suicide for him was a blessing.

He had probably thanked Hardy before he had squeezed the trigger.

Chapter 37

The sun rose like blood from a fresh wound.

Phoebe awoke to the sound of churning rotor blades overhead. At first she didn't know where she was. Then she remembered. She was in the Shell hotel on the Strip with Meredith and Courtney.

Phoebe had been sleeping on one of the sofas in the hotel lobby. She sat up on the vinyl upholstery that had a slit in it. Yawning, she felt hungry.

The chopper was still out there, she decided. Or maybe it was a different chopper that had taken the place of the one last night. She looked around the lobby. Meredith and Courtney were both sleeping. Courtney lay on her side on a sofa. Meredith sat on a worn leather recliner, her head canted to the side, her mouth ajar.

Phoebe didn't know how any of them could have slept with all the racket from the chopper going on. She figured it was because they were played out from stress and from the adrenaline it triggered.

She angled across the lobby to the restroom to empty her bladder.

She looked at her reflection in the mirror. She was a mess. She felt like the world was a hammer that kept beating down on her without letup.

What was the point of fixing her bedhead? she wondered, picking at her hair with no interest. She lowered her hand and left the bathroom.

She wandered back into the lobby in her rumpled clothes.

Courtney had woken up and was standing at the front door gazing at the chopper hovering over the street.

She caught sight of Phoebe out of the corner of her eye.

"I never seen anything like this before," said Courtney, ticked off. "They always leave during the night. What's with these guys?"

"You're finally pissed off, huh?" said Phoebe.

"They're cutting into my business by keeping everyone off the Strip. How am I supposed to make a living if the johns can't come here to see me."

"Maybe you should get a decent job like the rest of us," said Meredith, waking up and yawning.

"I got a decent job," said Courtney, resentful. "I'm a working girl. I'm not a bag lady living off handouts."

"Prostitution is illegal the last I heard."

"The people who made the law are jealous of my assets," said Courtney, looking down at her ample breasts.

"There are plenty of legal ways to make a living."

"What gives you the right to insult my profession?"

"I'm telling you like it is."

"You act like a queen because you save mutts for a living. Big deal. What makes you better than me?"

"I invested years of study into my profession. Not everyone can do my job."

"Not everyone can do *my* job either. If *you* tried it, you'd go broke."

"You'd be up on charges if you tried being a veterinarian. They'd throw you in jail for cruelty to animals."

"What difference does it make?" said Phoebe, tired of their arguing.

"I'm losing money with those cops, or whatever they are, out there," said Courtney, fuming. "They should be long gone by now."

Phoebe tried her cell phone.

"My cell phone's still not working," she said.

Courtney and Meredith tried theirs.

"Same here," said Courtney.

Meredith shook her head after trying hers.

"Where's the manager of this place?" said Phoebe, glancing at the deserted front desk. "Doesn't he ever show up?"

"He doesn't live here," said Courtney. "He must've gone home last night and can't get back here because of the cops."

"The only thing I can figure is they're closing off traffic because they're looking for a criminal who's at large on the Strip."

"That doesn't explain why they're shooting people on the street," said Meredith.

"They don't have to explain themselves," said Courtney. "They're cops. They do whatever they want."

"That's a cynical way of looking at it," said Phoebe.

"Cynical and true."

Meredith became pensive.

"Maybe we should try talking to them," she said.

"*Not* a good idea," said Phoebe, alarmed by Meredith's suggestion. "You saw what they did to those people on the street. And don't forget, they shot at us and blew up my Mini."

"What makes you think they'd be willing to talk to us?" said Courtney.

"Why not?" said Meredith. "We're tax-paying citizens. Don't we have the right to know what's going on?"

"I'm telling you, they don't care about getting approval from us for their actions."

Chapter 38

"We need a white flag," said Meredith, and commenced roaming around the lobby in search of a piece of white cloth. "Anybody got a handkerchief?"

"You're not seriously proposing to go out onto the street and yell questions at them," said Phoebe.

"Why not?" said Meredith, drawing up in front of Phoebe.

"It's dangerous. They could blow your head off if you set foot outside."

"I don't have a weapon."

"Neither did those people they gunned down in the street."

"They were in the act of running away."

"But they were unarmed—like you. Are you forgetting they shot at *us* too?"

"Because we were running away. That could be considered resisting arrest. If we act like we're surrendering to them, they won't shoot us."

"Man, you're putting a lot of faith in corrupt cops," said Courtney.

"We can't be sure they're corrupt," said Meredith.

"They come here all the time and shoot people. They want their shakedown money."

"Cops only do that sort of stuff on TV crime shows."

Courtney shook her head in disbelief. "You've led a sheltered life. This is the real world we're talking about. Open your eyes, honey."

"I guess you don't want to walk out there with me."

"Duh. Whatever gave you that idea?"

"There must be a better solution," said Phoebe.

"I'm not gonna stay locked up in this hotel for the rest of my life," said Meredith. "I have sick patients waiting for me today."

"The cops aren't gonna stay here forever," said Courtney. "They better not."

Meredith found a white antimacassar draped over the back of one of the sofas. She waved the antimacassar above her head.

"How's that look?" she said. "Does it look like I'm surrendering?"

"They don't care if you're surrendering or not," said Courtney. "They'll shoot you dead either way."

"The point is we can't go on hiding in fear in this hotel. We have to establish a line of communication with them."

"Better to wait till they leave," said Phoebe. "There's a difference between being scared and being prudent. We're being prudent, not scared, by staying hidden."

"When *will* they leave?"

"When they've finished what they're doing."

"Which is?"

"Well, they didn't come here to kill us. That's for sure. We just happened to be in the wrong place at the wrong time."

"Story of my life," muttered Courtney.

"We've got to hold it together," said Meredith.

"I don't think they came here to kill us specifically, but it looks like they came here to kill someone without firing a warning shot or identifying themselves," said Phoebe.

"Which is illegal."

"Stop with the 'illegal,'" said Courtney. "If the cops do it, it's legal."

"Wrong. That's why we have laws, so stuff like that doesn't happen."

"Laws," scoffed Courtney. "Laws are for lawyers. The only reason they exist is to make lawyers rich."

"You don't understand this country at all. Everybody is equal in the eyes of the law."

"You're the one that doesn't understand this country. You live in an ivory tower and don't know zilch about the real world."

"This isn't a third-rate banana republic. It's America. It's a democracy with a constitution and laws to protect the innocent."

"A lot you know," scoffed Courtney. "They can put anyone they want in jail. They can put the friggin' president of the United States in jail, if they want."

"Let's stop arguing," said Phoebe, "and find a way out of this."

Chapter 39

"I say, we find out what they want," said Meredith, holding out the antimacassar in her hand.

"You're too brainwashed by your college 'education'"—Courtney made air quotes—"to make a good decision."

"If you're accusing me of making an educated decision, I plead guilty."

"I'm not comfortable with your going out there without any means to defend yourself," said Phoebe.

"If I go out there with a gun in my hand, they'll shoot me on the spot, no questions asked," said Meredith. "It would defeat the purpose of my going outside waving a white flag."

Phoebe worried her lower lip. "We can't even be positive those are cops in that chopper."

"Who else would be shooting from a helicopter?"

"Do you really trust them not to shoot you after they know you've seen them in action?"

"I don't trust anyone," chimed in Courtney. "That's why I'm still alive on the Strip. A lot of the girls working here die young. Lying dealers hook them on drugs. I don't trust those crooks."

"I don't trust anyone either," said Meredith. "If I had my druthers, I prefer the company of animals. But we're in a situation here caused by the government. We need to trust that they know what they're doing."

"Ha. That'll be the day."

"The government is there to help us. We need to trust them."

"The government's run by people," said Phoebe. "Who you don't trust."

"I know, but we don't have a choice anymore," said Meredith. "I have to get back to my office. Lives depend on my being there. Let's hope, if these people are working for the government, they'll do the right thing and talk to me. I'm an American citizen like them."

Resolute, antimacassar in hand, Meredith made a beeline for the shattered door.

Phoebe intercepted her and stood in her path.

"You're my best friend, Meredith. I don't want to lose you."

"You're not gonna lose me. They wouldn't dare shoot me if I'm carrying a flag of truce."

"You have no idea what people are capable of till you've lived on the Strip," said Courtney, half to herself.

"If you care at all for me, you won't go outside," Phoebe told Meredith.

"Of course, I care for you, Bea. We need to get out of here. I have patients waiting for me. Their lives are hanging in the balance. They need me."

"I wish I could say the same," said Phoebe, her visage glum.

"People need you. What about your husband?"

"What about him? He's the reason we came here in the first place."

"He cares for you, and so do I," said Meredith, and hugged Phoebe.

"I think I'm gonna break into tears," said Courtney.

Phoebe couldn't tell if Courtney was being sarcastic. Phoebe didn't care. She didn't want to lose Meredith.

Meredith pulled away from Phoebe. "The bottom line is we can't stay here cowering like chickens."

"But giving up isn't the right answer," said Phoebe. "We can't lose faith in ourselves. We can figure out a better answer than surrendering."

"I'm not surrendering. I want to talk to them to find out what the hell is going on. We need to clear the air."

"Mark my words," said Courtney. "You can't trust the cops in these parts."

"Cops are people too. There are good cops and bad cops, just like there are good people and bad people."

"Coming from the person who doesn't trust anyone," said Phoebe.

Meredith gave her a look. "The government has a reason for doing this. We have to find out what it is."

"*Good* cops?" said Courtney. "I'd have to see it to believe it."

"In your illegal profession, you think *good* is bad and vice versa."

"I have a necessary job," said Courtney. "The world's oldest profession. If it's so awful, why's it still around after all these years? Huh?"

120

"I'm not arguing anymore. Unless somebody has a better idea, I'm going outside."

A better idea, thought Phoebe. She had learned the hard way that every decision she made was wrong. How was she expected to come up with a better idea? All she knew for sure was she didn't want to lose her BFF.

"What am I gonna do without you?" she said.

"I'm not leaving the Strip. I'm just gonna have a talk with the cops. Then we'll leave together—you and me."

"It'll be the last talk you ever have," said Courtney, her face grim.

"Come on. You guys sound like undertakers. It's not the end of the world."

"Then why are they shooting defenseless people?" said Phoebe. "Gunning them down like rabid dogs in the street."

"You always think the worst," said Meredith. "Maybe that's the problem. Maybe that's why you think everything you do is wrong."

"I don't know about you two, but I need a drink," said Courtney. "When in doubt, pour some stout. That's what I always say. I just made that up. I like it," she added, smiling.

She disappeared behind the front desk and rummaged around behind it.

"Where's the manager keep his booze?" she said to herself.

"That's not an answer," said Meredith. "It's a delaying tactic."

"*Be always drunken. Nothing else matters*. Isn't that what Baudelaire said?"

"You read poems?" said Meredith, dumbfounded.

"You don't have to have a college degree to be able to read a poem, smarty-pants. Poets love pleasure, and sex is pleasure. I'm a poet in my own right in my profession." Courtney raised a bottle of red wine in triumph. "What do we have here?" She read the label. "Cabernet Sauvignon. I knew the old geezer liked his hooch."

"That's your plan for everything—getting soused."

"At least, I don't sit around feeling sorry for myself."

"Neither do I. I face a problem and take care of it."

"Or it takes care of you."

"I'm not gonna end up hiding behind booze like you," said Meredith, and faced the front door, her mind made up.

Phoebe couldn't think of a way to get Meredith to stay inside.

121

"Be careful," said Phoebe, her voice cracking.

She could feel her eyes well with tears.

Meredith emitted a brief laugh. "You act like I'm going to a funeral."

Phoebe didn't laugh. "I wish I could talk you out of it."

"Pshaw."

Chapter 40

Phoebe watched Meredith head out the door onto the sun-splashed street.

As Meredith strode onto the tarmac, she raised the antimacassar above her head and waved it at the hovering chopper. She squinted her eyes in the bright sunlight.

Phoebe picked up on the AR-15 barrel swinging in Meredith's direction from the bottom of the cockpit. She knew Meredith could see it too.

Phoebe felt her heartbeat accelerate. Beads of sweat rolled out of her armpits down her flanks, tickling her ribs. She knew Meredith was beyond the point of no return. Meredith must proceed, willy-nilly.

"Hello," Meredith called out. "I come in peace. I want to talk to you. I'm not armed. Are you the police?"

She held up her arms to show she carried no weapons.

Adrenaline crashing through her veins, expecting the worst, Phoebe saw Meredith address the chopper. The apprehension was almost too much to bear. Phoebe thought she might black out any second. *Come back, Meredith*, she wanted to say. But the words caught in her throat, and she stood speechless, her eyes glued on her best friend.

Nobody in the chopper responded to Meredith's question.

"I need to leave and return to my office to treat my patients," Meredith yelled at the cockpit, trying to make herself heard above the din of the whumping rotor blades. She waved the antimacassar above her head. "Let me leave with my friend in peace."

Phoebe's heart was pounding in her mouth as she watched Meredith. It wasn't a good sign that nobody in the helo was answering Meredith, decided Phoebe.

"Come back, Meredith," she cried, fearing for Meredith's life.

She saw with mounting dread the AR-15 barrel trained on Meredith. She couldn't see any of the crew thanks to the cockpit's tinted Plexiglas. She had no idea how they were reacting to Meredith.

The crewman operating the AR-15 opened fire and stitched a bloody ellipsis across Meredith's chest.

Meredith's knees buckled. She collapsed on the tarmac.

"No," screamed Phoebe.

She started to dash into the street in complete disregard for her safety to save her friend when Courtney grabbed her from behind and held her back.

"Let me go," said Phoebe, trying to break free.

Courtney held fast to her. "You can't help her now."

Slumping, Phoebe burst into tears.

"I should've stopped her," she said, lowering her head in dejection.

Chapter 41

Meredith didn't know why her legs had folded under her. She knew she couldn't stand anymore. She knew something was wrong with her.

The sunlight was blinding her as she lay on her back. She could not move. How could the sun be so bright? It had a preternatural brightness. She had never seen it this bright. It was overpowering her as if sucking the life out of her.

She could not rest here. She had to return to her office to treat her animal patients. What would they do without her? They were waiting for her with their diseases and broken bones or whatever other problems they had that she could treat.

She mustn't be late. One of them could die if she was late. It would be on her conscience forever if she let one of her patients die, especially if she could have saved them by being on time for their appointment.

She was supposed to see the grey French Bulldog Bella today. Bella was seven years old and was throwing up her food every day. Meredith had to determine what was wrong with Bella. She had been treating Bella ever since she was a puppy. She couldn't let anything happen to Bella. And then there was twelve-year-old Charlie the Beagle. Charlie had arthritis in his knees and had lost his appetite. She needed to be at her office so she could write out his prescription.

She mustn't be tardy. She needed to get up and get going. But she couldn't move. What were you supposed to do when you couldn't move? she wondered. She told her body to move, but it paid no attention to her.

This was what she got for trusting someone, she decided. The police in this case. But you couldn't live distrusting everyone. It was impossible. You would think you could trust the police if not anyone else.

Something was happening with the sun. It was darkening. Was the helicopter in front of it? No, the moon must have been blotting out the sun. A lunar eclipse? A solar one? She did not know the difference. Astronomy was never one of her long suits. It had to be a total eclipse, in any case. The darkness was increasing.

She couldn't see her body. Where was it? What had happened to it? she wondered. How was she supposed to move if she couldn't see her body?

The eclipse was conquering the sky, turning it sable.

Something hurt.

She wasn't sure where the pain was coming from. It was washing over her as if coming from everywhere all at once.

And then the darkness. Total. Impenetrable. Nothing.

Maybe it was a dream. Maybe she would wake up soon. But it wasn't.

Chapter 42

Parked in a black Honda Civic in a liquor-store parking lot, Declan Hardy used his cell phone to call Jason.

"It's done," said Hardy.

"I told you not to call me about this."

"I thought you wanted to know."

"We need to be sure nobody can connect me with you."

"You worry too much," said Hardy, stifling a yawn.

"I can't be connected to this in any way. My career's at stake."

"Something else is at stake too I heard."

There was a pause on the line.

"What's that supposed to mean?" said Jason.

"Before he died by a gunshot to the head, he—"

"By a gunshot," cut in Jason, his voice edged.

"You heard me."

"I told you to make it look like an accident," said Jason, fit to be tied. "Now there's gonna be a murder investigation, and all sorts of questions are gonna be asked—"

"Hold your horses. You didn't let me finish. Accidents are hard to control. The target might survive if I cut the brake line of his car so his car crashes, say. You never know what's gonna happen in an accident. Understand? Too many things can go wrong."

"I don't want a murder investigation hanging over my head. There's no telling what the cops might find when they sniff around."

"There's not gonna be a murder investigation."

"A bullet to the head? No murder investigation? In a pig's eye."

"Listen to me. I made it look like he committed suicide."

"The cops'll figure it out. What did you do? Put the gun in his hand after you shot him? That only works on *CSI*. And it never works there either."

"I'm a pro. The suicide wasn't staged. He shot himself."

"How could you get him to do that?" said Jason, his voice ringing with skepticism.

"Do you really want to hear the details?"

"Just tell me you have proof he won't bother me again."

"What kind of proof?"

"I told you when I hired you."

Hardy couldn't remember anything about proof. Stalling for time, he said nothing.

"I need proof he's out of my hair for good," said Jason. "If he's still alive, he's gonna keep blackmailing me."

"He's not alive."

"Bring me his right thumb. That's the only proof I'll accept. That was our agreement."

Hardy had forgotten the goddamn thumb.

"I have something better," he said.

"A deal's a deal. I'm not accepting substitutes."

"You will when you hear what it is."

"I doubt it," said Jason, but didn't argue the point.

"How about his cell phone?" said Hardy, eager to hear Jason's reaction, knowing the phone contained sensitive pictures of Jason.

"Give me it," said Jason, his tone cold.

"Of course."

Hardy wondered if there was some way he could get leverage over Jason by using the photos. It was a shame he couldn't access them since he didn't know Jones's password for his phone, decided Hardy. However, Jason didn't know for certain that the phone needed a password to open it. Hardy might be able to gain some leverage yet, leverage in this case leading to more shekels.

"How do you know Jones didn't store his photos in the cloud?" said Hardy.

"So what if he did?"

"Other people could see them."

"Not unless they have his password."

"Was he married?" said Hardy, waiting for the other shoe to drop.

Jason took a deep breath. "I don't know much about the guy. All I know is he works for Uber."

"You see what I'm getting at?"

"Somebody else might have Jason's password to the cloud?"

Hardy knew Jason hadn't got elected mayor by being stupid.

"That someone needs to be dealt with if you want this nastiness to disappear," said Hardy.

"How many people do you give your phone's password to?"

128

"Me? Nobody. I learned long ago never to trust anyone."

"Not even your wife?"

"I'm not married."

"You see, Jones probably didn't give his password to anybody either."

"*Probably* doesn't cover all the bases the way *certainly* does."

Hardy watched customers entering empty-handed and leaving the well-lit liquor store with full bags. The owner wouldn't go broke if this was a typical night, Hardy decided.

"OK," said Jason. "Look into it. See what you can dig up on Jones's personal life."

"It will cost you extra."

"I'll throw in another ten grand for your efforts."

"That's not enough if you want someone else to disappear."

"We'll cross that bridge when we get to it."

"Fine with me. It's your money."

"Give me Jones's phone before you do anything else."

"Sure."

"We don't want it to fall into unfriendly hands."

Hardy wanted to have copies of the photos of Jason with the hooker—just in case Jason tried to send him up the river. After all, Hardy had been active in this game long enough to know never to trust a politician. Hardy liked to cover himself from as many angles as possible when dealing with his rich and powerful clients.

Chapter 43

"Why did they shoot her?" said Phoebe, sobbing. "She just wanted to talk to them."

"These cops are the worst ones I've ever seen," said Courtney, holding Phoebe's shoulder in case Phoebe tried to run to Meredith's body sprawled on the tarmac.

The chopper descended closer to Meredith.

"Now what are they doing?" said Phoebe.

"Inspecting the body?"

"Why?"

"Why anything? This is the Strip. You live here, you're screwed. That's all."

Setting her jaw Phoebe made up her mind. "I'm going out there and give them a piece of my mind."

Courtney strengthened her hold on Phoebe. "No way. Don't go out there. You saw what they did to your friend."

"That's why I have to go."

"Do you want to commit suicide?"

"This has got to stop."

"Well, you're not gonna do it by yourself, honey."

"Who's gonna help me? If those guys really are cops, we can't call the police for help."

"No, we can't do that."

"Then who's gonna help us?"

"I ask myself that same question every day," said Courtney, looking forlorn.

"What's your answer?"

"I can't come up with one. Nobody's gonna help me. Nobody ever has. I gotta get by by myself."

"It can't be that bad. Not everybody is rotten."

"If you scratch their skin deep enough, you'll find they are just that."

"I don't believe it. Look at poor Meredith out there," said Phoebe, her eyes welling with tears again. "She helped save the lives of thousands of pets. You couldn't find a better person than her if you looked for twenty years."

"Not here, you can't," said Courtney, shaking her head. "No wonder they killed her. Nice guys finish last, and all that."

"You're hopeless."

"Cash is king here. If you ain't got it, you better get it PDQ. Or they'll find ways to destroy you. You can take that to the bank."

The helo ascended and continued hovering on station above the street, its rotor blades clattering in a nerve-grating cacophony.

"You think we can buy our way out of this?" said Phoebe, unconvinced.

Courtney fetched a sigh. "Could be. You can buy your way out of most things on the Strip."

Phoebe gazed up at the helo "Those guys aren't shooting people for money. Who would pay them to do such a thing?"

"They're not doing it for sport."

Phoebe saw movement on the other side of the street.

A disheveled young woman was staggering down the sidewalk. She was wearing a grey hoodie, her face half-hidden.

"Oh no," said Courtney. "Somebody should tell her to go inside. Didn't she hear the bullhorn?"

"She looks plastered," said Phoebe, squinting to get a better look at the woman.

The chopper crew spotted the derelict. They flew toward her.

"Look out," Phoebe screamed at the woman. "Go inside."

Either the woman didn't hear Phoebe or she didn't care. She kept lurching down the sidewalk.

"Run," cried Phoebe, cupping her hands around her mouth to help her voice carry.

The woman halted and gazed at Phoebe, who realized with a start that it was Val looking more bedraggled than ever, barely recognizable, in fact.

Phoebe didn't know what to think. If they shot Val, Phoebe's troubles would be over. She wouldn't have to pay Val off or scare her out of town to keep her from seeing Jason again.

Part of Phoebe wanted them to shoot Val and be done with it. But the idea of shooting someone in cold blood didn't agree with her.

"Run, Val, run," Phoebe yelled.

Val stumbled around, looking disoriented.

Then a strange thing happened.

131

Chapter 44

From the bottom of the chopper hovering over Val, a steel mesh net lowered toward her.

Val continued stumbling, unaware of her peril.

"Is she on drugs?" said Phoebe from the hotel doorway.

"Everybody's on something on the Strip," said Courtney, standing behind Phoebe and peering over Phoebe's shoulder at Val.

"What is that net for?"

"Are they trying to capture her?"

"Why is she getting special treatment? They shot everyone else."

Phoebe was convinced her peripheral vision had picked up on movement by Meredith on the tarmac. It might have been a trick of the light or a floating dust mote near her eye that she had seen. There was only one way to find out.

"Meredith's still alive," she said.

"She couldn't be," said Courtney.

Taking advantage of the chopper crew's preoccupation with Val, Phoebe bolted into the street making for Meredith, who wasn't moving at the moment.

"Don't," gasped Courtney, trying to grab Phoebe but missing because she hadn't reacted fast enough to Phoebe's abrupt departure.

Phoebe reached Meredith as the chopper crew continued to try to capture Val. Breathing hard, Phoebe knelt next to Meredith.

"Are you OK, Meredith?" said Phoebe. "I'll help you."

Meredith didn't respond. She lay supine with her eyes shut, blood smearing her shirt.

Phoebe snatched one of Meredith's arms, stood up, and dragged her toward the hotel, where Courtney waited for them, her eyes bulging with apprehension.

"Leave her," cried Courtney. "She's dead."

Meredith sure looked dead, decided Phoebe and halted to feel for a pulse in Meredith's neck.

So far the chopper crew hadn't picked up on Phoebe thanks to their single-minded concentration on capturing Val.

Phoebe couldn't feel a pulse.

"Breathe, Meredith," she said, all but begging Meredith to breathe.

"Look out," cried Courtney. "They're coming."

Phoebe glanced at the hovering chopper. Unsuccessful at capturing Val, the crew was heading toward Phoebe. The AR-15 was pointing toward her out of the cockpit.

Terrified, Phoebe abandoned Meredith's corpse and sprinted for the hotel, where Courtney stood beckoning to her.

Gunfire erupted.

The AR-15 strafed the tarmac around Phoebe with 9mm bullets. Several of them ricocheted off the pavement a few inches from her sneakers. Dragging the empty net below it, the chopper chased Phoebe.

Phoebe gulped air. She ran faster. Her lungs felt like they were on fire. She backed and filled to throw off the shooter's aim.

"Hurry," yelled Courtney.

Another burst from the AR-15 coughed.

Phoebe sprang into the hotel as bullets tore into the doorjamb, chewing it to pieces. Storming into the hotel, she brushed past Courtney and all but knocked her over.

Chapter 45

"Halt," said a gruff male voice through a loudspeaker on the chopper.

"Why didn't they use their net on me?" gasped Phoebe between breaths in the hotel lobby.

"They didn't get a good look at you," said Courtney.

"You think it would've made a difference?"

"Your guess is as good as mine."

"They got a good look at Meredith, yet they shot her."

The chopper returned to hover over Val, who staggered aimlessly, lost in her stupor, oblivious to danger.

The crew maneuvered the steel net to entrammel Val. They were trying to knock her legs out from under her so she would fall into the net, but she managed to keep her balance, enough so as to avoid the trap.

"Do they know she's a murderer?" said Phoebe, catching her breath as she watched the proceedings from the doorway.

"They let a murderer live and kill a veterinarian?" said Courtney, screwing up her face in bafflement. "Am I missing something?"

"They must not know or care."

"Then why are they trying to capture Val instead of killing her like everybody else?"

"They better watch out when they capture her. She's a wild animal when aroused. She tore the throat out of one of her johns."

"That doesn't sound like the Val I know."

"You didn't hear the sounds coming out of her room that I heard last night."

"Oh, honey, those are just sex sounds."

"Screams of horror are sex sounds?"

"You know, johns get carried away. They're into play-acting and stuff. It's all harmless."

"She threw furniture around her room and broke her walls with her victim's head. She was killing the guy in there. I'm sure of it."

Courtney waved her off. "You have an overactive imagination is all."

134

"I saw with my own two eyes the dead body in an alley. The stiff had its throat ripped out."

"A coyote did it or rats. They found a dead wino and started eating."

"Then why are the cops capturing Val with a net like she's a wild animal?"

Courtney thought about it. "She might not be paying them their piece of the action. The cops want in on everything going down on the Strip. If it makes money, they want their take."

Phoebe eyed the chopper. "We don't know for sure those are cops up there."

"Who else would they be? Circus hands looking for a new act? Be real."

"Circus hands wouldn't go around shooting people."

"I was joking."

Much as Phoebe was loath to admit it, it bothered her that the cops hadn't shot Val. It meant Val might talk to them after they captured her. Phoebe didn't want Val to spill the beans about her relationship with Jason. Phoebe couldn't bear the idea of a scandal.

She doubted Jason's mayoralty could survive one. His reputation as being incorruptible was on the line. To show him in the opposite light would make him a laughingstock when the scandal burst into the news cycle. The papers would hound him and have a Roman holiday in their ruthless singlemindedness to sell copy.

Phoebe would become a talk-show punchline for being married to a cheating husband.

Phoebe had to reach Val before she talked to the cops. Val had to be prevented from blabbing.

No telling what Val would say in the condition she was in. Maybe she was on fentanyl, decided Phoebe—not that she knew much about drugs. It didn't take an expert to see Val's coordination was impaired. Any fool could see Val wasn't acting normal.

Could the chopper crew's mission be to take Val and stop anyone that got in their way? wondered Phoebe. But why Val?

"Maybe the cops'll leave after they capture Val," said Courtney, striking an optimistic note.

"I'm thinking the same thing," said Phoebe.

"Why so glum then?"

135

"What are they gonna do to Val?"

"That's *her* problem. She doesn't give them their take, this is what happens. She should've known better than to stiff the cops."

Her problem is my problem, thought Phoebe, but didn't say.

"I hope the rest of the city isn't this corrupt," she said.

"As long as the cops leave in their chopper, and they open up the Strip, that's all I care about."

"What about all those dead bodies in the street?"

"I didn't put them there."

"Nobody's gonna want to come here if you have dead bodies scattered all over your street."

Courtney scoped out the corpses strewn on the boulevard.

"I see what you mean," she said, her face sullen. "The least they could do is clean up their mess."

"Is that all dead bodies are to you? A mess?"

"*I* didn't kill them. Don't put this on me."

"Poor Meredith," said Phoebe, her gaze gravitating back to her friend. "She never would have come here if it wasn't for me."

"Look. They finally got Val into the net," said Courtney, pointing at Val, who sprawled inside the net. "Why are they using a steel net? It looks like something they use on a grizzly bear."

"They must know how vicious she can get."

Val struggled to escape the net. She climbed it and scrabbled around in it, searching for a means of escape, but it was hopeless. She could have been a fly trapped in a spiderweb for all the good it did.

The chopper rose into the sky carrying its live cargo beneath it.

136

Chapter 46

Jason exited City Hall and strode into a pool of reporters gathered in anticipation of his arrival.

"Mr. Mayor, are you planning on running for another term?" said a thirtyish brunette with a pageboy cut.

A boom operator shoved a live mic above Jason's head.

"You know I am. You all read the press releases I submitted to you," said Jason, all smiles. "I'm a winner, and I'm gonna win again. It's my destiny."

"Do you really think you have any chance to win?" said an Asian reporter in her early forties, looking concerned.

"I love my polls. The polls are telling me I'm a winner. This election is mine to lose."

A cropped black reporter pushing thirty raised his hand. His hair was cut so short you could barely see the stubble.

Jason called on him.

"What about reports we're hearing that the Strip is being closed down?"

"The Strip?" said Jason, taken aback. "I haven't heard anything untoward about the Strip."

"We're getting reports that the Strip's exits and entrances have been closed. There's no way in or out."

"Nobody has informed me of any problems on the Strip. I'll have someone look into it."

"Honestly, do you think you have any real chance of reelection?" said Pageboy.

"I sure do—unless your paper's polls are lying," said Jason, enjoying the back and forth with the reporters, happy to score a point against them.

"Does your wife want you to run?"

"My wife?" said Jason, caught off guard by the question.

They didn't normally ask about his wife, he decided. He didn't understand why they should start now. Why would they ask about his wife? Had she been talking to the press without his knowledge?

"Yes, your wife Phoebe," went on Pageboy. "Does she want you to run for office again?"

He enjoyed sparring with reporters, but he considered his wife off limits. As a rule of thumb, reporters agreed. For some reason, today was different. He wondered why. Or was he making something out of nothing?

"Of course, she wants me to run," he said, unleashing another one of his killer smiles that won female voters. "In fact, she's the one who encouraged me to run in the first place."

There, he had recovered nicely, he decided. He hadn't lost any of his poise under pressure, he was grateful to realize.

Phoebe. How the hell had Phoebe become a topic of concern to reporters? he wondered, thinking about Jones and the scandalous photos on the blackmailer's cell phone. Had Jones leaked the photos to the media without letting him know? Had the bastard reneged on his deal to keep the photos to himself if Jason paid him? Was Jones still alive? Hardy had said the guy was dead. How could the photos have leaked if Jones was dead?

The Strip. Why had that reporter brought up the Strip, of all places, during the news conference? wondered Jason.

He wondered if sweat was visible above his upper lip. He didn't want to break into a sweat in front of the cameras. Bad optics. He remembered how Nixon had sweated in front of the cameras when he had debated the polished JFK on live TV. There were those who said Nixon's sweaty performance had cost him the election.

Had Hardy lied to him about getting rid of Jones? wondered Jason. He had no way of knowing. Hardy hadn't turned over Jones's cell phone to him yet, nor had a report of Jones's death been circulated on the TV newscasts.

There could be a logical explanation, such as Jones's body hadn't been discovered and ID'd yet, decided Jason.

He had used Hardy before. He trusted Hardy—as far as you could trust a guy who made a living fixing clients' problems, a guy who had no compunction about breaking the law to achieve his end, a guy who, in fact, was a criminal.

Such a guy could be dangerous on account of the secrets he kept, decided Jason.

Yet Jason had no proof Hardy had exposed him.

Then again, why was the press bringing up Phoebe, a subject they steered clear of as a matter of course?

Was concern showing on his face? He had to make sure it wasn't. He smiled.

"Come on," he said. "You guys can do better than that. None of you have scored a sound bite yet. Is that the best you can do?"

He had them rattled, he decided. He had them eating out of his hand. They were on the defensive, as he had turned the tables on them with his witty riposte.

He felt himself recovering his equanimity. He pranced around in front of the press pool, trying to project invincibility.

It was time to leave, he decided. Quit while you're ahead.

He broke away from the pack of jackals as they busied themselves thinking of another question to destroy him and sabotage his career. He knew as well as they did, they wanted blood. Politics was a blood sport. The pols knew it as well as the hacks who covered them. Blood, not smiles, sold copy. Any hack worth his salt who thought otherwise would go begging for another profession. Any politician who wasn't willing to joust with the bloodsuckers would join the homeless living in blue tents on the streets.

Dissembling a sigh of relief with a triumphant smile, he strutted away from the feeding frenzy and returned to City Hall.

"Cradle robber," a woman called after him in an accusatory voice.

He wondered if it was one of the reporters or an onlooker. He decided to ignore the remark. There was nothing wrong with May-December marriages as far as he was concerned. So what if Phoebe was much younger than him? It wasn't like she was an underage teen.

Once inside the lobby, he produced his cell phone and called Phoebe. It went straight to voicemail.

Why wasn't she answering her phone? he wondered. Where was she anyway? Could Jones have contacted her about the photos he took? It wasn't like her to go without contacting him for such a long time. Jason and Phoebe liked to keep in touch with each other. He sensed something was wrong.

Could Hardy have contacted her about the photos? wondered Jason. Did Hardy know what was in the photos? Maybe he shouldn't have employed Hardy to take care of this. Where the hell was Phoebe?

Chapter 47

Phoebe watched the chopper that had trapped Val leave. Phoebe was thankful for the silence. Maybe the worst was over. Then she heard the whump-whump of another chopper approaching.

The black helicopter stationed itself above the body-strewn street, taking the place of the chopper bearing Val away.

"Now what?" said Phoebe.

Courtney watched the new chopper, trying to understand what was going on.

"This is new for me," she said. "I've never seen them stay for more than a day."

Something protruded from the bottom of the chopper cockpit.

It looked like some sort of barrel, decided Phoebe. Not a rifle barrel but similar.

A long flame shot out of the barrel and incinerated one of the corpses lying on the street. The stench of burning flesh mingled with burning hair filled the air.

Phoebe widened her eyes. She felt like running onto the street and retrieving Meredith's body before they cremated her. Meredith deserved a decent burial, and her body needed to be ID'd by the police when her death certificate was filled out.

Another flame shot out of the chopper and incinerated another corpse on the street.

They were destroying all evidence of the murders that had taken place, decided Phoebe. Murderers covering up their crimes. Without evidence of murders, the killings would never be investigated. And Meredith. They were going to burn Meredith next.

Phoebe felt compelled to run onto the street to drag Meredith's body to safety. Her murder must not go unpunished, Phoebe decided. She would not let the evidence go up in smoke.

"You'll never make it," said Courtney, reading Phoebe's mind. "They'll kill you too."

Another flame streamed from the chopper and struck Meredith's body.

Phoebe felt her throat tighten with both fear and rising anger. She didn't want the thugs to get away with killing Meredith. They needed to pay for their crimes.

The reek of burning bodies nauseated her.

"Why are they burning the bodies?" said Courtney.

"They're covering up their murders. No corpus delicti means no crime."

"The cops have never bothered to do that before. They're the police. What do they have to be afraid of? Nobody busts cops."

"Cops can get busted like everyone else."

"Not on the Strip."

"Somebody's gonna report them to the authorities. You'll see."

"That'll be the day."

Phoebe watched with revulsion as Meredith's body burned. An overpowering lust for vengeance raged inside her. The chopper crewmen needed to pay for what they had done to Meredith.

Phoebe was the mayor's wife. She could get things done. Courtney, of course, didn't know Phoebe's true identity. As the mayor's wife, Phoebe could throw her weight around. She could persuade Jason to initiate an investigation into these senseless murders and their cover-up—if she ever got out of here alive. Or was she going to end up like Meredith, burned to a crisp?

If she could find out what was really going on here, maybe she could figure out what to do. On the other hand, the success rate of her decisions hadn't been too high of late. She had to accept the fact that it was her decision to bring Meredith with her to the Strip that had cost Meredith her life.

It wouldn't do her any good to kick herself for past decisions, decided Phoebe. Self-pity accomplished nothing.

Chapter 48

A middle-aged short man with frizzy grey hair burst out of one of the buildings, screaming and shaking his fists at the helo, his face flushed and contorted with rage. He spat gobs of saliva out of his mouth as he bellowed incoherently at the chopper crew.

Phoebe wondered if the crew could hear him what with the racket their chopper was ginning up. In any case, you didn't have to hear him to know he was infuriated at the aircraft crew.

She thought the man was acting berserk. He could have been on speed the way he was carrying on, jumping up and down and screaming his lungs out.

She couldn't blame him for being enraged. But it looked like he would have killed the crew with his bare hands if he got ahold of them. He had a manic amount of energy, which energized his leaps as he tried to punch the chopper that hovered far out of his reach.

She thought the guy was going to suffer a heart attack if he couldn't pull himself together. She had never seen anyone blow their stack like this guy. Sure, he had good reason to be upset, but he had to calm down. His psychotic energy was unsustainable.

He looked like he believed he could jump up to the chopper and punch a hole in its fuselage.

She saw a crewman's hands training the barrel of the flamethrower on the bellicose man.

Phoebe yelled a warning at the man.

The guy picked up on her and bolted toward her, continuing to fume, gnashing his teeth, foaming at the mouth, and grimacing.

"Why's he coming over here?" said Courtney, fear in her eyes.

"Take cover," Phoebe cried at him.

Apoplectic, the man shook his fist at her. Gouts of phlegm shot from his mouth as he screamed in rage.

"What's his problem?" said Courtney.

"He's acting like Val did the night she killed her john. That's how she was screaming."

"We're the ones trying to help him. Why's he getting mad at us?"

142

A stream of yellow flame erupted from the flamethrower's muzzle and arced toward the crazed, running man.

Frothing at the mouth he leaped up and started shaking in the air like he had palsy, screaming and spitting as the flame engulfed him.

"Oh no," screamed Phoebe, raising her hands to cover her mouth, aghast at the dreadful sight.

The man ran toward her, pumping his fist, his clothes and flesh in flames, his hair blazing like a golden crown. As he burned alive, somehow he kept running. Exhaling smoke he slowed down until he was slouching forward, hunching over.

The flamethrower erupted again, shooting another streak of fire at him, igniting what remained of his burnt clothes and melted flesh.

Courtney turned away in horror.

The man collapsed, screaming in agony and impotent rage, which died in his smoke-filled throat.

"Those bastards," muttered Phoebe, staring at the smoldering man.

"Why did he go out there?" said Courtney. "They warned everyone to stay inside the buildings."

"He was angry at them. He looked rabid. He must've been on drugs."

"Yeah. He was a crackhead who couldn't take being shut in anymore. It's like prison here."

"We have to make contact with those crewmen somehow. Meredith had the right idea, but she went about it the wrong way." Phoebe racked her brains for an answer. "We have to contact them somehow without going outside."

"They kill everyone who goes outside."

"Everyone but Val."

"Maybe they're killing her now. How do we know what they're doing to her?"

"We don't. But why not torch her like they did everybody else? What's so special about her?"

Courtney slapped the side of her head in frustration. "What are we supposed to do?"

"I wish we had a bullhorn like they have. Then we could make ourselves heard."

"Wishes never come true. Jiminy Cricket was so full of shit. The Strip is where dreams come to die."

Phoebe mulled it over. "Maybe there's method to their madness."

"What do you mean?"

"Maybe they're shooting people who are angry."

"And that's a good reason to kill them?"

"I'm not saying that. But it's a reason."

"Meredith wasn't mad at them."

"No, but she was excited. She was scared, no doubt."

"Maybe they shoot you if you're afraid. Who knows? I think they're killing everyone they see on the street."

"But there has to be a reason. Unless the chopper crews are escapees from a loony bin."

"That's what they are. They're called *cops*."

To Phoebe's surprise, a late-model metallic red Ford Mustang convertible with its black nylon top down tooled down the street beneath the hovering chopper.

Chapter 49

"Look," said Phoebe, pointing at the Mustang.

"I see it," said Courtney, puzzled. "I thought the cops had barricaded the Strip so nobody could watch them in action."

"Maybe the car was already parked on the Strip when the driver started it."

Courtney nodded. "I guess."

"Let's run out there and get a ride before the Mustang passes through."

"I have nowhere to go. This is my home. I'm not leaving."

"You don't want to end up dead and cremated by those butchers in the choppers, do you?"

"What makes you think they'll let you hitch a ride in that Mustang?"

Phoebe shook her head in irritation. "I dunno. I don't understand what's going on. I'll think about it later. I'm gonna make a run for the Mustang before it's gone."

The Mustang slowed down as it drove past the heap of ashes that used to be Meredith piled in the street.

Sporting three days' growth of stubble, the dark-haired driver was in his late twenties, wearing Ray-Ban shades. His blonde girlfriend was several years younger and wore oversized bug-eyed sunglasses that dominated her thin, good-looking face. The driver and his girlfriend beamed with happiness.

When he gazed at the heap of ashes in curiosity, his mood changed. He sniffed the air with disgust.

Maybe the smell of burning flesh lingered in the air near the ashes, decided Phoebe, watching him.

Phoebe was fixing to run toward him when she felt Courtney grab her wrist.

"Wait a minute," said Courtney. "I saw something."

"He's slowing down," said Phoebe. "I need to leave now to reach his car before he drives away."

Then she saw what Courtney was talking about.

Four people hiding inside the buildings had the same idea as Phoebe. They charged out onto Cimarron Street toward the

Mustang, yelling and flailing their hands. Foaming at the mouth they rushed the car from different directions. Phoebe didn't know which building they had come from. They must have come from different buildings.

In any case, they didn't look friendly. They reminded her of the maniac who had shaken his fists at the chopper just before the crew had incinerated him.

The two men and two women, all between twenty and forty years old, converged on the Mustang.

The driver wondered what was going on. Watching them his girlfriend latched onto his arm with fear.

The four newcomers ran full bore at the car. Phoebe couldn't believe how fast they ran. Like the crazy man before them, they looked like they possessed manic energy, which enabled them to practically fly to the Mustang.

Screaming gibberish, a blond, powerfully built six-foot guy in the group lunged at the driver, clasped the driver's arm, and hauled him out of the car, spraying saliva everywhere as his face twisted convulsively.

A brunette in her thirties grabbed the girlfriend's hair and yanked her out of the shotgun seat. The enraged brunette shook her head, her teeth chattering, her face a twisted mask of loathing.

Phoebe couldn't believe her eyes when she saw a middle-aged man trudging toward the Mustang, his arms extended. It looked like the guy in the alley, the john Val had killed. At least, Phoebe *thought* she had killed him. Yet there he was staggering toward the Mustang, his face working, that part of his throat missing where Val had torn it out with her teeth.

"That's the john Val killed," she gasped.

"I guess not," said Courtney. "He's alive and breathing. You were mistaken about Val. I didn't think she could kill anyone. I know her too well."

"But look, part of his throat's missing."

"The coyotes' handiwork."

"How can he be alive with that gaping wound in his throat?"

"Seeing is believing."

One of the incensed mob had succeeded in dragging the Mustang driver out of his seat and was in the process of biting the man's shocked face.

146

A crazed redhead pushing thirty climbed over the trunk into the backseat of the convertible, reached over the back of the shotgun seat, and commenced throttling the girlfriend, who screamed in terror as another attacker continued to pull her hair. The redhead chewed the girlfriend's left ear off, chomped on it with relish, and continued strangling her.

The chopper flew toward the Mustang.

A crewman with an AR-15 opened fire from the cockpit. Bullets slammed into the mob in and around the Mustang, stitching bloody holes in their bodies, which jerked on impact. Screams of anger and of terror from the falling bodies suffused the air.

Struck by a bullet to his head, Val's victim crumpled on the tarmac.

Phoebe wondered if he was really dead this time. She didn't understand how he could even be walking around after what Val had done to him. Maybe some people were just hard to kill, decided Phoebe, lamely.

Chapter 50

"Why did they all charge the car like that?" said Phoebe.

"They wanted to get out of town like you," said Courtney.

"But did you see their faces? They looked like they were tripping on crack or crystal meth."

"I'm telling you, there's a lot of both here—and more stuff you've never even heard of."

"Drugs turn them into killers? I never heard of a drug that does that. Did you see what they were doing to the driver and his girlfriend?"

"Yeah. It didn't look like they wanted to hitch a ride," said Courtney, taking in the scene of carnage around the Mustang with a wave of nausea engulfing her.

Phoebe scoped out the motionless bodies sprawled on and around the Mustang. The driver's dead girlfriend sat in her seat with the attacking redhead's hands clasped around her throat as the redhead sat without moving in the backseat, her head hanging forward.

The driver's blood-streaked body lay supine on the tarmac five feet away from the Mustang driver's-side door that hung ajar. He had lost his sunglasses in the struggle and stared up into the sky with glassy eyes that never blinked.

"What was their crime?" said Phoebe, flabbergasted at the senseless mayhem.

Courtney glanced at the chopper. "Are they killing everyone who's on drugs? If that's true, they're gonna wipe out the entire population on the Strip."

Phoebe stared at the Mustang.

"I bet that Mustang'll still run," she said, her eyes widening with eagerness.

"They'll cut you down before you get within ten feet of that car."

"I'm not on drugs."

"Neither was the driver and his passenger. Now look at them."

"The car motor is still running. I can hear it. All I have to do is jump in the driver's seat and drive, and I'm outa here."

Phoebe psyched herself up, preparing to dash to the Mustang.

A flamethrower pointed out from the bottom of the cockpit and unleashed a thirty-foot-long streak of flame at the car. The Mustang burst into flames. It exploded when the fuel tank caught fire. Dense black smoke spewed upward from the burning car and mushroomed into the sky. The bodies in the car caught fire, looking like immolated wax statues.

The arc of the steady flame from the chopper spread from the car to the bodies that lay scattered around it on the tarmac, torching them.

"You're not going anywhere in that car, honey," said Courtney.

"Shelter in place," announced a chopper crewman with a bullhorn. "Attention. Do not go outside. I repeat. *Do not go outside.* Violators will be shot. This area is under lockdown by order of the United States government. No one is to enter or leave the quarantine zone under any circumstances."

"Quarantine?" muttered Phoebe.

"A bad case of syphilis?" said Courtney. "Wow. It's never been so bad that they quarantined the entire Strip."

"They wouldn't quarantine the area for a venereal disease. It must be some kind of virus like Covid."

"Another Covid outbreak? That's all we need. I'm gonna go bankrupt. You have no idea how many customers I lost during the first Covid outbreak. I could barely get by on what I made. I thought for sure I was gonna end up living on the street with a motheaten blanket over me."

"I don't understand. If it's some kind of virus, why are they shooting people? Why don't they take them to the hospital and treat them?"

"You saw how crazy those people who ran into the street acted. Maybe they were infected."

"Yeah," said Phoebe, remaining in awe. "They attacked the guy in the Mustang and his girlfriend for no reason at all. But is shooting the infected the only treatment?"

"Who are we to argue with the government?"

I'm married to the mayor. I'm part of the government. Where does that put me? Right now it puts me in the crosshairs of their 'cure' like everybody else on the Strip.

"The virus must attack the hosts' brains, driving them berserk," she said.

"Can't the syph do that to you?"

"Tertiary syphilis could. But I've never heard of the government blowing away patients infected with syphilis. This must be something else."

"How long is this quarantine gonna last?"

"I can't stay here forever. I have to get out of here," said Phoebe, thinking about Jason.

She produced her cell phone and tried calling him. No dice.

"Mine doesn't work either," said Courtney, watching her.

"We have no way to tell them we're not infected. We have to let them know somehow."

"If we try to talk to them like Meredith did, they'll shoot us," said Courtney, looking out at the corpse-strewn street. She paused and, turning ashen, faced Phoebe. "How do you know we're not infected?"

The question sent a frisson down Phoebe's spine.

"Well—uh—we don't feel sick," she said.

Sick with fear maybe, but not from a physical ailment.

Unconsciously, she felt her forehead to see it she was running a temperature. It seemed OK.

Courtney coughed.

Phoebe widened her eyes with concern. "Are you OK?"

"Oh, yeah. My throat's dry. I need some water, is all."

"Are you running a temperature?"

Phoebe shook her head no. "I'm OK. Just thirsty."

She retreated to the coffee table, scoffed up her half-full water bottle, and took a long pull.

Phoebe turned her gaze outside.

The chopper had retreated from the Mustang and was hovering at a higher altitude now.

The flames engulfing the car were dying down. However, a thick column of smoke continued to rise from the vehicle into the sky.

Under the wafting smoke, the charred bodies around the car lay motionless—

Except for one, that of the brawny blond guy, whose body had been only partially consumed by flames. His face hadn't been touched by them. Nevertheless, Phoebe could see from his blood-splotched shirt that the bullets from the chopper's AR-15 had found their mark.

She could have sworn she saw his leg twitch.

Chapter 51

Was he still alive? she wondered.

She doubted it. Too many bullets had riddled his chest full of holes. At least one of them must have found his heart. His shirt was soaked with blood.

But if there was any chance he was alive, shouldn't she try to help him? Under ordinary circumstances she would run to him and give him whatever aid she could manage. *Ordinary circumstances.* Nothing could be farther from the truth, she decided. Today was anything but ordinary.

She was certain his leg had moved again.

How could he be alive with all those bullets in his chest? she wondered. The chopper crew might not have succeeded in incinerating him, but they had certainly shot him to death. There was no way he could be alive.

To her amazement, he was getting up.

She gasped.

"What's wrong?" said Courtney, approaching her.

"One of them is alive."

Courtney looked at the blond getting uncertainly to his feet. Then she looked at the chopper.

"Not for long," she said.

"How can he be alive? Look at all the blood he lost. His shirt's dripping with it."

"He looks alive to me. The flamethrower burned only one of his legs and missed the rest of him."

"Those bullets didn't miss him. We should help him."

"Are you crazy? You saw what the chopper did to the others. The shooter will do the same to us."

The blond staggered around in a daze.

"Can you imagine?" said Phoebe. "Being killed because you're infected with some virus. And it's not even your fault."

"The government doesn't give a damn about people. They care only about staying in power. This virus threatens their grip on power."

"The government isn't *that* bad," said Phoebe. And then to herself added, "It can't be."

"You're right. It's worse."

Phoebe tried to get the stunned man's attention by motioning to him to come over to the hotel.

He continued stumbling around, looking lost. He reminded Phoebe of Val's victim, who had also been bumbling around after surviving certain death with his throat ripped out. She thought of Val.

"Do you think Val is infected?" she said.

"Maybe," said Courtney. "She didn't look good. I know she does drugs, but I've never seen her look as strung out as she did when they put her in that net. She looked worse than any junkie I've ever seen. She looked even worse than junkies who shoot up that new skin-rotting zombie drug that's going around."

"Maybe that's why they captured her—to study the virus's effects on her."

"Why her and not the others out there lying dead in the street?"

Phoebe scratched her head. "I can't answer that."

The blond tripped over his own feet and fell on the tarmac.

"What a klutz," said Courtney.

"Doesn't he know he should be dead?"

"He must be infected. That's why they shot him and tried to burn him."

He shambled to one of the charred dead bodies and inspected it. He pulled a face, looking disappointed.

Phoebe continued beckoning to him.

He was too disoriented to see her.

"Stop doing that," said Courtney.

"Why?" said Phoebe. "Maybe we can bandage his wounds."

"The chopper crew will see you and come over here. That's why."

"We're safe as long as we don't leave the building."

"You think? I don't know about that. Anyway, I have to admit I don't like the looks of that guy. He's messed up bad."

"Because he's hurt. How would you feel with all those bullets in you?"

Courtney grabbed Phoebe's motioning hand and pulled it down. "I don't want him over here."

"Look at his face. It's white as a sheet."

153

"Like a cadaver, you could say."

"He's not gonna last much longer. I can't figure out what's keeping him up."

Phoebe had second thoughts about inviting him over now that he was looking in their direction. The ghostly pallor of his face was disconcerting. It appeared devoid of blood. His eyes had a milky glaze and were focused on nothing—as if he was, yes, she decided, as if he was dead.

"That guy gives me the willies," said Courtney.

"He must have one foot in the grave. I doubt anyone can help him now."

He flailed his arms and lurched in circles, each step uncertain.

The helo commenced flying toward him.

"Uh-oh," said Courtney. "They must've spotted him."

Phoebe picked up on the flamethrower's barrel as a crewman aimed it out of the bottom of the cockpit at the reeling blond.

She wanted to yell a warning at the blond. But his looks were so off-putting the yell died in her throat. If the chopper crew didn't kill him, he would be dead soon from loss of blood. She had no idea what was keeping him up.

The flamethrower shot an arc of steady fire at the addled guy. This time they didn't miss. His body burst into flames. He bellowed in pain and swiped at the chopper with his blazing arms.

Phoebe looked away from the stomach-turning sight.

When he stopped screaming, she knew he was dead—for good this time. Ashes couldn't come back to life.

Chapter 52

"That guy was a walking corpse," said Phoebe.

"What kind of government would kill its own people?" said Courtney.

"He had to be dead even though he was walking around. Did you see his face? It was the face of a cadaver."

Courtney dropped her jaw. "You know what you're saying?"

"Yeah."

"I'll say it for you. He's a freaking zombie."

Phoebe clutched her forehead. "I know. It's impossible. But he couldn't be alive. You saw him. Was that the face of a living man?"

"I don't want to go there."

"Maybe that's why they're burning the corpses. Because if they don't, they come back to life—if you can call it life."

"Zombies? They only happen in grindhouse flicks."

"Let's look at the facts. We know there's a quarantine. Which means people are being infected, probably with a virus of some sort."

"How do we know that?"

"There are millions of viruses out there mutating constantly. According to the laws of probability, sooner or later the viruses will produce a combination that starts infecting people. It's inevitable."

"You're scaring me."

"It's science. Viruses are everywhere. Where was I?"

"The virus starts infecting people."

"Right. Now what are the symptoms? It looks like people go berserk and try to kill each other—and . . . eat each other. That's what happened at the Mustang."

"And you said Val went berserk and killed someone in her room last night."

Phoebe nodded yes. "OK. Let's think this out from what we saw. Next stage, the bodies of the victims burn out from raging fever, and the victims die. During the following stage—unless their infected bodies are incinerated—they rise from the dead and stumble around—"

"Looking for human flesh to eat, if I'm reading you right."

"Exactly. That explains why me and Meredith saw Val hunched over the torn throat of her victim. She had been eating his body."

"So she was infected with the virus."

"I can't say for sure any of this is true. I'm just trying to analyze what we've seen."

Courtney took a swig from her water bottle, polishing it off. "So how do we get away from these infected zombies?"

"I wish I knew."

Courtney slumped her shoulders. "I thought you were gonna tell me how we escape."

"I'm trying to analyze the situation before we decide what to do. We can't make the right decision until we know what we're dealing with."

Here she was talking about making the right decision—something she had rarely been able to do her entire life, decided Phoebe with wry amusement. Nothing seemed sillier to her than to hear herself lecturing about making the right decision. What a joke.

"I don't want to get infected," said Courtney. "I'm young. I got my whole life ahead of me. You're not supposed to die when you're twenty-five."

"We're not infected yet."

"How do you know?"

"We're not experiencing any symptoms."

"Maybe we *are* infected, and the symptoms will come later."

Quite possible, decided Phoebe with dismay. But she didn't want to let on to Courtney her true feelings. She kept her demeanor calm.

"We need to get off the Strip to have any chance of survival," she said.

"But this is where I live."

"Then it's time to move."

"I was an army brat. I moved around a lot when I was a kid. I was always the odd kid out at school because I was new in the neighborhood. As soon as I made friends, our family moved, and I had to start all over as the outsider in a new neighborhood. I didn't like it at all. I got to the point where I hated moving. And that's where I am now."

"It's not safe to live here. This area is contaminated with a virus, so we're quarantined."

"That's what those guys in the chopper say. How do you know we can believe them?"

"They work for the federal government."

"That's what I mean."

Phoebe had never met anyone as suspicious and as cynical as Courtney, who especially distrusted the government—of which Phoebe was a part. Naturally, she wasn't going to tell Courtney that bit of information. It would undermine their relationship, which was rocky as it was.

"They're concerned about our health," said Phoebe.

"Then why are they shooting all those people in the street?"

Phoebe frowned in thought. "They must have a reason."

"This quarantine bullshit could be some kind of government cover-up. Maybe it's a pretext they're spreading to justify their killing of everybody who lives on the Strip."

"Why in the world would they want to do that? Government officials aren't monsters."

"I'm not so sure about that. You saw what they did to those people on the street."

"I know. It doesn't make sense," said Phoebe in frustration, mystified by the chopper crew's actions. "All I know for sure is, we're not safe here."

"As long as that chopper's out there, nobody can go anywhere."

Phoebe wished she could contact Jason. He must know what's going on. If anyone would know, he, the mayor, would.

A full-throated new Rosso Scuderia Ferrari convertible roared down the street, a tall fortysomething man with dark curly hair at the wheel. Wearing black-tinted designer sunglasses he drove past the smoking Mustang and the piles of ash that were once human beings, paying little attention to them.

He braked to a halt in front of the Lavender Whip Resort Casino and hopped out of his vehicle.

A score of people burst out of the buildings and belted after the Ferrari, screaming and shaking their fists at the driver.

Taken aback at the riot, he strode apprehensively to the casino entrance in a white linen suit.

Baring their teeth the enraged mob charged after him, hissing flecks of spittle.

He broke into a run.

Chapter 53

"Another car got through," said Phoebe, watching the Ferrari park in amazement. "Who is that?"

Courtney scoped out the guy. "Muldoon, the owner of the Lavender Whip. He's a big shot in these parts. A lot of juice."

"The infected aren't impressed. It looks like they want to tear him apart."

"I can't believe how many are infected. The disease must spread fast."

"All the more reason to quarantine the area."

The frenzied throng reached the Ferrari and blew past it toward Muldoon, who stormed into the lobby as the plate-glass door whooshed shut behind him. He locked it behind him, barring the rioters from entering.

Fearless, they crashed into the door, indifferent to the pain the impact inflicted on their infected bodies. The bulletproof glass withstood their blows.

"They must've let his car onto the Strip 'cause he's the boss," said Courtney, glancing at the chopper, surprised the AR-15 hadn't opened up on him.

"They haven't fired yet at the infected either."

"They're waiting for Muldoon to get off the street before they start firing. They don't want to kill a honcho."

As if listening to Courtney, a crewman in the chopper fired a burst at the mob right after Muldoon had reached safety inside the casino.

Bullets strafed the sidewalk in front of the casino and ricocheted higgledy-piggledy.

"Didn't he get the message the Strip is quarantined?" said Phoebe.

"He doesn't care. Nothing can separate him from his money. He's a big wheel. He can do whatever he wants. Probably friends with the mayor."

"Not to my knowledge."

"Huh?" said Courtney, staring at her.

"Uh—I read the papers. I never saw him with Jas—the mayor."

159

If Muldoon was friends with Jason, Phoebe had never met him at one of Jason's parties. Maybe Jason didn't want to be seen with the guy, she decided. It would make sense if Jason did know him. The guy was loaded and would be a generous donor to Jason's reelection campaign.

On the other hand, some people, like Jason's religious backers, might not cotton to the idea that the mayor was accepting money from the shady operator of a casino nightclub on the Strip. In which case it was a good idea for Jason to conceal the friendship from inquiring minds.

Though Jason was a savvy politician who didn't want to alienate anyone, decided Phoebe, he also didn't want to pass up bundles of moolah that could aid his reelection. But what if it was an illegal contribution? Would he accept an illegal contribution?

She was finding out things about Jason that she had never suspected. He had a dark side. The closer she looked at it, the darker it became.

"Who are you?" said Courtney, searching Phoebe's face.

"I'm—I'm. I had a start-up. It went belly up. I lost everything. I had to sell my car. I was going bankrupt."

Phoebe had no intention of telling Courtney she was married to the mayor.

"You drove here in your car," said Courtney.

"I had to lease that Mini after I sold my Mercedes."

"If you're bankrupt, how did you get credit to lease a car?"

"Ironically, credit card companies want to give you their cards after you declare bankruptcy."

Phoebe didn't want to tell Courtney that Jason had saved her from filing for Chapter 7 by giving her a loan. Phoebe let Courtney go on believing she had declared bankruptcy.

"Sounds weird," said Courtney. "Maybe you belong on the Strip with me. It's full of losers."

"If you were really a loser, you'd be living in a pasteboard box on the street."

"There are all types of losers in this world. They're not all homeless."

Right after Muldoon disappeared into the casino lobby, the chopper advanced toward the frantic, gyrating mob that had gathered around the entrance. A male and a female teenager were lying on the sidewalk on their backs and spinning around like they were trying to break dance, snapping their heads back and forth and growling as they used their feet to propel them. They yelled gibberish at the rest of the mob and punched the air in anger.

A stubble-faced guy pushing thirty wearing jeans, suede cowboy boots, and a fringed leather vest was brandishing a pistol. He commenced firing at the lobby entrance, pocking the bulletproof glass but not penetrating it with his bullets.

His jerky, uncoordinated movements threw off his aim. Foaming at the mouth he shook his head and growled in frustration, dismayed he hadn't hit Muldoon. He shook his head so fast and hard Phoebe thought he might suffer a concussion.

The shooter in the chopper opened fire on the throng, riddling the sidewalk with lead.

Seeing the wounded bleeding, the rest of the mob turned on them, aroused and agitated by the sight of fresh blood. They sank their teeth into the bleeding cuts of the wounded.

"Holy shit," said Courtney, watching them, frozen with terror in the hotel doorway.

"What if we make a break for it now that the chopper isn't watching us?" said Phoebe.

"The infected will come after us like they did Muldoon."

Courtney could be right, decided Phoebe. The infected charged anyone who ventured onto the street. They had attacked the Mustang driver and Muldoon. Hundreds of them could be hiding inside the buildings chomping at the bit to stampede out and attack at a moment's notice.

If the infections had started yesterday, they must be spreading at a blazing rate of speed, infecting hundreds—maybe even thousands—overnight, decided Phoebe. No wonder the government was so quick to quarantine the area.

She wondered if you could contract the disease by breathing the air on the Strip. If so, she and Courtney were doomed.

"I bet Muldoon's sorry he came here," said Courtney, darkly amused. "Now that he's here he can't get out because of the quarantine. He's trapped with the infected like we are."

"If he's as rich as you say, he might have his own chopper and a helipad on his roof he could use to escape."

"Or he'll grease the palm of some politician to help him get out of here."

The chopper swooped lower enabling its shooter to fire the AR-15 with increased accuracy. He mowed down the infected, turning them into bullet-riddled corpses splayed on the tarmac and on the sidewalk.

The cowboy with the pistol tried to return fire, but he had little control over his reflexes and struggled without success to aim the gun at the chopper and bring it down. Automatic-rifle bullets shattered his head, catapulting shards of his skull through the air along with gobbets of his infected brain.

"If we run now while the chopper's distracted, we might make it," said Phoebe, sick of watching the butchery taking place.

"Run where?" said Courtney.

Phoebe knew Courtney was right. If they ran down the street away from the Strip, the chopper would spot them before they reached the end of the quarantine zone. And what was at the end of the zone awaiting them? Phoebe wondered. Squad cars with armed cops blocking the street waiting to gun them down with orders to shoot the infected, no doubt.

"What's Plan B?" said Courtney.

"We have to let them know that we're not infected."

"Supposing we're not—and I don't know how we can be sure—how do we let them know? And why should they believe us?" said Courtney, her face pallid.

It was clear to Phoebe that Courtney couldn't stomach watching wounded bodies twitching in their death throes on the bullet-raked street. Courtney retreated into the lobby, plugging her ears with her fingers to blot out the ungodly screams of the dying.

Phoebe couldn't blame her.

"Shelter in place," boomed the bullhorn in the chopper. "All violators will be shot by order of the federal government. Do *not* go outside."

Chapter 54

Ensconced in his spacious, well-appointed casino office, Muldoon produced his cell phone and tried to put through a call to the authorities. Nothing doing. He figured the cops were jamming the cell phones on the Strip as part of the quarantine.

He tossed his cell phone onto his desktop in frustration, walked around to the other side of the desk, pulled open a drawer, and withdrew his satphone.

Knowing the satphone worked only outside where it could connect with a satellite, he strode onto his office balcony and punched out the mayor's number.

The call went straight to Jason's direct line, bypassing his secretary.

"Hello," said Jason.

"This is Rick Muldoon. What the hell's going on here?"

Jason paused in astonishment. "Hello, Mr. Muldoon. I don't know what you're talking about."

"The Strip is under quarantine. Choppers are flying all over the place shooting people. The road in and out of here is blocked by feds, cops, and patrol cars. They wouldn't let my car out. I'm goddamn trapped."

"It's news to me."

"You mean, you didn't order the quarantine?"

"No way."

"What? Didn't the feds tell you?"

"No, they didn't. And they better have a damned good reason to shut down part of my city without telling me. This is unheard-of."

Muldoon balled his large fist in aggravation. "Tell them to get out of here. My casino's losing money hand over fist."

"I'll look into this."

"With all due respect, Mr. Mayor, I suggest you hurry up about it, or I'm not donating another nickel to your reelection," said Muldoon, seething.

"The feds aren't under my authority. They must have authorized an emergency health mandate without contacting me. My hands are tied."

"It's *your* city. This has to be unconstitutional."

"The governor must know about it. The feds wouldn't take action without his knowledge."

"Then tell the governor to end the quarantine. I can't make a living in a quarantine zone. And another thing. The motherfuckers are jamming cell phone signals so nobody here can contact anyone. They're causing a massive disruption to our gaming business. We can't take bets over the phone."

"Then how are you calling me?"

"I'm smarter than them. I'm using my satphone," said Muldoon, gloating as he looked up at a chopper hovering over the main drag, tempted to give them the finger.

"They're not closing down my city without telling me. This has got to stop."

"Do you have any idea what's going on here?" said Muldoon, taking in the corpses sprawled on the street.

"A quarantine, you said."

"They're fucking shooting everybody on the street. I'm lucky to be alive."

"What?" said Jason, flabbergasted. "Say again."

"You heard me."

"This can't continue."

"We understand each other," said Muldoon, and ended his call, his face contorted with rage.

He took leave of the balcony and returned to his office. He realized he was still wearing his sunglasses. He removed them and hung them by one of their black plastic bows on his shirt's neckline.

He flipped open the cigar box on his desktop and withdrew a Montecristo White Toro. He guillotined the tip, inserted the cigar into his mouth, and lit it with a wooden match he withdrew from a matchbox lying on the desktop.

The Montecristo would help relax his nerves. The idea that the feebs would shut down his operation with a quarantine galled him. They thought they could do whatever they wanted when they declared their health mandates the way they had succeeded in shutting down the entire country during the Covid outbreak. Now they were shutting down the Strip and killing everybody who tried to leave. In the name of a *health mandate*? *What a joke.*

It was all about power with the feds, and they loved exerting it, Muldoon knew. He didn't know how he could fight back. How could he defy a health mandate, a fucking quarantine for Chrissake?

He had to do something. He wasn't going down without a fight. These clowns had to be stopped. He had built his billion-dollar gaming empire with bribes in the right places and making people who wouldn't cooperate disappear. Another bribe here and there wouldn't bankrupt him. The question was, who did you bribe during a quarantine?

Albright didn't know what he was doing, decided Muldoon. The feds were walking all over the mayor by not telling him anything.

Muldoon would have to go higher up than the mayor. He would have to grease the palms of the governor or maybe higher. He didn't know. How should he know? His nightclub casino had never been locked down in a quarantine zone before.

He blew a smoke ring across the office, contemplating his next move.

Even his lucrative prostitution ring was shut down by the health mandate. He had no money flowing in. There was nothing worse than having no money flowing in. Money was like blood flowing in his veins. No money meant no life.

Somebody had to pay for this, he decided.

He hadn't gotten this far in life by being a weakling. If somebody had to be taken out, Muldoon wasn't loath to order the hit.

Maybe the mayor thought playing patty-cake was the way to make it in the big leagues. Muldoon knew otherwise. If greasing palms didn't work, leaking blood would. The Colombian cocaine cartels had an expression for it—*plata o plomo*, popularized by the legendary drug kingpin Pablo Escobar. Silver or lead. Bribery or a bullet.

Enough said.

Chapter 55

Jason put down his cell phone, doing a slow burn. He hated being cut out of the loop. This was his city, and nobody had bothered to tell him the feds were quarantining the Strip. If the casino boss Muldoon hadn't told him, Jason would still be in the dark about it.

He was the mayor. It was unconscionable that he wasn't notified before the quarantine took place. Not only that, the feds had yet to notify him.

The media were certain to hear about the quarantine soon—if they hadn't already. They would want to know why he had covered it up when they had asked him about the shutdown of the Strip at the press conference. The truth was he didn't cover it up. You couldn't cover up what you didn't know.

But it made him look like an ignoramus. A mayor who hadn't a clue about what was going down in his own city. And it had happened at a televised press conference for all the public to see and hear.

He slapped his head, feeling miserable about the optics.

He summoned his press secretary to his office over his intercom.

Yvette Pontchartrain bustled into the office, clutching a yellow legal pad to her chest. Clad in a mauve pencil dress, she was a slender, shiny-faced African American woman in her early thirties who had graduated from Columbia's prestigious School of Journalism. She wore her hair short to fit her businesslike demeanor.

"The feds have quarantined the Strip without my knowledge, Yvette," said Jason. "We need to spin this to make me look on top of the situation even though they didn't consult me before they acted."

"Does anyone know they didn't consult you?"

"Nobody but you and—uh, one other guy," said Jason, thinking of Muldoon. "I don't think he'll let the cat out of the bag. He doesn't like publicity."

Everything was under the table and in the shadows with Muldoon, Jason knew. The guy liked keeping his association with Jason private. The feeling was mutual.

"What did you tell the press pool during your conference?" said Pontchartrain.

"I said I had no idea about it. When a reporter asked me about the Strip being shut down, I told them the truth, that it was news to me."

"Yes, I remember now."

Pontchartrain turned over possible responses, keeping her own counsel for a few moments.

"In this case," she said at last, "it might be better to tell the press that you knew about it, but were ordered not to talk about it. That was the reason you denied knowing about it at the press conference."

"They'll accuse me of a cover-up."

"You tell them you were following orders to cover it up."

Jason nodded yes. "Yeah, this is all the feds' fault anyway." Jason shrugged, grim-faced. "But a cover-up is a cover-up, no matter how it happens. The public's not gonna like it."

"It's better than having you look like an imbecile who doesn't know jack about what's going on in your own city."

He liked Pontchartrain's candor even though she had just insulted him. It was why he had hired her in the first place. She could cut to the heart of the matter better than anyone else he knew, and she wasn't shy about laying it on the line.

"Point taken," he said. "But I'd rather come out of this smelling like a rose than opening myself up to a charge of a cover-up. That was how they got Nixon, you recall."

"Nixon was covering up a crime by the Watergate plumbers. You're covering up your ignorance of a quarantine. There's a big difference. The latter isn't a crime."

Jason stroked his chin. "Still, a cover-up has negative connotations."

"I'm not gonna deny that, yet it's the lesser of two evils, in my opinion. You're the mayor. I'm not telling you what to do. My job is to give you politically expedient options."

"You're probably right," said Jason, not happy about admitting to a cover-up to his archenemy the media.

"Remember. The cover-up wasn't your idea. It was the feds'. The public will blame them for the shutdown of the Strip."

Jason's expression brightened. "Yeah. I had nothing to do with the shutdown. And I'll tell my constituents I'm angry about it just like them. They'll vent their wrath against the feds. Perfect."

"I would suggest making an announcement ASAP clearing you of blame for the quarantine. You want to look on top of the situation."

"Ladies and gentlemen, I've just been informed of a federal quarantine of the Strip," said Jason, practicing his announcement, gesturing as he paced around his office.

Pontchartrain watched him, admiring his ability to adapt to any situation and always to appear in charge.

He caught her eye.

"This is gonna work," he said, smiling. "Set up a press conference for me."

"Yes, sir," said Pontchartrain, spun on her heel, and hustled out of the room.

Jason produced his cell phone and called Hardy.

Chapter 56

Hardy took the call at a zinc counter in a pub with maroon banquettes and cherrywood tables.

"Have you got it?" said Jason.

"Got what?" said Hardy, watching the head foaming in his mug of Guinness.

"The proof that the problem has been removed."

"Isn't my word good enough?" said Hardy, peeved.

"It's not that I don't trust you, but I have too much riding on this to accept anything without verification."

In other words, Jason didn't trust him, decided Hardy, decoding Jason's words.

"Haven't the cops found the body yet?" said Hardy, nursing his Guinness.

"They're busy elsewhere."

"Too busy to find dead bodies?"

"Haven't you heard?"

"Heard what?"

"The feds closed down the Strip, and they're using the local police to help enforce the quarantine."

"Quarantine?"

"An outbreak of a virus."

"You don't say. Hasn't there been a report on the news of a dead body with a bullet in his head found in a car in an alley?"

"Nothing. The only dead bodies with bullets in them that the cops are finding are on the Strip."

"What's happening? Is it a riot?" said Hardy in astonishment.

"The feds aren't talking to me. The only reason I know anything about it is because of a friend who's on the Strip."

"What do you want me to do?"

"I want you to give me the proof. The cops are all on the Strip."

"I told you I got his phone."

"Is your line encrypted?"

"Of course."

"We agreed on the right thumb."

The right thumb, decided Hardy. Now he was beginning to remember his first meeting with Jason. The right thumb for proof of Jones's death.

"Uh—somebody interrupted me," said Hardy. "I had to leave the area before they spotted me near the objective."

"I'm not giving you the rest of the payment till you give me the proof."

"I can't believe you're questioning my word," snarled Hardy.

"This isn't personal. It's business. I'm always thorough in business agreements."

"When the cops find his body, that will be adequate proof."

"You're not listening to me," said Jason, raising his voice. "The cops are busy elsewhere."

"Don't worry about it. I'll give you his cell phone."

"How am I supposed to know it's his?"

Good question, decided Hardy, since Jones's phone had a password and Jason wouldn't be able to open it.

"Because I took it from him," said Hardy.

"How do you know he didn't have someone else's phone on him?"

"Why the hell would he be carrying someone else's phone?"

"I'm done arguing. The fact is we can't be sure whose phone you took."

"Then I'll put it back on his body," said Hardy, grinning.

"No," said Jason hurriedly. "Don't do that."

"If it's someone else's phone—"

"Stop dicking around. We agreed on the thumb. And give me that phone too. Or don't you want the money?"

Hardy didn't fancy Jason's tone.

Hardy resented having to return to the scene of the crime. It was an old adage that criminals returned to the scene of their crime. Which was why a lot of them got caught, decided Hardy. Knowing better, Hardy never returned to the scenes of his crimes.

"The thumb's not a good idea," he said.

"Are you reneging on our deal?"

"The situation has changed."

"A deal's a deal."

Hardy didn't want his rep as an A-list fixer tarnished. Jason could spread the word if he thought Hardy had screwed him.

"The body will be found," said Hardy. "All you need is patience—"

"I want this taken care of now."

Maybe he could pull it off, decided Hardy, if as Jason said, all of the cops were on the Strip. Which would mean none of them would be near the alley where Jones had blown out his brains in his car. Still, Hardy didn't believe it was worth the risk. Hadn't that passing woman seen Jones's body in his car? Why hadn't she reported it?

"What if I can prove the phone is Jones's?" he said.

"The only way you can do that is if you open it with his password."

"Maybe I know a guy who can hack the phone—"

"The answer's no. I want the right thumb and the phone."

"You figure you can open the phone yourself with his thumbprint, huh?"

The reason Jason specified the right thumb, decided Hardy. The left thumb wouldn't open the phone.

"You're not paid to tell me what I think," said Jason. "Do your job and stop wasting time. Or . . ."

"Or what?"

"Or I won't employ you in the future, and I'll spread the word about your lousy service. A lot of would-be clients won't employ you either."

"I don't respond well to threats."

Jason hung up.

Hardy wondered how much Phoebe would pay to see the pictures on Jones's phone. The problem remained that he couldn't open the phone. He wondered if the phone could indeed be opened by Jones's thumbprint.

He fished the phone out of his trouser pocket and inspected the display window. He noticed a circle on it that was a fingerprint reader. Jason had probably noticed the reader as well when Jones had paid him a visit to initiate his blackmail scheme and had showed him the incriminating pictures on the phone.

Now Jones's thumb as proof made sense, decided Hardy. And it had to be the right thumb.

If he returned to the corpse, he could use Jones's thumb to open the cell, decided Hardy, twiddling the phone absently. And he could cut Jones's thumb off for Jason. Maybe he could see how much Phoebe was willing to pay for the phone after he examined the contents of the photos. Then he could double his money.

He took a pull on his Guinness.

He liked having options, and he had many if he was able to open Jones's cell, he decided, wiping beer from his lips with the back of his wrist.

One thing bothered him. Why hadn't that woman who had heard Jones's gunshot and had entered the alley reported the corpse to the cops? Or had she reported it, but the cops weren't taking any calls because they had deployed their entire force to quarantine the Strip?

Chapter 57

Phoebe couldn't believe her eyes when the elevator opened and her father Sam Spillane stumbled out of it, rubbing the back of his head.

"Dad," she exclaimed.

She ran over to him.

He blinked his eyes in a daze, trying to focus on her.

"What are you doing here?" she said.

He was having difficulty standing up.

"He's infected," cried Courtney. "Get away from him."

Phoebe felt a shiver run down her spine. No, Courtney was wrong, she decided. It couldn't be. Her dad couldn't be infected.

"What?" said Sam. "What's she screaming about?"

"Nothing," said Phoebe. "What happened to you?"

"I came here to ask questions about Val Lewton like you asked," he said, wincing and continuing to rub the back of his skull.

"Get away from him," said Courtney, her eyes wide with fear. "He's got the virus."

Sam looked at her in puzzlement.

"What happened to your head, Dad?" said Phoebe.

"I went to knock on a door to ask about Val and somebody coldcocked me from behind. I don't know how long I've been out."

"Have some water," she said, retrieving a water bottle from the coffee table and handing it to him.

He knocked back the water.

"I can't believe how thirsty I am," he said, becoming steadier on his feet.

"You don't know about the choppers?" said Phoebe.

"Choppers? I think I hear one outside. What about it?"

"You were blacked out the whole time?"

"What are you talking about? What whole time?"

"The Strip is under quarantine."

Sam narrowed his eyes with concern. "For what?"

173

"They didn't say. But the feds in charge of the quarantine are killing people."

"*Killing* people? What the hell?"

"They're shooting the infected."

"You must be mistaken," said Sam, shaking his head. "They can't do that. We have laws."

"Yeah, laws," scoffed Courtney, keeping her distance from Sam, continuing to suspect he might be infected.

"Who's she?" said Sam.

"Courtney," said Phoebe. "She lives here."

"I haven't been able to dig up much on Val. She's a hooker. She seems to be quite popular—"

"We think Val got infected," cut in Phoebe.

"Infected with what?"

"We don't know. They're not telling us. They took her away in a net like a wild animal."

Sam couldn't get his head wrapped around it.

"She got lucky," said Courtney. "They're blowing away everyone else in the street and burning their bodies."

"Wait a minute," said Sam, befuddled. "You're coming at me from the *Twilight Zone*."

"It's true, Dad. The government is shooting everyone who goes outside. They even shot Meredith," said Phoebe, sobbing.

"Why did they shoot Meredith?" said Sam, appalled.

"She walked onto the street to talk to them so they would let us leave. She needed to return to her office to treat her patients—"

"And the chopper crew shot her dead," said Courtney.

"Why for Chrissake?" said Sam.

"They never said anything," said Phoebe. "We don't know for sure. They must have thought she was infected, but she was no more infected than you or me."

"This has got to be illegal."

"Whatever the feds do is legal," said Courtney.

"Look, I'm a journalist. I'm telling you this is illegal. Shooting defenseless people in the street in cold blood? That's not how you treat infected people."

"It's how they do it here."

Sam made a beeline for the front door and scoped out the street strewn with smoldering skeletons lying around the charred hull of a Mustang. He couldn't help but notice the gutters running with blood. Additional skeletons that still had portions of burned flesh on them sprawled in the gutters and on the sidewalk in unnatural positions in front of the Lavender Whip casino.

His jaw dropped.

Chapter 58

Sam glanced up at the chopper hovering in the cloud-dappled azure sky above the street. Dark wisps of smoke from the torched Mustang lingered among the clouds like torn cobwebs.

"I need to find out what's going on here," he said, his face gaunt. "This reeks of government overreach. Abuse of power. Call it what you will. The public needs to hear what's going on. And I'm the one to tell them."

"We need to be careful, Dad. They're shooting everyone who goes outside."

Sam shook his head in disgust. "This is all wrong. This isn't America. It's a third-world dictatorship. The public needs to know what's happening here." He looked up at the chopper. "I need to talk to them."

"No, don't, Dad," said Phoebe, grabbing Sam's elbow with alarm. "That's how Meredith got shot. She tried to talk to them."

"They don't talk," said Courtney. "They just shoot." She paused. "How do we know you're not infected?"

"What?" said Sam.

"You stagger around like you're in a stupor. That's how the infected walk."

"I told you I got hit in the head."

"Why would someone hit you in the head?"

Sam shrugged. "Maybe I was asking too many questions about Val. I found out people don't like answering questions in this place. They're close-mouthed. Have you noticed that?"

"That's because they think you're a cop when you pump them with questions."

"I'm no cop. I'm trying to find out the truth. That's what journalists do. It's my job."

"Maybe you got somebody's pimp nervous with all your questions."

Sam waved it off. "I can't worry about getting beaned every time I ask a question. Otherwise, I'd get nothing done."

"You might live longer."

Sam shot Courtney an awed look. "It can't be *that* bad."

Courtney jacked her eyebrows, but didn't answer.

Sam turned to Phoebe. "I'm sorry, dear, but this quarantine story takes pride of place. This story is gonna make my name. I smell a Pulitzer. I happen to be in the right place at the right time. That's how you score a scoop in the news business. A lot of it is plain luck. Your questions about Val will have to wait."

"The chopper crews shoot first and ask questions later, Dad. Asking them anything could be hazardous to your health. You should have seen poor Meredith out there."

Phoebe's eyes filled with tears.

"They're not gonna shoot me," said Sam. "I'm the press. The feds don't like messing with the fourth estate. Free speech is protected by the First Amendment. It's the basis of our country."

"Spare us the speeches," said Courtney. "Believe me, honey, the Strip ain't about free speech. In fact, nothing's free here. Everything's got a price. If you can't afford it, take a hike."

"Do you want to be in my article?"

"I'll deny everything I told you."

"Do you have anything to say about the quarantine?"

"It's costing me business."

Sam typed out a note on his smartphone. "Can I quote you?"

"No."

"Does your cell phone work, Dad?" asked Phoebe, watching him.

"I can't call out if that's what you mean," answered Sam. "I can write notes to myself though."

"Just don't go outside to ask your questions," said Phoebe.

"How else are the feds gonna hear me?" said Sam, standing on the shattered glass in the doorway and gazing up at the helo.

"I already lost my best friend. I don't want to lose you."

"They're not gonna shoot me. I'll show them my press pass," said Sam, reaching for his wallet in his back trouser pocket and digging out his press pass.

"You think that little piece of paper will stop a bullet?" said Courtney, amused.

"You don't understand this country, do you?"

"You're the one who doesn't understand it. I'm living in it. I ought to know."

"I'm living in it too. Freedom of the press is the bedrock on which our democracy is built."

"If that piece of paper is all you got for a shield, I wouldn't go out there if I was you."

"Nonsense. I have a job to do." Sam studied the hovering chopper. "That helo has no markings on it. How is anyone supposed to know it's a government aircraft?"

"Somebody with a bullhorn said it was the feds," said Phoebe.

"If they shot all of those people dead in the street, they've got some explaining to do. The people have a right to know what's going on, especially when it comes to their health."

"How have you managed to live this long?" said Courtney, baffled.

"Seeking the truth is a noble profession. I'm proud of my job."

"You know what they say about pride."

"You can't find the truth if you're afraid to look for it," said Sam, puffing out his chest.

"They *will* shoot you, Dad, if you go outside," said Phoebe with a worried expression.

"They wouldn't dare shoot a member of the press. Our government knows better."

"Let's stay inside the hotel and think it over before you go."

"There's nothing to think over. I have to find out the truth. That helo crew knows what's going on. It's their duty to tell me, an agent of the press."

"What if they think you're infected?"

"I'll tell them I'm not."

"Remember what you told me as a kid?" said Phoebe.

"What?"

"You said, 'Never be afraid, but never be stupid either.'"

"I can't believe that our government would shoot someone for no reason."

"Don't you see those charred bodies out there?" said Phoebe, worn out from arguing with him. "The chopper crew killed them."

"I'm not armed. They won't blow me away."

"Meredith said the same thing before they pelted her body with bullets."

"They wouldn't dare do that to a member of the press. The *Courier* would raise holy hell."

"Look, Dad, I know you have a low opinion of my decisions because my start-up went belly up, but in this case you need to listen to me," said Phoebe. She got into Sam's face. "It's not safe to go outside with that helicopter up there."

"I don't have a low opinion of you," said Sam in surprise. "Whatever gave you that idea?"

"I was ready to file for bankruptcy."

"It's not the end of the world. I wasn't always rich and successful," he said, and laughed at himself, knowing he was anything but rich. "Nobody gets rich trying to tell the truth as a journalist. Journalists aren't rock stars. The truth is usually unpopular."

"The fact is the truth can get you killed."

"Nevertheless, it's my job to find it—wherever my search leads me. The crew in that chopper know what's going on here what with all their killings and the street gutters running with blood."

"I have only one father. I don't want to lose you."

"You're not gonna lose me. This is my job. I haven't lasted this long in my profession without knowing what I'm doing. Our government respects the rights of journalists."

"Won't you listen to reason?" said Phoebe, becoming angry at his stubbornness.

"If they dare shoot a reporter like me, the news will spread over the Internet and over the airwaves like wildfire. The government will never get away with it."

"They have so far," said Courtney. "Just look at the stiffs littering the street."

"They can't possibly have orders to shoot everyone. What would be the point?"

"They're preventing the virus from spreading," said Phoebe.

Sam stared at her in shock. "That's not how we treat the sick in our country. I'm done arguing. I'm going outside to question the crewmen of that chopper. We the people deserve an explanation."

His jaw set with determination, Sam strode over the glass shards in the doorway out onto the street. He held his hands over his head as he approached the chopper. In his right hand he brandished his press pass.

The better part of twenty feet ahead of him he caught sight of Meredith's half-burned corpse sprawled on the street.

Chapter 59

Gritting her teeth Phoebe watched Sam with a racing heart, expecting the worst to occur at any moment. She had already lost her best friend. She didn't think she could stand losing her father on the same day.

"Be careful, Dad," she yelled.

"Press," Sam cried so he could be heard over the racket of the chopper's rotor blades as he gazed up at the chopper, standing beneath it. "Press. I'm a reporter for the *Courier*. I have questions for you about this quarantine."

Nobody in the crew responded.

It didn't feel right, decided Phoebe. Why weren't they talking to him? It was their job as government workers to keep the media informed of their actions. This was the same thing that had happened to Meredith. Instead of talking to her, the crew had shot her dead.

"What is the quarantine for?" asked Sam. "What is the name of the disease? How is it spreading? Who is giving you your orders?"

No answer.

"What are your orders?" he demanded.

Silence from the crew.

"The public has the right to have more information about the quarantine," said Sam. "I have heard eyewitness accounts of your shooting people dead. How can you justify murder in cold blood?"

"Be careful, Dad," hollered Phoebe, her rapid heartbeat thundering in her ears. "Come back inside."

She doubted he could hear her above the commotion whipped up by the hovering chopper's rotor blades. She was tempted to run onto the street and bring him back inside. The crew might shoot her if they saw her running toward him. They were targeting anyone on the run.

Even though Sam wasn't running, she feared for his safety. The trigger-happy crew could cut him down in a split second. Unarmed, he was at their mercy.

"The public demands answers," yelled Sam, shaking his hand above his head at them. "Your silence is damning. What do you have to hide? Why are you murdering innocent people?"

You're pressing your luck, Dad. Don't make them angry.

With frazzled nerves she saw the AR-15 barrel projecting from the chopper cockpit.

She wished she could help him somehow. But how? She didn't have a weapon.

"Run, Dad, run," she yelled, cupping her hands around her mouth.

"Are you infected?" said the bullhorn from the chopper.

"No," said Sam.

"You do not have permission to be in the quarantine zone."

"I'm a member of the press. I have the right to find out what's going on here."

The burst from the AR-15 turned Phoebe's stomach. She felt her knees buckle.

Courtney caught her from behind. "You warned him not to go out there. It's not your fault he didn't listen."

"Why did they shoot him?" said Phoebe, grief-stricken.

"I keep telling you they're cops. They do what they want."

"This has to be reported to the authorities," said Phoebe, bursting into tears.

"The authorities are the ones doing the shooting."

Phoebe didn't know how much more of this she could take. Disaster followed disaster. She was losing all of the people that meant anything to her.

"He told them he wasn't infected," she sobbed.

"I guess they didn't believe him."

"Or they didn't want him to tell anyone via the news the horror that's happening on the Strip." She couldn't control herself any longer, venting her anger. "They're monsters."

But it wasn't over.

The barrel of the flamethrower projected from the cockpit and unleashed a flame that ignited Sam's and Meredith's lifeless bodies.

Numb and disoriented from the loss of her father and of Meredith, Phoebe stood in shock, her face streaked with tears.

She watched in a daze as her father's body burned.

Courtney gathered Phoebe and ushered her away from the devastating sight. Phoebe could barely stand. She collapsed on the sofa.

"Can it get any worse?" she muttered, her face ashen.

"Their idea of a quarantine is wiping out everybody on the Strip."

Her head muzzy from her funk, Phoebe struggled to marshal her thoughts.

"I wonder how long we'll be safe inside," she said.

"It's only a matter of time before they come for us. I don't know why they haven't started entering the buildings and blowing away people."

"Maybe they're afraid of resistance."

"They're armed to the teeth and they're afraid?" said Courtney, and shook her head no.

"They could be afraid of becoming infected."

"This virus or whatever it is must be awful if they're going to such lengths to stop its spread."

"They want us all dead. They'll start going house to house soon and wiping us out."

"I don't want to die," said Courtney, sitting beside Phoebe on the sofa.

"Losing people you care for is worse than dying," said Phoebe, crestfallen, her mind replaying her dad's brutal murder.

"At least you had someone who cared for you. Nobody ever gave a damn about me."

Phoebe felt rage smoldering inside her. "We have to fight them. We can't let them get away with this."

"How? They control the street."

"There must be some way. It looks like they're assuming everyone in the quarantine zone is infected even if you tell them otherwise. They're not taking any chances to let the disease spread."

"Great." Courtney paused. "Maybe dying's better than getting that disease and going nuts and eating people—if those are our options."

Screwing up her face Phoebe could smell the stomach-turning stench of burning flesh wafting in through the broken front door. Her father's flesh. As if she needed to be reminded of his immolation. Her father had said he smelled a Pulitzer. She smelled death.

Their leaders were going to lay waste to the quarantine zone and everyone in it. Was Jason one of the leaders who had ordered this holocaust? she wondered. Did he know she was here? He knew Val was here, and they had taken her away. Spared her because she was his lover?

Jason wouldn't have any part of this if he knew his wife was here, decided Phoebe. He would put an end to it. Then again, he couldn't overrule the feds if this was their idea. Jason must not know she was here. How could he? She hadn't told him.

Chapter 60

Hardy drove his nondescript black Honda Civic to the cul-de-sac where Jones had shot himself. Hardy owned a new Porsche Carrera S, but he never drove it while on a job. The luxury car turned heads, and he didn't want to be noticed while working.

He tooled past the cul-de-sac, checking it out.

Jones's Toyota was still there. Hardy couldn't tell if the body was inside it. He didn't want to linger near the alley, knowing it would invite suspicion.

Hardy kept driving. He parked in a strip-mall parking lot a half mile away from the cul-de-sac and walked back.

When he reached the cul-de-sac, he smelled garbage, redolent of rotting oranges mixed with a fertilizer-like stench. He sniffed the air to detect the scent of a corpse. Maybe the odor was present, but he couldn't be sure. If it was there, the overpowering stench of the garbage in the Dumpsters was masking it.

In any case, he needed to go to the Toyota to retrieve Jones's thumb.

He didn't see anyone in the blind alley and he didn't notice anyone paying attention to him on the sidewalk.

He stole into the cul-de-sac toward the Toyota, pricking up his ears listening for approaching strangers.

He knew Jones's stiff was in the car because he could see it slumped over the steering wheel. If the lady he had seen turn into the alley last night to investigate the gunshot had seen Jones, she must not have reported it, Hardy decided. Or maybe she hadn't seen Jones. After all, it was dark at the time. Or could it be that Jones hadn't shot himself, that he was still alive? he wondered with apprehension. Had Jones fallen asleep on the steering wheel? It made no sense. How could the guy fall asleep knowing his daughter was in danger of being shot?

Hardy was wearing khaki cargo pants. From one of his deep pockets he withdrew a pair of purple latex surgical gloves. He slipped them on. From another pocket he fished out a pair of stainless steel bone-cutting forceps, which had cost him over six hundred bucks when he had bought them online a few years ago.

Jason wasn't the only client who had demanded fingers to ID victims.

Hardy knew ordinary scissors weren't effective on human fingers. The forceps sliced through bones with ease.

The stainless steel glistened in the sunlight as he held up the forceps.

He opened the Toyota passenger's-side door and slid onto the shotgun seat. The odor of the rotting cadaver hit his nostrils. A musty stink tinged with garlic. No worry. He didn't plan on being there long. The stench would get much worse four days after death.

A jagged fragment of Jones's skull covered with hair clung to the headliner like a rodent, glued there by his coagulated blood. Blood splatters on the dash, on the driver's-side window, and on the windshield were due to Jones's skull exploding when struck by the slug.

Unfortunately, the Ruger was still in Jones's right hand, making the removal of the right thumb problematic, decided Hardy. He didn't want to remove the pistol from Jones's hand, since it confirmed death by suicide with Jones's prints on the gun and with gunshot residue on Jones's hand. Moving the pistol would disturb the presence of the GSR, possibly rubbing it off, which would look suspicious to the trained eyes of forensics cops, who might suspect a staged suicide.

Hardy could amputate the thumb without removing the pistol from Jones's hand. He would just have to be more careful. It was a matter of pulling the thumb far enough away from the pistol so he could get the blades of the forceps around the digit without causing the pistol to fall out of Jones's hand.

As luck would have it, Jones's forefinger was inside the trigger housing and holding the pistol in place. The problem was rigor mortis had set in overnight. He would have to snip off the thumb without prying it away from the gun stock. It made his job more difficult, but not impossible.

The top joint of the thumb protruded enough from the gun stock for him to work the forceps around the digit and snip through it.

The severed thumb fell onto the front seat and bounced into the driver's-side foot well. Craning his neck Hardy cast around for the wayward digit. He used his cell-phone flashlight to pinpoint it.

"Damn," he said under his breath.

Whenever he dropped something, it always ended up bouncing into the least accessible place. Was that a law of physics?

Chapter 61

As Hardy retrieved the thumb and sat up, he realized Jones's thumbless hand presented a problem. Not that the thumb stump was bleeding. Livor mortis prevented bleeding.

No, the problem was the cops were going to wonder why Jones was missing his thumb. They were going to suspect foul play. Why would he cut off his thumb to shoot himself? It made no sense. And where was the thumb? The obvious conclusion was somebody had taken it. Which would lead to more questions.

The son of a bitch Jason was screwing up Hardy's perfect murder thanks to his demand for the thumb, decided Hardy in frustration. He deposited the thumb in one of his cargo pockets.

This called for a change in plan.

Hardy swore under his breath.

He ought to charge Jason more money because the guy had botched a job. A perfectly executed job. Nobody would have suspected a thing. Now all bets were off.

Hardy told himself to calm down and think of a solution.

He saw only one way out. He would have to torch the car.

If the cops discovered Jones had one thumb in the burnt wreckage of the Toyota, they would think he had lost the other to the fire and would not become suspicious.

Hardy wondered if he should remove the gun from Jones's hand since the death scenario had changed. If there was no gun in the car, the cops wouldn't suspect murder—unless they found the bullet. But what were the chances they would find it? If the slug was lodged inside Jones's skull, the chances would be pretty good. But the slug had blown out a fragment of parietal bone, which meant the slug had exited Jones's skull.

If Hardy removed the gun and the bullet from the Toyota, he would be home free. The cops would suspect the car caught fire and Jones was burned alive. Case closed.

Hardy eyed the Ruger in Jones's hand. He hated tampering with his perfect crime. Everything had worked to a T. Nobody would have suspected murder. And then Jason had to spoil everything by demanding Jones's thumb. There was no way Hardy could talk Jason out of it.

The more Hardy stared at the gun, the more he dreaded tampering with his masterpiece of murder.

He saw no other options, though. The missing thumb was evidence of a murder. Why would Jones cut off his thumb and kill himself? It defied explanation.

A fire was the only solution to covering up the missing thumb, decided Hardy. Of course, if the cops examined Jones's corpse close enough, they would find out that he hadn't died from smoke inhalation or from wounds caused by the car's explosion, but from a bullet to the head.

Hardy could only hope they wouldn't examine the corpse closely. Why should they? There was no reason to suspect murder. The car blew up and killed its driver. An obvious accidental death.

So where was the bullet that killed Jones? wondered Hardy. He wasn't going to waste a lot of time searching for it. He had to blow up the car and beat it.

Using his cell phone's flashlight to find the bullet, he cast around the driver's-side footwell and around the headliner near the clump of hairy skull and brains stuck to the headliner. No bullet.

He needed to get moving.

He glommed onto the blood-spattered suicide note from the console and pocketed it.

With lingering reluctance he seized the Ruger from Jones's thumbless hand and deposited it in one of his cargo pockets. He looked around for something flammable that he could insert into the gas cap.

He checked out the backseat. He picked up on a copy of the *Courier* lying on it.

He scoffed up the newspaper and clambered out of the shotgun seat.

He surveyed the area making sure nobody was watching him. He heard a noise and started. Rooted to the spot, he gazed in the direction of the clatter.

A rat the size of a small cat was clawing its way out of the Dumpster, scratching the metal with its claws as it pulled itself over the Dumpster's lip. Twitching its whiskers it scoped out its environs. Satisfied it was safe, it jumped off the Dumpster and scampered away.

Hardy sneered at the ugly rodent. He hated rats.

He rolled the newspaper into a cylinder, unscrewed the gas cap, and stuck the paper into the fuel tank.

He would have preferred dousing the newspaper in lighter fluid to make sure it burned all the way down into the gas tank, but he hadn't brought any. He was ad-libbing now. Which he never did, knowing it courted disaster.

But he had no choice. He removed his lighter from a cargo pocket and ignited the newspaper. He made sure the paper was burning well and would continue to burn as the fire proceeded down into the fuel tank.

The car should blow any second, he decided.

He stole toward the cul-de-sac's entrance.

He hoped the blast wouldn't attract a crowd thanks to the car's hidden location. Since the cops were at the Strip, maybe the Toyota would burn for a long time without interruption. Yet the fire department could respond—unless they too were at the Strip for the quarantine.

Hardy saw no witnesses in the area. A stroke of good luck for him.

The best thing in the world was luck, he knew, even better than meticulous planning, which he prided himself on. If he had luck, he might succeed. But he never counted on luck. It wasn't dependable. He counted on his professional skills.

He was near the cul-de-sac's entrance when the explosion rocked the earth, deafening him. His ears ringing, he emerged onto the sidewalk and headed back to his car parked at the strip mall.

People on the sidewalk were looking around, startled by the explosion. However, they weren't sure where the blast had emanated since Jones's flaming Toyota was out of view. Unable to locate it, they dismissed it from their busy minds and continued on their errands.

Hardy looked around like everybody else, saw nothing untoward, and kept walking to his car. To ignore the blast would have looked out of the ordinary. People might take note. Hardy wanted to fade into the background like an extra at a movie shoot.

He climbed into his Honda and felt Jones's thumb in his pocket. He realized he could open Jones's cell phone with it. He smiled.

189

It was time to make Jason pay for ruining Hardy's masterpiece of undetectable murder. Hardy considered himself an artist at his craft. He didn't take kindly to his works being destroyed, especially when he was forced to destroy them himself thanks to the whims of a thankless client.

Chapter 62

Using Jones's severed thumb Hardy sat in his Honda and opened Jones's password-protected cell phone.

He tapped the Photos icon and inspected Jones's recent photos. He instantly saw the photos of Jason grabbing the ass of a heavily made-up, shapely woman clad in a skintight black leather microskirt and in a pair of black fishnet stockings while leering at her. The woman was not Jason's wife.

The tabloids would launch a bidding war to acquire the rights to publish the photos once Jones had informed them of their existence. Which was obviously his plan if Jason didn't pony up the blackmail money. No wonder Jason had him removed.

Didn't Jason know Hardy would be able to open Jones's cell phone once he had possession of Jones's thumb? wondered Hardy. Or hadn't it crossed Jason's mind? Didn't Jason think Hardy would be able to figure out why he was so intent on possessing the thumb? Did Jason think that by explaining he wanted the thumb to ID the corpse he was providing a thick-enough smoke screen to prevent Hardy from seeing Jason's real motive of wanting to access Jones's photos?

It was never wise to underestimate the intelligence of a professional you employed to do a dirty deed in your name, decided Hardy. It was even less wise to tick off that professional. Hardy hadn't become a master of his craft by being stupid or timid.

He now had leverage he could use against Jason in any way he wanted, such as raising the price of their contract.

Wondering if Jones had contacted any of the tabloids, Hardy scrolled through the list of contacts on the cell phone. It came as a surprise to see Phoebe Albright's name on the list. Had Jones attempted to contact Phoebe about the photos before he died? He wasn't supposed to if Jason forked over the blackmail money. However, Jason hadn't paid up at the time of Jones's death.

Maybe Jones suspected Jason might double-cross him and had taken precautions. Maybe he had told Phoebe about the photos, but didn't say what was in them, decided Hardy.

Curious, Hardy tapped Phoebe's name on the cell phone to put through a call to her. He wasn't sure what he was going to say to her—if anything. He harbored a wild idea of kidnaping her, holding her for ransom, and doubling his fee for his services to Jason. Not a good way to get future assignments from Jason. But maybe Hardy would retire after this project.

Hardy chuckled at the thought. It would serve the bastard right for spoiling a work of art, for that was what Hardy's professional services were—works of art. As such, they didn't come cheap. Each objet d'art was perfect in its own way.

Hardy didn't feel like retiring yet, though. He still had the urge to continue working.

The call went straight to voicemail.

Maybe it was for the best, decided Hardy, and terminated the call without leaving a message. Why wasn't Phoebe answering her phone?

He couldn't very well kidnap her if he didn't know where she was. How could he ask her her whereabouts if she didn't answer her phone?

Undeterred, Hardy was full of ideas. He could always come up with another idea in his brain that was teeming with them.

Jason owed him at least two million bucks at this point, and he better be willing to pay.

Whoever said crime didn't pay didn't know much about the business, decided Hardy. Some bottom-feeder bank robber that got caught, no doubt.

Jason had everything to lose, and Hardy was the only one who could save the player's career and marriage or could, just as easily, deep-six them.

Hardy liked having power over the rich and famous like the "incorruptible" mayor of Costaguana. Hardy smiled. The "incorruptible" part amused him. Life was full of ironies.

192

Chapter 63

Hangdog, Phoebe was staring out the hotel front doorway at the hovering chopper wondering what to do when her eyes bulged in terror at the sight of a screaming middle-aged bald man foaming at the mouth on the other side of the street hurtling through a window and shattering its glass as he plunged four stories to the tarmac.

"What was that scream?" said Courtney, approaching Phoebe from behind.

"Some guy jumped out a window," said Phoebe, trying to assimilate what had happened.

She saw the bald man's body sprawled on the street, his legs bent at unnatural angles.

"Did he kill himself?" asked Courtney.

"Looks that way," answered Phoebe, visibly shaken. "I didn't see anybody push him. He ran through the window at full throttle."

"I can't say I blame him. Maybe he's got the right idea."

"I don't know if it's *that* bad. We still have a chance," said Phoebe, but wondered if she meant it.

"A chance of what? Getting infected or getting shot? Some choice."

"I saw foam on the guy's mouth. He must've been infected. This virus causes people to go nuts and become violent."

"I don't understand how people are getting infected."

"We need to get out of here," said Phoebe, gazing at the bald man lying motionless in the middle of the street.

"Easy-peasy. Let's hitch a ride on the chopper."

Phoebe didn't laugh at the joke. Her eyes were widening as she watched the bald man slowly sit up.

"Courtney?" she said in horror.

"What?"

"That guy's still alive."

"How could he be? He jumped to his death."

"Look. He's standing up."

The bald man got to his feet and staggered around on broken legs in a daze. Phoebe didn't know how he could stand on such mangled legs, which he had broken in his fall.

"He has risen," said Courtney, dropping her jaw.

"Like the other infected. They turn into homicidal raging cannibals, die, and come back from the dead."

"I'd rather they stay dead. Leave resurrections to Jesus."

Snarling, the bald man snapped his jaws. He looked in Phoebe's direction and shambled toward her, lurching on his fractured legs.

"Can he see us?" said Courtney. "It looks like he's coming over here."

"We can see him. It figures he can see us."

"Even with his dead eyes? Look how his eyes stare out of his head like they're blind."

"He's got dead legs and he can walk, so why can't he see with dead eyes?"

"I suggest we hide instead of waiting for him."

"If only this door wasn't broken, we could lock him out," said Phoebe, knitting her brows.

She noticed the chopper descending and flying toward the bald man, who swiped at it awkwardly with his arm as if the chopper was a giant fly annoying him. Maybe it was the machine's racket that bugged him, she decided.

Becoming disoriented by the chopper, he slogged around in a circle. He kept swiping his arms at the chopper trying to get it to fly away from him. The chopper closed in on him. The crew's AR-15 opened fire. Bullets slammed into his skull, felling him.

A crewman trained the flamethrower on the guy and incinerated him. Ragged gold flames danced on his inert body as they consumed his flesh.

"They wouldn't burn him if they didn't think he was infected," said Phoebe. "You know what that means?"

"It means he's finally dead now?"

"It means he got infected inside a building on the Strip. Which means *we* can get infected while we're inside too."

"The virus is spreading inside the buildings?"

"It must be. That's why they shoot anyone who goes outside. They figure if you're inside you're infected, and they don't want you to come out—or else."

Courtney scoped out the lobby anxiously. "We can get infected just by being inside?"

Phoebe eyed the grill covering the air duct in the wall. "Maybe the virus is spreading through the air ducts."

"Then they're condemning us to death by keeping us cooped up."

"I hope I'm wrong. But it would explain a lot of what's happening."

Who was she trying to kid? decided Phoebe. She was always wrong. Every time she made a decision, it turned out bad.

"Next thing you know, they're gonna go door to door to shoot all of us. They won't have any problem getting in here," said Courtney, nodding at the broken door.

"Maybe we would be safer outside."

"How could we be safer? The chopper will kill us."

"The fresh air might keep us from going insane with the virus."

"Didn't you hear me?"

Phoebe rubbed her brow. "I'm trying to come up with a solution."

"Not every problem has a solution. There's no cure for cancer."

"Something will come to me," said Phoebe, not really believing it, but not giving up either.

She wished she had a better track record of making good decisions. It would give her confidence in making another one. Best not to think about it. She needed to get out of here and warn Val to leave Jason alone.

Speaking of Val, where was she? What had they done to her after they had captured her?

Phoebe looked out the doorway at the Lavender Whip and noticed Muldoon's Ferrari was parked outside it, all in one piece. The rioters hadn't trashed it when they charged Muldoon. All they cared about was feasting on his flesh. The luxury car meant nothing to them.

But to Phoebe the Ferrari represented a means of escape.

Phoebe wondered if Muldoon had left the keys in the ignition. It depended on how big a rush he was in to get inside the Lavender Whip, which depended on when he had picked up on the infected stampeding toward him in a feeding frenzy. As she recalled, he was in a rush when he leapt out of his car. Which meant he could have left the keys in the ignition.

If she could reach the Ferrari, she could drive away from this horror hotel and never come back. Of course, she would have to survive the trip to the Ferrari with the killer copter hovering overhead.

"The Ferrari's over there," she said.

"How nice," said Courtney indifferently, without looking out the doorway. "Why don't you take a picture of it?"

"You don't understand. It's our ticket out of here."

Courtney strode to the doorway, her interest piqued.

"I wonder why they didn't torch it like the Mustang?" said Phoebe.

"Because Muldoon's top banana in these parts. They're not gonna burn his toys."

"Or the infected didn't enter it like they did the Mustang, so there was no reason to burn it." Phoebe squinted in the sunlight. "Part of its front fender got scorched by the flamethrower, but the tires look intact. I bet it still works."

"All we have to do is walk over there without getting shot by the chopper. Looking good," Courtney deadpanned.

"I know it won't be easy, but at least it's a chance for us to escape."

Phoebe started. She heard a loud noise behind her and whipped her head around.

Chapter 64

A stocky sixtyish man with his shoulder-length thick white hair combed back over his head and curled around his ears like ram horns launched himself out of the opening elevator at her and Courtney. His face spasming and contorting, drooling, he reached his hands out toward them.

Courtney screamed and darted behind one of the sofas.

Adrenaline coursing through her, Phoebe thought fast and broke off a shard of glass from the broken front door's steel jamb, cutting her finger. She brandished the jagged glass fragment in front of her, flinging drops of blood through the air.

"I'll cut you," she said. "Don't think I won't."

The man slowed down and growled at her, grimacing.

Courtney retreated to the manager's office and searched for a weapon behind the front desk.

Phoebe swiped the glass back and forth in front of her to ward off the attacker.

He was either on drugs or infected, she decided. Either way she didn't like her chances. The glass fragment wasn't going to scare him off. Drug addicts and the infected had no fear. She had seen the infected at work with her own eyes when they had butchered the couple in the Mustang.

Baring his teeth and emitting a guttural sound, the man reached toward her throat.

Phoebe slashed his hand with the glass fragment, cutting herself in the process as she gripped the glass hard so as not to drop it. She managed to slash his forefinger.

He howled in pain and withdrew his hand.

He could feel pain, decided Phoebe with elation. Maybe she would have a chance against him, after all. She had thought from their berserk actions on the street that the infected might be impervious to pain. She didn't think he was on drugs. She had never seen anyone on drugs turn into a homicidal maniac.

This guy wanted blood. He must be infected, she decided.

Undeterred by his slashed hand, he stabbed it toward her throat. She slashed his wrist, managing to cut an artery. His blood jetted ten feet into the air.

Her heartbeat hammering, she backed away from him toward the front desk, where Courtney was casting around for a weapon, yanking out drawers and rummaging through them in frantic haste without any clear idea what she was searching for.

Phoebe backed toward her, fending off her attacker with swipes of her blood-smeared piece of glass.

Every time the infected reached for her she stabbed his hand, drawing blood. Apropos of nothing, she wondered if the infected continued to bleed after they had risen from the dead. This guy hadn't died yet. He was in the initial stage of infection, where the victim went berserk and became homicidal.

The virus was in the process of killing him by burning him up with fever and driving him mad, decided Phoebe. She wondered how much longer he could go on living as his temperature continued to soar. Sweat was pouring out of his forehead and streaming down his flushed face. He gazed at her with bloodshot, dilated green eyes brimming with bloodlust.

"Get back," she cried at him, backing toward the manager's desk swiping the glass in front of her.

He showed no fear. He kept advancing on her as his hand spurted blood.

She could only hope he would bleed out soon from loss of arterial blood. But he was in such an adrenaline-charged state he might be able to go on living with scarcely any blood in his body. Then he would die and return to life as a shambling ghoul. For now, he was pulsating with life and hellbent on killing her.

Courtney dashed out from behind the front desk, something in her hand, Phoebe noticed. She couldn't make out what it was. She was too preoccupied with warding off her attacker.

"Keep him busy," said Courtney, approaching Phoebe.

It looked like a letter opener in Courtney's hand, decided Phoebe.

Courtney launched her attack.

She managed to slash the infected guy's bleeding wrist, drawing blood, which seeped out as his blood pressure continued to drop due to a faltering heartbeat.

Phoebe knew neither Courtney nor she could let their guards down since the guy was jacked up by adrenaline and could kill both of them with ease.

Courtney saw an opening and lunged at the guy from his flank, thrusting the steel letter opener into the guy's temple. The guy reeled back in agony, clutching his impaled temple, letting loose an unnerving scream that sent shivers down Phoebe's spine.

Phoebe hoped Courtney had pierced the guy's brain, killing him.

Hanging his mouth open the guy shook his head with blinding speed. He had to be burning himself up with fever, decided Phoebe. There was no way he could go on living much longer.

"What's he doing?" said Courtney, awed by his shaking head which had become nothing but a blur at this point.

"Dying, I hope," said Phoebe.

The guy pitched forward on his face onto the floor and lay motionless.

"Holy shit," said Courtney, bloody letter opener in hand. "I thought we were dead for sure."

"Don't hold your breath."

"What?"

"It's not over. You saw those infected rise from the dead in the street."

"Look at the blood all over the place. He can't be alive without any blood."

"I don't know how it works," said Phoebe, disconcerted as she eyeballed the guy's body that lay prostrate in front of her.

"I once saw a movie where you kill a zombie by destroying its brain. I'm sure I stabbed that guy in the brain."

"You saved my life," said Phoebe, blood dripping from her wounded hand as she looked at Courtney.

"I saved *my* life. Oh, you're hurt. Did he bite you?" said Courtney suspiciously.

"I cut myself on this glass." Phoebe dropped the blood-smeared glass fragment onto the carpet. "The glass cuts both ways."

Courtney heaved a sigh of relief. "That was close. I thought we were goners."

"We're no safer inside than outside."

"Can you get infected from an open wound?"

"I have no idea how you get infected. A lot of people around here are, though."

Phoebe cast a wary glance at the closed elevator door.

"There might be more of the infected upstairs," she said.

Courtney wheeled around to face the elevator. "How are we gonna keep them from coming down in the elevator?"

Phoebe strode to the elevator and pushed its button. She waited with apprehension for its door to open.

She felt relieved when she saw the elevator was empty. She cast around the lobby until her gaze landed on a planter containing a philodendron in the corner. She retrieved the planter and set it in the elevator's doorway. When the door slid to close, the planter blocked it, disabling the elevator.

"How do we keep them from coming here off the street?" said Courtney.

"The chopper will do that."

Chapter 65

Jason sat behind his desk in his office at City Hall, concerned about Val. Was she quarantined on the Strip like everyone else? he wondered. She must be.

He produced his cell phone and called her. The call went to voicemail.

He had found out the feds were jamming cell phone signals on the Strip, which would explain Val's not answering since she must be quarantined. He had wanted to tell her they shouldn't meet again until the quarantine had blown over.

He tapped Phoebe's number. Voicemail again. He was becoming worried about her. She should have contacted him by now. Something must have happened to her.

He started when his phone vibrated in his hand.

It was Hardy.

Jason took the call. "Is it taken care of?"

"There's been a change in plans."

"What?" said Jason, puzzled.

"It turns out he didn't commit suicide. He was in a car accident."

"Whatever. As long as it looks kosher. Why the change?"

"Because of the thumb you wanted."

Jason detected a trace of anger in Hardy's voice. "I need it for ID."

Silence on the line.

"Hello. Are you there?" said Jason.

"Yeah. I know why you want it."

"Because I just told you. Now bring it and the phone to me. You do have his phone?"

"No problem. It has some interesting photos on it."

Jason froze. "You opened it?"

"I was curious."

"That wasn't part of the deal."

"I risked my life for this phone. I wanted to know why it was so damn important."

"It's none of your business," said Jason, managing to bridle his anger. "Your job now is to give it to me with the ID."

"Not so fast."

"I want them *now*."

"You changed the deal. I had to remove the target twice because you wanted the ID."

"The ID was always part of the deal. It's your problem you don't listen to instructions."

"It's gonna cost you double because I had to risk my life twice to do the job."

"No way," said Jason, flabbergasted. "We had an ironclad deal. You can't make changes in it."

"You should have thought of that when you demanded proof. The proof doubled my risk of getting caught. You should have known you don't need proof when you hire me. I always get the job done."

"I'm not paying you any more money until you hand over the thumb and the phone."

"Are you gonna pay me double like I deserve?"

"No way. You can't change the terms of the deal."

Hardy hung fire.

"I wonder what your wife would say if she saw these photos," he said.

Jason felt his heart skip a beat. "You wouldn't dare."

"I have her cell phone number. I could e-mail her the photos."

Seething, Jason ground his teeth. "Don't do that."

"Do you agree to the change in terms?"

Jason didn't appreciate being backed into a corner. "Word will get around if you pull this stunt. Nobody's gonna want to hire you when they find out you're a double-dealer."

"I wouldn't tell anyone that if I was you."

"You're committing career suicide."

"Your wife . . ."

"What about my wife?"

"Might disappear."

Jason couldn't believe his ears. "Are you threatening my wife?"

Hardy hung up.

In a state of shock Jason called Phoebe again. Voicemail. Had Hardy kidnaped her? Jason wondered. Was that why she wasn't answering her phone? The guy had been reliable in the past. Now he was playing games—life or death games.

Not only did Jason have a virus outbreak to deal with, he had his fixer blackmailing him. And where was Phoebe? How could Hardy have found her so quickly when even Jason didn't know where she was? Wait a minute. Hardy had never said he had her. He had said she "might disappear." But if Hardy *did* have her, he would have taken her cell phone. And she wasn't answering her phone.

Chapter 66

"I can't believe how hungry I am," said Courtney.

Phoebe could smell lavender-scented perfume wafting off Courtney borne on the breeze blowing through the shattered front door.

Phoebe realized her empty stomach was growling. She couldn't remember how long ago she had eaten. This day seemed to be lasting an eternity.

"Doesn't the manager have something to eat behind his desk?" she said.

"I thought I saw a bag of roasted peanuts back there. I'll check it out."

Courtney brought up when she reached the corpse sprawled in its own pool of blood on the carpet.

"Are the corpses contagious?" she said, leering at the stiff she had impaled with the letter opener.

"Why would they incinerate them unless they were contagious?"

"How do we prevent ourselves from getting infected by this stiff?"

"The only way to be sure is to burn the body."

"The building will catch fire and so will we."

"We'll have to move the body."

"Where? If we take it outside, the helicopter will shoot us."

Phoebe chewed it over. "Maybe if we drag the body outside, the chopper will incinerate it for us."

"Before or after they shoot us?"

"If we burn the body in here, we could die of smoke inhalation—if we don't burn the building down in the process."

"If we don't burn the body, we'll get infected with the virus and turn stark raving mad like those people who ran into the street and rioted."

"We could burn it in the bathtub and prevent the building from catching fire, but we can't stop the smoke from spreading into the lobby and poisoning us."

Courtney backed away from the corpse. "Maybe if we keep away from the body, we won't get infected."

Phoebe shook her head no. "I don't like our chances. You saw how quickly they cremated the bodies on the street. The corpses must be highly contagious."

Grimacing, Courtney backed farther away from the corpse.

"Maybe they're only contagious after they rise from the dead," she said, becoming hopeful. "This guy can't come back to life because I killed his brain."

"According to a horror movie you saw."

"Well, yeah. So?"

Phoebe frowned. "We can't take that chance. If he comes back to life here with us, we'll be his lunch."

"If we drag him outside, they'll shoot us."

Phoebe had to make a decision even if it was the wrong one. The infected body had to be dealt with.

She retreated to the manager's office and inspected his bathroom. It had a white porcelain bathtub that could accommodate the body. But it didn't have a window for ventilation. It had only a round five-inch-wide vent, which had been painted white scores of times, in the ceiling above the tub. Some of the thick paint had sealed spaces in the grillwork that covered the vent. She flicked on the light switch and listened for a fan. Nothing. She doubted the partially clogged vent would be adequate to draw out all the smoke from a burning corpse.

She closed the bathroom door and inspected the gap between the bottom of the door and the floor. Smoke would escape through the wide opening under the door. She could block the gap with a bath towel.

Of course, they wouldn't be able to use the bathroom if they burned the corpse in the tub.

What if the smoke could infect people? she wondered. If it could, it could seep into the lobby and infect them.

She opened the bathroom door and entered the lobby.

"We might inhale smoke that would leak out of the bathroom," she said. "The smoke could infect us. We don't know enough about this virus to take any chances."

"If we burn the body outside, how do we know the wind won't blow smoke into the lobby?" said Courtney.

"Hopefully, the wind will dissipate the smoke and make it harmless."

"How do we know the smoke will infect us? You're just making it up."

"I'm trying to think of the safest thing we can do to protect ourselves from the virus."

"I say you're overreacting."

"Better to overreact than underreact. We know nothing about how this virus spreads."

"It spreads when one of the infected bites you."

"But it may also spread in alternate ways."

Courtney threw up her hands in frustration. "I'm sick of thinking about it. Maybe we should leave the stiff where it is. Touching it could infect us, for all we know. We can't move it without touching it."

"We could wrap our hands in towels so we wouldn't expose them to the corpse when we move it."

Chapter 67

Phoebe had to make a decision. Even if it was the wrong one. Her decisions were always wrong, she knew from experience. Which didn't mean she could go through life without making another one. You could never play it safe in the game of life. Decisions had to be made every day.

When she made her decision, she had to stick to her guns, even if she made the wrong one. If she gave up making a decision, someone else would make it for her. Then she would be nothing more than a slave following orders, a puppet on a string.

Phoebe wasn't going to be anybody's slave, not if she could help it. It was decision time. Her life depended on it.

"How do we know the disease can't spread through cloth?" said Courtney.

"We don't. But we can't leave the infected body here with us. It could come back to life. It needs to be incinerated."

"I don't want to go near it."

"It could be contaminating the air with germs even now."

"You can't be sure of that."

Phoebe couldn't wait any longer for Courtney. "I'm taking it outside—with or without your help."

Phoebe returned to the bathroom, grabbed two white hand towels, wrapped them around her hands, and approached the cadaver. Bending over she latched onto its two arms and dragged it toward the front door. It was hard to get a good grip with the towels wound around her hands.

What made it worse was the guy's weight. He weighed well over two hundred pounds, maybe close to three hundred. Her back was killing her as she strained to haul him along the carpet. The wound in her hand opened up. She noticed her blood seeping through the towel around her hand.

"He's bleeding on you," cried Courtney. "Don't let his blood get on you."

"It's *my* blood. Don't worry."

"You're spreading his blood underneath him all over the floor."

"It can't be helped. We have to get the body out of here."

207

Courtney darted over to her. "Give me one of those towels. Not the bloody one. I'll help."

Phoebe unwrapped her good hand and handed Courtney the clean towel.

Courtney wrapped the towel around the corpse's arm and clutched it with two hands. Phoebe did the same with her blood-streaked towel around the corpse's other arm. They dragged the body to the door.

It was much easier with Courtney's help, decided Phoebe.

Hearing the chopper overhead, they paused at the door and straightened up.

"Are you sure you want to go out there?" said Courtney, glancing up at the chopper.

Her mind made up, Phoebe snagged the corpse's towel-wrapped arm with both hands and proceeded to drag the body down the short flight of concrete steps and across the sidewalk into the street by herself. Courtney rushed over to her and helped.

Phoebe could hear the helicopter become noisier as it approached. Her pulse raced. She wasn't going to risk going any farther into the street.

"Let's go," she said, releasing her hold on the corpse's arm.

Courtney followed suit.

Phoebe bopped back to the front door, dreading the sound of automatic-rifle fire from the chopper. She hadn't run this fast in her life. It was only twenty feet to the door, but it seemed like it was taking forever to reach it.

The clatter of the helicopter was becoming deafening. It sounded like it was on top of her. The shooters couldn't miss from such close range.

She heard the shooter in the cockpit open fire.

The blood drained from her face. So this was how it ended. Shot in the back while running for her life.

She didn't care how many bullets were riddling her body. She kept running.

Incredibly, she made it through the door. She didn't feel any pain in her body. Maybe her surging adrenaline was masking it. Or maybe they had shot Courtney.

Phoebe craned around in search of Courtney.

Her face flushed from running, Courtney was all in one piece behind her.

208

But the gunfire, thought Phoebe. Puzzled, she looked outside.

The shooter in the chopper was pelting with 9mm Parabellum bullets the corpse Phoebe and Courtney had left in the street. The corpse shook and vibrated as the slugs struck it.

A half minute later the flamethrower stuck out of the cockpit and torched the corpse.

"Why didn't they shoot us?" said Courtney, watching the cadaver flaming on the tarmac.

"I don't know. Maybe they think we're not infected because we dragged the infected body into the street."

"Then let's surrender to them," said Courtney, her eyes brightening.

"Or maybe they wanted to take care of the infected body before they killed us."

Courtney pouted. "Let's not surrender."

"Bottom line is we can't trust them."

Phoebe had no idea why the chopper crew hadn't shot them before shooting the corpse. She wasn't going to push her luck by going outside again. She could still see her dad and Meredith being cut to pieces by bullets. She would be seeing their deaths in her dreams for the rest of her life.

"Can we get infected from the stiff's blood?" said Courtney, staring at the bloodstained carpet, careful not to stand on the stains.

Chapter 68

Jason was seething from his conversation with Hardy when he put through a call to Thomas Vitti, the governor of California. The guy had the nerve to quarantine his city without notifying him.

"With all due respect, Mr. Governor, I don't agree with your methods of implementing the quarantine of my city," said Jason.

He could see the fifty-five-year-old Vitti now with his bushy white hair, his Botoxed forehead, his fake tan, and his matinee idol handsome looks.

"If it ain't the old cradle robber himself," said Vitti.

Vitti loved teasing him about his wife, decided Jason.

"My wife is younger than me," he said. "OK. I plead guilty."

"A lot younger than you, huh?" Vitti chuckled. "She could be your granddaughter. Ah, don't get your knickers in a twist. I like 'em young, too. You'll get no argument from me."

"Can we stick to the subject?"

"It was an emergency, Mr. Mayor," said Vitti, becoming serious. "I had no time to inform anyone. I have the power to declare a state of emergency. It needed to be done."

Jason wasn't buying it. "You had time to notify the FBI. They knew about it before me. Why am I last in the loop? *It's my city.*"

"Actually, you have it in reverse. The bureau notified me of the virus and advised me to take protective measures immediately."

Jason gripped his cell phone tighter. "You're mishandling the quarantine."

"What?" said Vitti, not sure he had heard Jason right. "The Strip in your city is on complete lockdown. The virus is contained. Everything is perfect."

"Then why am I hearing reports that people are being shot on the Strip?"

"If the infected attack other people, the state police have orders to shoot the infected to protect healthy citizens."

A neat way to spin it, decided Jason.

"That's not what I'm hearing," he said. "I'm hearing people are being gunned down in the street by your people patrolling the area in helicopters."

210

"You have no idea what you're talking about. You can't conceive how dangerous this virus is."

"Let me understand this, Mr. Governor. You're telling the state police to *kill* everyone who is infected?"

"The infected go berserk and become violent. They kill everyone in sight and eat them."

"Eat them?" said Jason, aghast.

"You heard me."

"Don't you even try to cure them before you kill them?"

"As of this time, we don't have a cure. The virus doesn't even have a name yet. It's like nothing we've ever seen before. It spreads faster than your wife spreads her legs. If we don't contain it in your city, California's doomed, and the entire country's next. It's *that* dangerous."

Jason didn't appreciate the wisecrack about his wife. "Leave Phoebe out of this."

"I meant no disrespect. She's a beautiful woman. But this virus is hellacious."

"So that gives you the authority to gun down my citizens like it's a turkey shoot?"

"We have to do everything we can to stop the spread of the killer virus."

"I'm hearing reports that hundreds of people are being shot. Not only that, state police are incinerating the bodies."

"There's a reason for that, I'm afraid. In this peculiar virus, the infected die and then come back to life. We're burning their bodies to keep them from returning from the dead and spreading their disease. Their flesh must be burned to a crisp, or they will continue to infect others."

"Jesus Christ. And that gives you the right to kill all of my city's citizens?"

"What's one city compared to the thousands of cities in this great country? Are you so selfish that you don't want to save America? God bless America."

I get it, thought Jason. *You're running for president already. Never let a crisis go to waste.*

"You're using the crisis to launch your run for president," he said. "Is that it?"

"What kind of a disgraceful remark is that? How dare you? I'm trying to save this great country, and this is the thanks I get?"

211

"Wait till the press gets wind of this."

Vitti sucked in his breath noisily. "What I just told you doesn't leave your office."

"The people of my fair city have the right to know you're ordering the state police to execute them."

"I'm the one *saving* your city," said Vitti, exasperated. "You should be thanking me."

"You're a mass murderer, and you want my thanks? You must be as nuts as the infected."

"When the people know the truth, they'll agree that I'm doing the right thing," said Vitti, regaining his composure.

"*You're* the one who's infected. You're berserk."

"Is that your way of saying you're handing me your resignation?" said Vitti in a stern voice.

Jason's blood boiled. "I'm not handing you squat. The people of my city elected me. I don't work for you."

"You might want to reconsider."

"What are you talking about?"

"I've heard rumors from the CDC investigators at the scene of zone zero who are tracking the source of the outbreak."

"What rumors?"

"Nothing definite yet, but nobody in your city is allowed to leave the city limits. That includes you."

"This is outrageous. I'm the mayor. You can't order me around."

"Nobody is above the law. I've declared a state of emergency. Nobody is to leave your city until the virus has been eradicated. *Nobody* means nobody."

"Are you afraid I'll run against you in the next election? Is that it?"

"Tread carefully, Mr. Mayor. I have resources. You don't want to tangle with me."

Vitti hung up.

Chapter 69

Jason chafed at the bit. The problem was Vitti was right. He *did* have the right to declare a state of emergency and lock down the entire town of Costaguana.

Jason felt like he was being squeezed not only by Hardy but by Vitti as well. Vitti had taken over his town and locked him inside it, and Hardy was threatening to kidnap his wife—if he hadn't already.

There was one good thing about the quarantine, decided Jason. He could blame the whole thing on Vitti, who outranked him. Jason could wash his hands of the debacle.

He hoped the lockdown would come back to haunt Vitti. He wondered if there was a way he could accelerate Vitti's downfall.

Was that Vitti's plan—to lock Jason in Costaguana in hopes Jason would become infected? Jason wouldn't put anything past the duplicitous governor. Everything the guy said was a lie calculated to advance his political career.

Maybe there really wasn't a virus epidemic, decided Jason. Maybe the whole thing was a scam to sling mud on his reputation and prevent him from challenging the governor for another term. A mayor with a quarantine in their city was bad optics. Infected people running around berserk and killing everyone in sight ruined a city's image. Who would want to live in a city rife with infected citizens? Who would want to vote for the mayor of said city?

Jason had to get the quarantine lifted off Costaguana as soon as possible. But he had to locate his wife even sooner to prevent Hardy from kidnaping her.

How was he supposed to find her if she never answered her phone? Jason wondered.

The phone on his desk rang, interrupting his thoughts.

"Yes," said Jason through the speakerphone.

"Sir," said his secretary, "I just got a call from a concerned citizen who is worried about your wife Phoebe."

Jason locked his gaze on the phone, his heartbeat accelerating. "Why is he worried, Yvette?"

213

"It's a she. She says Meredith told her she was going to the Strip with Phoebe today."

"What?" said Jason, taken aback.

"She's worried because they never returned. Meredith is a veterinarian, and she didn't show up at her medical office today. She didn't call in sick, and nobody knows what happened to her."

What was Phoebe doing on the Strip? wondered Jason. It was the last place she would visit. And Val. Val on the Strip too.

He felt his knees going weak. Could Phoebe possibly know about his seeing Val? He didn't see how Phoebe could have found out about her. Phoebe and Val were both quarantined. Could Hardy have contacted Phoebe already and told her about the photos of Jason with Val on Jones's cell phone? But how could Hardy contact her while the state police were jamming everybody's cell phone on the Strip?

It was bad no matter how Jason looked at it.

His knees continued to wobble.

He tried to find a bright side. If Phoebe *was* on the Strip, it meant Hardy didn't have her, Jason decided. On the other hand, it meant she could be infected with the killer virus. She might even have been shot dead by the state police who were killing the infected.

The tension bottled up inside him was too much. He screamed and slammed his fist against his desktop, sending pencil holders and papers flying. His Styrofoam cup full of coffee with cream and sugar fell over and spilled onto his desk blotter.

His secretary rang his office.

"Mr. Mayor, are you all right?" she said, her voice fraught with concern.

I'm fucked is what I am. My career and my marriage are falling apart. My life's in a tailspin.

"I spilled my coffee, is all," he said.

His cell phone chimed.

"Hello," he snapped into it.

"It's me," said Muldoon. "Lift this goddamn quarantine, or I'm not gonna contribute another dime to your reelection campaign."

"It's the governor's quarantine. My hands are tied."

"Are you so afraid of him that you won't stand up for your own city?"

"Afraid?" said Jason, fit to be tied. "Who's afraid?"

214

"You are. You're afraid to tell the governor to take his dirty paws off your city."

"I told him. But he's the governor. He declared a state of emergency, which gives him the power to lock down any place in California, no questions asked."

"My business is going to pot without any customers. *Your* people are shooting them in the street. There are stiffs all over the place."

What if one of those stiffs is Phoebe? Could they have shot her?

"They're not *my* people," said Jason. "They're the governor's."

"Are you scared?" said Muldoon with a needling laugh.

"If you're so brave, you talk to him," said Jason, raising his voice, his face flushing.

"Tell him he's not gonna get another penny from me for his goddamn campaign. You know as well as me he wants my money so bad he'd get down on his hands and knees and give me a blowjob for it."

"You tell him. I'm not your messenger boy."

Jason terminated the call, livid. The idea of a corrupt casino boss telling him what to do galled him.

His cell phone chimed again.

He didn't answer it.

Muldoon could rot in hell for all he cared.

Chapter 70

In his Honda Hardy studied the pictures of Jason with the hooker on Jones's phone and decided it would be a good idea to pay Val a visit on the Strip.

Hardy could use her as leverage against Jason to increase the amount of the blackmail payment he sought from Jason. Photos were incriminating, but Jason could claim they had been doctored. Actual testimony from the hooker would seal the deal, forcing Jason to pony up.

Hardy put down Jones's phone and drove to the Strip.

He was puzzled by the numerous helicopters flying over the area. Something was up, he decided. Then he saw the roadblock up ahead. California state police had blocked the street with their patrol cars.

The quarantine, he decided, recalling his conversation with Jason, who had said something about an outbreak of a virus on the Strip.

Hardy took a detour, having no desire to meet up with cops. He had paid numerous visits to the Strip and knew of alternate ways to enter it. He also knew the hotels where most of the hookers stayed.

Hookers had no moral qualms, he decided. They cared only about money. It should be easy to enlist Val's aid in his blackmail scheme.

He tooled down the side streets until he found a place to park.

He got out of his car and looked up at the crowded sky.

It must have been a serious outbreak to attract so many helos, he decided. And it was the state cops, not the local ones, blocking the entrance.

Dressed in a navy blue suit, Hardy set out for the main drag of the Strip. He passed a strip mall and spotted cruisers blocking the road that intersected the Strip.

He was glad he had parked his car. He wasn't going to be able to access the Strip in it. The state troopers looked like they meant business. They weren't letting any cars in or out of the cordoned-off area. He doubted they would let a pedestrian pass.

He turned left and walked another block.

Having spent a lot of time on the Strip to enjoy the fruits of his labors, he was familiar with the area. He knew there was a cul-de-sac on the upcoming block. He hung a right and walked down it.

There were small stucco bungalows with red-tiled roofs on this block. At the end of the cul-de-sac was a grey-painted cinder-block noise barrier that kept out sound from the raucous nightclubs and casino on the other side of it. The foot-wide barrier stood over ten feet tall preventing people from looking over it into the neighborhood.

He walked all the way to the noise barrier and circumvented it. On the other side of it was a narrow alley barely wide enough to accommodate pedestrians. Drunks used the alley to piss on the noise barrier when they exited the nightclubs.

He didn't see any cops. They must not have known about the alley. Which wasn't a surprise. Few people did.

Wincing at the reek of stale urine in the area, he entered the alley and made his way to the Strip, which was unusually quiet thanks to the cops shutting it down. The only sound he heard was the ruckus of the choppers hovering overhead.

At the mouth of the cul-de-sac he slowed down and scoped out the area, getting his bearings.

He was surprised to see the charred remains of a fire-gutted car in the middle of the street. The car could have been a Mustang, but he wasn't sure on account of its extensive fire damage. Scattered around the car were heaps of ashes. He could make out human skeletons lying in the heaps.

There were more ashes and skeletons lying in front of the Lavender Whip entrance. To his right he saw the smoking remains of a man. The stiff was sprawled in front of the hotel that most of the hookers called home, which was where he was headed.

He tried to figure out what was going on. Why were there burned bodies everywhere? It must have had something to do with the outbreak.

Hardy looked up at the choppers. Could the choppers have burned the corpses? A crewman with a flamethrower could reach all of the corpses from a chopper. But why would the choppers burn the corpses? Who had killed the victims in the first place? Or had the victims died by fire?

Out of the corner of his eye he picked up on two middle-aged men and a young woman bolt out of a building and charge into the street, foaming at the mouth, gesticulating wildly, their eyes popping out of their heads that they were shaking back and forth. Hardy had never seen anyone run so fast. He wondered if they were high on crystal meth.

A crewman in one of the choppers opened fire on the three crazed rioters, cutting them down with a long burst from his AR-15.

Hardy watched in awe. The shooters were in the choppers. It was the cops shooting everybody.

Hardy shook his head, trying to figure out what was happening. Why were the cops shooting people? Because they were rioting? Had riots broken out because of the virus? To hell with it, he decided. He had a job to do.

He came here to see Val. Now that the killer choppers were distracted, it was a good time to make a break for the hotel, Hardy decided.

He sprinted toward the hotel, glancing overhead to make sure the choppers hadn't opened fire on him. He pumped his legs furiously, breaking into a sweat. He had no idea why the cops had shot those three rioters in cold blood, but he was a witness and could testify to the fact.

Breathing heavily, he realized he was almost at the hotel entrance. He spotted one of the choppers flying toward him. Adrenaline shot through his body. He had to reach cover inside the hotel. The crewman would fire a burst any minute now and take him out.

The chopper moved in for the kill.

Hardy wished he had worn his sneakers. Instead, he was wearing patent leather shoes to go with his suit. His feet were killing him. He hoped he didn't slide on the shoes' leather soles and break his neck.

He heard gunfire erupt.

He dove through the shattered plate-glass door of the hotel. Parabellum bullets tore into the doorjamb, sparking off the steel frame and ricocheting either into the hotel lobby or out onto the street.

He wondered if he had been hit. He couldn't tell. He couldn't feel anything while on his adrenaline high.

Another burst of slugs flew through the door.

218

Hardy tumbled onto the floor and ducked away from the door. He saw two women gaping at him. One of them clutched a bloody ice pick or letter opener in her hand and looked like she was getting ready to pounce on him.

She had legs up to her neck and wore black fishnet stockings.

Gasping for breath, kneeling on the floor, Hardy blinked his eyes several times to make sure he wasn't dreaming. Standing beside the woman was the mayor's wife Phoebe. He couldn't believe his luck.

Once in a blue moon he got lucky. He guessed there must be a blue moon in the sky above all those choppers. This couldn't have worked out better if he had planned it. She was just the woman he wanted to see. Val could wait, he decided. Wherever she was. He didn't need her anymore.

He got to his feet and brushed glass shards off his trousers. He had torn a sleeve on his jacket as he had dived through the broken door, he noticed with disapproval.

"Don't move or I'll kill you," said Courtney.

Chapter 71

The woman looked like she meant it, decided Hardy. She had a wild look in her eyes.

"Are you infected?" she said.

"Infected?" he said, bemused.

"Do you have the virus? Answer me," she said, brandishing the bloody letter opener in front of her.

"I don't have any virus. Put that thing down before you hurt someone," he said, gazing at the letter opener.

"If you're not infected, why did the choppers shoot at you?"

"I have no idea why they shot at me. What the hell is going on here?"

"Don't you know?" said Phoebe.

Hardy shook his head no. "Why are all those choppers in the sky?"

"This is a quarantine zone."

"I just got here, so I'm not infected. What about you two?" he said, eying them with suspicion.

"We're not infected. If we were, you would know."

"How would I know?" he said, screwing up his face.

"The infected go berserk, attack people, and eat them."

Hardy widened his eyes. "Are we talking fucking cannibals?"

"Zombies. They rise from the dead after they die."

Maybe his luck wasn't so great, after all, decided Hardy. Getting stuck in a quarantine zone for a killer virus that turned its victims into zombies was luck he could do without.

"Why don't you tell the cops you're not infected so they'll let you go?" he said.

"My father tried to talk to them, and they shot him," said Phoebe, face glum.

"Did he tell them he wasn't infected?" said Hardy, baffled.

"Yeah."

"I guess they didn't believe him," said Hardy as if to himself.

"They shoot everyone who walks onto the street," said Courtney.

"Let me get this straight. They're *shooting* the infected?"

"Right. Then they burn their corpses."

"That explains those piles of ashes I saw out there. They must assume everyone in this area is infected."

"How do we know you're not infected?" said Courtney, glaring at him.

"I just got here." Hardy glanced at the bloody letter opener. "Who did you kill?"

"One of the infected attacked us." Courtney looked at the open elevator door. "He came from upstairs."

"We think everyone from upstairs could be infected," said Phoebe.

Hardy eyeballed the planter that was preventing the elevator door from closing. "How can you be sure?"

"We can't. But the guy who attacked us definitely was. He was foaming at the mouth and charged us with a crazed look in his eyes."

"We're not taking any chances by letting any more people from upstairs down here," said Phoebe.

"We shouldn't even let *you* here," Courtney told Hardy.

"Who are you, anyway?" said Phoebe.

"The name's Hardy. Who are you?"

"I'm Phoebe, and this is Courtney."

"Look, I want to get out of here as much as you do. Let's pool forces."

"Why did you come here?" said Courtney.

"Business."

Hardy wondered if Courtney knew Phoebe was the mayor's husband. Courtney had to be a hooker who worked the Strip like Val Lewton. Maybe they knew each other.

"What kind of business?" said Courtney.

"I'm looking for someone. Maybe you know her. Val Lewton." Nonplussed, Phoebe stared at him.

"Why do you want her?" said Courtney.

"I'm not at liberty to say," said Hardy.

"Are you a cop?"

"No. I'm a fixer. I fix people's credit."

"My credit sucks."

"You're in the same boat as a lot of other people. Not a problem. Times are tough. Do you know where I can find Val?"

"They took her away."

221

"Who did?"

"The guys in the choppers. Cops or whatever they are."

"Do you know why?"

Courtney hiked her eyebrows. "No idea."

"They trapped her in a steel net like a wild animal," said Phoebe.

"You said they shot a lot of people," said Hardy. "Why didn't they shoot *her*?"

"We can't figure it out."

Hardy produced his cell phone.

"Forget it," said Phoebe, watching him.

"What do you mean?"

"The cell phones don't work here. It must have something to do with the quarantine."

A monkey wrench in his plans, decided Hardy. He was going to hold Phoebe hostage and demand a ransom from Jason. No dice. He had no way to notify Jason that he was holding Phoebe hostage.

Chapter 72

Jason entered the medical biolab, which looked more like a prison. He was wearing a white hazmat uniform like everyone else. The entire biolab was painted white and was scrubbed so clean it sparkled as did the stainless steel chairs and desks it accommodated.

He was standing with a man and a woman gazing through a bulletproof Plexiglas window into what looked like a jail cell.

Hanging by her arms suspended by chains from the ceiling, a twentyish woman with disheveled blonde hair writhed in her manacles growling and frothing at the mouth. Blood trickled out of her ears. She was the only one not wearing a Hazmat uniform.

"What do you want to see me about, Mr. Mayor?" said the middle-aged man with thick black-framed glasses who turned to peer at him with deep-set brown eyes from behind a Plexiglas face mask.

Vincent Zandorf, a CDC pathologist, had a thinning-out widow's peak that reminded Jason of nothing so much as an aging Eddie Munster's hairline.

"I can't believe you're conducting experiments without asking for my approval," said Jason, hot under the collar.

It wasn't just the uncomfortable hazmat uniform that was burning him up. He was angry at being omitted from the power loop. Instead of asking for his approval, the CDC had gone to the governor to obtain approval for the quarantine.

"I work for the CDC," said Zandorf. "Which, as you no doubt know, is a federal department. We don't need his or your approval to conduct experiments in pathology."

"What about the quarantine on the Strip? I never authorized it."

"We needed the governor's approval to use the state police to enforce the quarantine."

"The local police are there as well, as I understand it."

"The sheriff was good enough to volunteer his forces to help us enforce the quarantine."

"Enforce? Is that your euphemism for committing murder? I've heard reports of cops in choppers shooting people in cold blood on the Strip," said Jason, outraged.

"We're dealing with a highly contagious virus that has a kill ratio of a hundred percent. Need I say more?"

"And that gives you the right to murder the infected?"

Zandorf looked glum. "We have no choice. The virus must be stopped. It spreads exponentially. It turns its victims into insane cannibals—"

"Insane cannibals?" said Jason, not believing his ears.

"That's not all," said Zandorf, holding up his hand. "After they die, they return to life and feed on living humans."

"Oh, sure," scoffed Jason. "You're talking zombies? Yeah, right."

"It's true, I'm afraid, Mr. Mayor."

"Can't you treat the victims with penicillin or something? I don't know. I'm not a doctor."

"There is no cure. The victims must be terminated and incinerated. They cannot be allowed to leave this city. Otherwise . . . ," said Zandorf, trailing off.

"Otherwise what?"

"Otherwise this entire country will be infected in a week."

"Jesus."

"I know."

"What about the president? Has he authorized you to murder the infected victims?"

"He has. And so has Governor Vitti. They both know the future of humanity is at stake."

Jason struggled to wrap his head around the enormity of the outbreak.

"Couldn't you at least have told me what you're doing?" he said. "I had to find out by myself, and it wasn't easy. I had to call in a lot of favors. Getting info about this was like getting a worker paid by the hour to work faster."

"The president told me to notify only Governor Vitti. As you can understand, the president wants to limit the number of people who know about this virus. The fewer people that know, the less chance of a leak. He doesn't want to spread panic among the populace. Nobody must know, and that includes the media— especially the media."

"I can see why you want to keep a lid on it. But couldn't you have told me? I'm the mayor of Costaguana. This is *my* city."

"I was following the president's orders." Zandorf stared hard at Jason. "Now that you know, you must promise not to tell another living soul."

"Or what?"

"I have orders to lock you in solitary confinement at 5880 CO-67 if you refuse to comply."

"Where's that?" said Jason, bemused.

"ADX in Florence, Colorado."

"*ADX*? That's a maximum security prison for the most hardened criminals. What the hell?"

"I can't impress enough on you how serious this outbreak is."

"This is insane."

His expression earnest, Zandorf gripped Jason's arm. "Do you agree to keep silent about the outbreak?"

Jason stared at him, thunderstruck.

"I didn't hear you," said Zandorf.

"I won't tell anyone. But I demand to know what's going on here," said Jason, attempting to reassert his authority as mayor. "I want to be apprised of everything you do."

"With all due respect, Mr. Mayor, you're stepping over the line. The control of the outbreak is not in your purview."

Jason had no desire to end up rotting away in ADX. He backed off.

"Can you at least tell me why you're hanging this poor woman from chains?" he said in an authoritative voice, intent on avoiding a tone of submission.

"We're treating her for the virus. Well—let me correct that— we can't treat her. There's no cure. We're studying her."

"I don't understand what the chains are for. It looks like torture."

Val commenced thrusting her legs like she was running in place.

"The infected have high metabolisms," said Zandorf. "They're literally burning out. We need to keep her in chains so she won't hurt anyone, including herself, and at the same time to allow her to burn off energy. The infected never rest. They have to be constantly in motion. Hanging her in the air allows her to burn off energy."

"Why is she squirming and running?"

"It's the virus," said Zandorf, gazing at Val. "It attacks the brain. She's in agony."

"Is that why she's grimacing all the time?" said Jason.

For some reason, she reminded him of someone. How could she? She looked like a filthy wino ravaged by DTs. He didn't know any bums.

"Yes," said Zandorf. "The virus causes extreme agony." He turned to face Jason. "Do you know how ants burrow into the ground and create tunnels?"

"Sure. Like rabbits."

"Exactly. That is how the virus attacks the human brain. It eats through the brain tissue, boring tunnels into the victim's brain. To use your analogy, the infected brain looks like a rabbit warren."

Jason grimaced at the image. "The pain must be unbearable."

"The reason she's contorting her face in agony," said Zandorf, his face grim.

"It reminds me of an earwig. You know, how they're supposed to enter your ear and eat through your brain."

"That's a myth. This virus isn't a myth, I'm afraid."

"How can you do tests on her if she's constantly in motion?"

"It's not easy."

"What exactly are you trying to find out?"

"We're trying to discover patient zero. We have reason to believe it's her."

"Patient zero?" said Jason, studying the woman more closely.

"The first carrier of a communicable disease. The one who started the outbreak."

Jason's eyes widened as he gazed at the woman. He did a double take.

He recognized her even in her manic, disheveled state.

It was Val.

Chapter 73

Jason gaped at her as if in a trance.

"Are you all right, Mr. Mayor?" said Zandorf.

"Uh—uh—yes. She's the one who infected everyone?" said Jason, barely able to speak through his tight throat.

This can't be happening.

"We believe so, but our investigation is not conclusive, which is why we're continuing to subject her to tests."

And I had sex with her. Does that mean I'm infected?

Alarm bells blared in his head, deafening him.

"She's contagious?" he managed to utter.

"Of that much we are sure. However, we're not a hundred percent sure she is patient zero. Another person might have infected her. Our tests are not conclusive. There could be another carrier out there we haven't found yet."

"How long does it take for symptoms of the disease to appear?"

"As far as we can ascertain, the symptoms appear immediately. The disease is in full swing as soon as it's transmitted. The victim's metabolism ramps up. They have superhuman speed. They froth at the mouth and go berserk. They become homicidal and crave living human flesh."

Maybe he was OK, decided Jason, sweating. Maybe Val hadn't infected him. Maybe she had become infected after they had had sex and therefore couldn't have infected him. Maybe he could relax. Too many maybes. His rapid heartbeat continued.

"There are no exceptions to that?" he said, hanging on Zandorf's every word.

"Not as far as we know." Zandorf shrugged. "But this is a new virus, and we can't be certain."

"Has V—, I mean, has she risen from the dead?"

"V?" said Zandorf, cocking a grizzled eyebrow. "You said V."

"Uh—uh—I was gonna say *victim.*"

Zandorf shook his head no. "She hasn't risen from the dead. Otherwise, we would've had to incinerate her. *Exterminate and incinerate.* That's how we control this nightmare virus."

227

"She's the one who infected everyone?"

"Well, not everyone per se. She infects someone, and that victim infects someone else and so on, you see. Are you feeling all right? You don't look well."

"I'm all right. It's this hazmat uniform. It's like being locked in a steam bath. I feel lightheaded."

Zandorf nodded. "It takes time to get used to them." He paused in thought. "Of course, we don't know for sure that the symptoms appear immediately. We believe that's the case. On the other hand, maybe it's different for each victim. You look white as a sheet."

Jason leaned against the nearest wall to prevent himself from collapsing.

"It's hard to breathe in these contraptions," he said, his face haggard.

"Been there," said Zandorf, nodding. "It took me a full week to get used to it."

"Can this virus be transmitted sexually?"

"It's highly infectious. To answer your question, yes. That's one of the ways it can be transmitted. Why do you ask?"

"No particular reason."

His knees feeling like jelly, Jason slid down the wall.

"Maybe you should leave," said Zandorf, watching him with concern. "I don't want you to pass out in that uniform."

Jason nodded.

Zandorf helped him to his feet.

"Can I talk to the patient?" asked Jason, watching Val writhe in torment in her chains.

"Her brain is scrambled. She can make only unintelligible sounds like growls and screams. We tried talking to her. She couldn't understand a word we were saying."

Then she probably hadn't recognize him, decided Jason, heaving a sigh of relief. And even if she had, she couldn't tell anyone about it. At least, nobody could connect a hooker to him and trash his career. That was one consolation.

On the other hand, he wished he could communicate with her. He wanted to know if she was infected when they had had sex. The only one who would know for sure was her. And she was a raving lunatic with her mind eaten away by a killer virus.

How could he tell if he was infected? he wondered.

"Is there a vaccine for this virus?" he said.

"No vaccine. No cure. Nada."

Jason tried to swallow, but his mouth was dry.

He couldn't have been infected, he decided. He would have shown symptoms by now. But he wasn't convinced.

"How can you tell if you're infected?" he said.

"We don't know. We haven't been able to get answers from any of the infected because they're not capable of answering. As soon as they become infected, the virus eats their brains, rendering them incapable of understanding the simplest question."

Jason unleashed a brief smile. It was all but undetectable.

"I can understand you fine," he said.

"What?" said Zandorf, puzzled by Jason's response.

"Nothing."

Jason had used a rubber when he was with Val. Maybe it had prevented him from becoming infected by her—if she *was* infected at the time. He didn't want to think about it. His mind would never shut down if he continued thinking about it.

"I hope you have the virus under control on the Strip," he said.

"We believe we've contained it so far. But new infections keep popping up. At some point we're going to have to go door to door to inspect everyone in the area. So far, we have been eliminating only the infected who exit the buildings."

"When you say 'inspect' everyone, does that mean 'shoot' everyone?"

Zandorf didn't answer.

A chill went down Jason's spine.

They were going to eliminate and incinerate everyone on the Strip, he decided. Zandorf's response was clear even though he had not voiced it.

Dear God. Phoebe's on the Strip.

Chapter 74

Phoebe was watching Hardy with suspicion. She didn't trust him. Even though he looked like an accountant and wore a suit with Italian shoes, he bothered her for some reason.

Why was he here? she wondered. Couldn't he tell from all the squad cars blocking the streets that the Strip was quarantined?

"I don't understand why you're here," she said.

"I told you I have business with Val Lewton."

"Why would you want to enter a quarantine zone? Didn't you see the black-and-whites blocking the main road?"

"It's important business. I'm not gonna a let a couple of black-and-whites deter me."

"What about the choppers? Didn't you see them shooting people?"

"Actually, no," said Hardy. "I never heard of a quarantine where they shoot everybody in the area. I couldn't believe it when they tried to waste me."

"You're willing to risk your life for your job?" said Phoebe in disbelief.

"Call me dedicated," he deadpanned.

"I call you crazy," said Courtney, waving the letter opener in front of her like it was a weapon.

Phoebe turned to Courtney. "I don't trust him."

"I don't either," said Courtney.

"It's immaterial to me," said Hardy, looking bored.

"Aren't you worried about getting infected?" said Phoebe.

"What kind of a disease are we talking about? If this is Covid, I got all my shots and boosters, so I'm not worried."

"Nobody has told us anything. We're cut off. Our phones don't work. We have no way to contact anybody. We're in the dark as much as you are."

"You can't get through the day worrying about every little thing. Why worry about things you don't know?"

"Because if you go outside, they're gonna shoot you dead," said Courtney. "We know that much."

"Well, the choppers had their chance, and they missed me."

"You sound like you're crazy. You must be infected."

"You're the one wielding a bloody letter opener. You whacked someone, didn't you?"

"He was infected and tried to kill us."

"I suggest you put that down. You're making me nervous."

He didn't look nervous, decided Phoebe. He had a cool attitude about him that didn't jibe with the unfolding cataclysm.

"I'm not putting anything down," said Courtney, brandishing the letter opener in front of her, "until I'm sure you're not infected."

"Oh yeah? I think you're about to change your mind," said Hardy, whipping out a Beretta 92 Compact from his shoulder rig concealed inside his jacket and training the muzzle on Courtney.

Which confirmed Phoebe's suspicions of Hardy. The guy was bad news.

Courtney started at the sight of the pistol.

"Drop it," said Hardy.

Courtney dropped the letter opener. "Are you one of the executioners?"

"Huh?"

"You're a spy from one of the choppers, is that it?"

"Are you kidding? They tried to blow me away."

"Maybe they shot at you to make us think you're not one of them."

"Really? And what's my mission since you know so much? Why did they send me to infiltrate your little group of two?"

"How should I know?" said Courtney, throwing up her hands. "Why are they shooting everybody in sight? Is killing people their idea of curing them?"

"So you think they sent *me* here to kill you?" said Hardy with undisguised amusement.

"Why else would you be pointing a gun at us?"

"I'm holding this piece in self-defense. You're the one who had a bloody letter opener in your hand. You were getting ready to attack me."

"She can't harm you now," chimed in Phoebe. "She dropped the letter opener. You don't need to keep pointing that gun at us."

"Is that right?"

"There's no need for the gun," said Phoebe, her gaze locked on the Beretta.

231

"How do I know you two aren't infected, Phoebe Albright?"

Phoebe's face turned pale.

Chapter 75

How could he know her name? Phoebe wondered, her mind in turmoil.

Courtney looked at her. "Do you know this guy?"

"I never saw him before in my life."

"Everybody knows her," said Hardy. "She's the mayor's wife."

"What?" said Courtney in astonishment.

"Don't tell me you didn't recognize her."

"How would I recognize her? I never seen her before."

"Don't you read the papers?"

Courtney pshawed. "Fake news. I don't go near that stuff."

"She and her husband are in the papers quite a bit. You know, the social pages."

"You're the mayor's wife, huh?" said Courtney, facing Phoebe. "You look awfully young to be his wife. Isn't he an old guy?"

Phoebe didn't like the idea of being seen on the Strip. It would sully her and Jason's reputations. Jason's career would crash and burn if it got out that his wife was seen in the city's red-light district. She decided to deny it. Probably a mistake since virtually all of her decisions were mistakes.

"He's mistaken," she said.

"Nice try," said Hardy. "I happen to know your husband Jason quite well."

Phoebe felt her pulse accelerate. Was this guy for real? How could he know Jason?

"I doubt it," she said.

"I do odd jobs for him, actually."

Phoebe didn't like the sound of that. *Odd jobs*? What the hell did that mean? she wondered. This guy was creeping her out.

"Good for you," she said. "I guess you're connected."

"Yeah, that's me. I know all the right people, the people with money, that is. And they like parting with a great deal of it when they hire me."

"You must be very much in demand."

"That's right. I'm a nobody, and nobody's ever heard of me. But I make a fortune at my job."

"That doesn't change the fact that I don't know the mayor," said Phoebe, tired of Hardy's bragging.

Hardy searched her face. "True, you don't know him even though you're his wife. He's good at keeping secrets from you."

"What?" she said, bowled over.

Hardy snickered. "Secrets. You've heard of the term *secrets*, haven't you?"

How much did Hardy really know about Jason? she wondered. Or was this a sick cat-and-mouse game he was playing with her?

How could he know Jason was seeing a hooker on the sly? Or had Jason told him about it? But why would Jason tell Hardy something personal like that? In any case, Hardy must think she didn't know about Val. Jason obviously thought she didn't.

"I don't know what you're talking about," she said.

Hardy frowned in thought. "The problem is if you don't know about your husband's secret life, why are you here on the Strip?"

This guy knew too much, she decided, getting edgy. "I go wherever I want."

"What's going on here?" said Courtney, cutting her eyes back and forth between Hardy and Phoebe. "Am I missing something?"

"Unless you found out about Jason's secret life somehow," Hardy told Phoebe. "That's the only reason I can think you'd be here. These people on the Strip ain't your kind of people."

"Too good for us?" said Courtney, eying Phoebe.

"He doesn't know what he's talking about. I'm not the mayor's wife."

"Deny it till your blue in the face," said Hardy. "I *know* who you are. Your husband's a piece of work, you know it?"

"*My* husband is a nice man."

"He's a control freak. He's trying to control *me*. I need to teach him a lesson. Now that I have you with me I can do just that."

"We need to get out of here before they kill us," she blurted. "They're killing *everyone*. We don't have time for your stupid games."

"She's right," said Courtney. "It's only a matter of time before those choppers land, and their crews go door to door shooting everybody."

Hardy looked out the front door with concern, listening to the nerve-grating whump-whump of the choppers flocking together overhead.

234

"What kind of cops would whack out innocent people?" he said.

Phoebe shook her head, irked at his refusal to believe what was happening.

"Why can't we leave the same way you entered?" she asked Hardy.

"Because they would shoot us as soon as we walked onto the street," said Courtney.

"It's true I *do* know a way out of here," said Hardy, gloating. "So you two better be nice to me."

"They'll cut us down on the street. Haven't you been listening? Unless—"

"Unless what?"

"Unless you're one of them working undercover. How could you have gotten past them to get into the hotel?"

"Have it your way," said Hardy with amusement, training his Beretta at her. "I'm one of them, and I'm gonna whack out both of you."

"Fuck you."

He squeezed the trigger.

Courtney screamed.

Chapter 76

Jason returned to his office, beset by problems. Phoebe must be quarantined on the Strip. How could he help her? The state cops weren't allowing anybody into the area. How did he know she wasn't already infected with the killer virus?

If that wasn't enough, he had to deal with Hardy. Had the idiot gotten rid of Jones, or was Jones still a threat because of the pictures on his cell phone? Knowing Jason was desperate, Hardy might pull a fast one. Hardy was clever in an underhanded way. How could you trust such a guy? And the bastard had seen Jones's photos of Jason with Val.

Standing near his desk Jason whipped his cell phone out of his trouser pocket and called Hardy. Jason needed proof Hardy had removed Jones. Where was Jones's thumb? The call went to voicemail.

Grinding his teeth Jason called Phoebe. Voicemail.

Why wasn't anybody answering? he wondered. He tossed his cell onto the desktop in exasperation. He rubbed his forehead. He felt a cluster headache coming on. The overhead light was blinding him. He needed to sit down.

He plunked down on the leather-upholstered sofa alongside the wall and lay on his back. The light continued to blind him. Covering his eyes with his hand, he shot to his feet, strode to the wall, and killed the light with the light switch.

He returned to the sofa and lay down.

The pain was insupportable.

It felt like a needle was burrowing into his ears and piercing his brain. Not a needle. An earwig eating through his ear into his brain, carving tunnels in it.

The virus, he thought with a start. Was he infected?

He had had sex with Val. Zandorf claimed Val was patient zero.

Had Val infected him? Jason wondered, his pulse running amok. Would he start screaming and writhing in agony like Val?

His face broke into a sweat. He wanted to scream on account of the pain in his head. He couldn't be infected. He had used a rubber.

But maybe the virus was passed in a way other than sexual transmission. In which case it might be eating through his brain even now.

Or was he suffering from a killer headache brought on by all of his problems? he wondered. The president and Vitti had quarantined the Strip. What if they quarantined the entire city of Costaguana? *His* city. They were destroying his city without even consulting him. Declaring a state of emergency the governor had the power to do anything he wanted, including destroying Jason's city. Was the bastard worried Jason might challenge him in the next gubernatorial election? Why else take such drastic measures like closing the Strip?

Jason writhed on the sofa, his face dripping with sweat. Was the virus boring holes in his brain? No. It couldn't be. It must be a headache. A stress headache. Things were happening to him beyond his control. He felt helpless. That was why his head was throbbing in agony.

Or was the virus driving him insane as it turned his brain into Swiss cheese?

He opened his mouth, gasping for breath.

What did it feel like to go mad? he wondered. Or were you even aware of it?

Pain could drive you mad, he decided. Your brain feeling like a colony of fire ants was tunneling through it could make you want to commit suicide.

He had to stop thinking about it. Too much thinking could drive you over the edge. Thinking. Thinking. Drilling. Drilling. Pain. *Pain.*

He felt like gouging out his eyeballs. Anything to stop the agony. Anything to stop the earwig from drilling through his brain tissue.

He ordered himself to stop thinking about it. He needed to make his mind go blank.

A bullet to his brain could succeed at that.

Stop thinking. Stop.

Concentrate on blackness. Nothingness. The brain fire would die out. It would. His crazed thoughts were fanning the flames. Stop the thoughts, stop the fire.

Stop.

Why did he have to go to Val in the first place? he asked himself. He already had a beautiful wife. Because he wanted to know what Val felt like. Women all felt different. Val got him hot with her long muscular white legs.

If he hadn't gone to her, he wouldn't have gotten infected. Or *was* he infected?

He didn't feel blood seeping out of his ears. If a virus was eating through his brain, wouldn't blood be streaming from his ear canals? Val's ears had been bleeding as she hung writhing from her chains bolted to the ceiling.

On a sudden impulse he felt his ear canals. He relaxed after a fashion when he didn't feel any fluid oozing from them.

Still, his headache was killing him.

Rest helped with a headache. If he could only get some rest.

Was something falling out of his ear canal? he wondered with apprehension. He jackknifed upward on the sofa. A damn earwig? It couldn't be. It had to be wax if anything. Cerumen. Nothing to panic about. He felt his ear canal again. Nothing.

Relieved, he lay down on his back in the darkened room. The curtains were drawn shut so the bright sun wouldn't exacerbate his headache. All he had to do was relax.

While the virus dug a rabbit warren in his brain.

Chapter 77

Phoebe thought she was going to die when she saw Hardy fire his pistol at Courtney. Being cooped up with Courtney, Phoebe had grown fond of Courtney. They were both stuck in this mess together.

The bullet whistled past Courtney's ear.

Courtney shivered in terror.

"Don't give me any lip," said Hardy. "I don't need you around."

Shaking, Courtney nodded, trying to gather herself.

"Is that why you want Val?" said Phoebe, every nerve in her body tense. "To kill her?"

Hardy nodded with admiration. "You're putting two and two together. I'm impressed. But the answer's no. Jason didn't hire me to remove her."

"Then why'd you bring the gun?"

"It goes with the territory. I have a dangerous job."

"Hit man."

"Fixer," he corrected her.

"You smell like a cop to me," said Courtney, recovering from her trauma of being shot at.

"I detect from your tone that you don't dig cops."

"Those guys in the choppers killing everyone are cops."

"I don't plan on dying here," said Hardy, fingering his Beretta.

"If we stay here, we're dead," said Phoebe. "If you know a way out, we need to take it now."

"How do you propose we do that with those choppers firing at us?" said Hardy, approaching the front door and peering out at the deserted street, gun in hand.

"You're the fixer. You must know the answer."

"I can't go up against the entire police force. If this is a quarantine, I bet the feds are outside too."

"If only there was some way we could convince them we're not infected," said Courtney.

"The way they're shooting everyone, they must be operating under the assumption that everyone on the Strip is infected," said Phoebe.

"Then we're screwed."

Hardy gazed down the street at the Ferrari parked in front of the Lavender Whip.

"Whose Ferrari is that?" he said.

"Rick Muldoon," said Courtney. "He owns the Whip."

Hardy thought about it. "It's too far away. Even if we reached the car, the roads are all blocked. We'd be boxed in."

Two men and a woman in either their twenties or thirties belted out of a restaurant across the street, grimacing and howling, foaming at the mouth.

"Jesus," said Hardy, watching the trio.

Jacked up with adrenaline, they ran at a lightning clip.

Wondering what Hardy was looking at, Phoebe headed to the door and picked up on the threesome.

"They're infected," she said. "The virus drives you insane."

"If we could run that fast, we might be able to make it to the alley out of here without getting shot."

As if on cue, the crewmen in the choppers trained their AR-15s on the three virus-crazed victims and pelted them with bullets. The bloody victims flailed their arms as they ran, arched their bodies, and fell to the tarmac, where they writhed and grimaced.

Phoebe heard a noise behind her.

She whipped her head around and noticed a jeans-clad, beer-bellied fortysomething guy wearing an olive drab wife beater barreling out of the elevator. Seeing the planter outside the elevator doorway, she realized what had happened. The constant nudging of the planter by the elevator door attempting to close had managed to push the planter out of its way, allowing the door to close and the elevator to rise to pick up a passenger on an upper floor.

Beer Belly was the passenger.

Shaking his head in a daze, his eyes wild, he spotted Phoebe and Hardy and charged them, growling. Spicules of spit shot out of his mouth as he howled at them.

"He's infected," yelled Phoebe, her eyes glued in fear on Beer Belly.

Hardy wheeled around and, gritting his teeth, fired at him and kept firing, knowing one bullet wouldn't be enough to fell the raging maniac.

"They have superhuman strength when they're infected," said Phoebe. "Make sure he's dead."

Lunging forward, Beer Belly latched onto Phoebe's arm and yanked it toward his gaping, salivating mouth. Phoebe screamed. She tried to pull free without success.

Hardy put two slugs in Beery Belly's forehead, which cracked like a cocoanut. Virus-infected brains leaked out of the back of Beer Belly's riven skull.

Gasping, Phoebe pulled her arm free from his grasp.

Beer Belly fell on his stomach on the floor, smashing his face against the carpet and breaking his two front teeth.

"Make sure he's dead," said Courtney, her eyes huge.

"I put two slugs in his brain for Chrissake," said Hardy.

"Sometimes they come back to life."

Another round of gunfire erupted from the choppers outside. Hardy slewed around to see what was happening.

The three bullet-riddled victims were rising from the street, coming back to life, and shambling around in search of food. AR-15 bullets tore their heads to pieces, hurling skull fragments hugger-mugger. Their heads pulverized, the infected collapsed on the tarmac.

Hardy watched, enthralled.

He spun around and put another slug in Beer Belly's head to make sure the guy wouldn't rise from the dead.

"If I hadn't seen it with my own two eyes, I wouldn't have believed it," said Hardy, stunned.

Thinking on her feet, Phoebe darted to the open elevator door and shoved the planter into the doorway to prevent the door from closing. She didn't want any more infected coming down to the lobby. The door struck the planter and retracted into the wall.

"The body needs to be burned," she said, eying Beer Belly.

"How come?" said Hardy.

"The choppers burned every stiff on the street with flamethrowers," said Courtney.

Hardy nodded. "That explains the piles of ashes I saw out there." He gazed out the broken door. "They torched a car, it looks like."

241

"There were people in it."

"I never heard of a deal where the government whacks out everyone who gets infected with a disease. The only cure is a bullet? Wow," said Hardy, hiking his eyebrows.

"Bullets and flames."

"That's why we need to burn this cadaver," said Phoebe.

"The lobby will catch fire if we do," said Hardy.

"He's contagious even when he's dead."

"We dragged another stiff out of here earlier," said Courtney, eyeballing the cadaver, "but this guy looks heavy. And we almost got shot when we dumped the other guy outside."

"How long do we have before he infects us?" said Phoebe, half to herself.

"The choppers burned those bodies fast on the street."

"Not long, then," said Phoebe, her face drawn.

Chapter 78

How did he get into this mess? wondered Jason with his agony-racked mind as he lay supine on his sofa. If he had just stayed away from Val, none of this would have happened. He wouldn't be on the verge of watching his career and his marriage nosedive in a death spiral. If that wasn't bad enough, Val could have infected him with a brain-eating virus. He hoped he just had a killer headache.

Or was the virus/earwig eating holes in his brain?

Would he soon go berserk like Val and foam at the mouth like a rabid dog? To hell with it. He could still think even though it was difficult arranging his thoughts through the vermilion pain permeating his mind.

He sat up and clutched his aching head. Spotting his cell phone vibrating on his desktop, he wondered if he could reach it. The idea of walking with his throbbing headache dismayed him. He needed to find out what was happening to Phoebe. Maybe she had escaped the quarantine.

He stood up unsteadily and staggered toward his desk. Reaching it he grasped the desktop to prevent himself from losing his balance and falling.

He regained his balance and answered his cell, eager to hear Phoebe's voice.

"I thought you were gonna blow me off by not answering," said Muldoon.

"This better be important," said Jason, struggling to keep his voice steady even as pain contorted his face.

"Are you OK, Albright? You sound like you're talking through a pillow."

"Get on with it, Muldoon. I'm a busy man."

"Busy doing what? Your city's being shot up by state cops, and you're doing nothing about it."

"They're not under my jurisdiction. Neither are the feds."

"The Strip is worse than ever. The sky is chock-full of helos. They're blowing away people in the streets. You call this a quarantine? I call it a fucking massacre."

243

"The governor's running the show. Tell him."

"I'm telling *you*. And if you don't do something quick, I'm gonna tell a whole lot of people things you want kept secret—like I'm paying you money so your cops don't harass my hookers. I guarantee you the media is dying to hear about the graft you're raking in."

"You'd be cutting off your nose to spite your face if you tell them. You're the payor of the graft."

"If you don't call off this quarantine, my business is kaput. I'm hemorrhaging money. What have I got to lose if I take you down with me?"

Jason rubbed his forehead. Why couldn't anything be easy? Muldoon was a necessary evil to keep Jason's reelection campaign in gear.

"Have you seen my wife Phoebe on the Strip?" said Jason.

"I hope not. Everybody I've seen on the street has gotten shot and charbroiled. People are dropping like flies. If she was out there, she's deader than your dried-up dick."

Jason had trouble standing. He braced his thigh against his desk.

Phoebe wasn't answering her cell phone. Was it because she was dead? he wondered. Would the state cops dare shoot his wife? Or were they shooting everyone in sight like Muldoon said? Or was Phoebe infected and in no shape to answer her phone?

Jason couldn't think straight with the throbbing pain in his head.

"How am I supposed to get Vitti to call off his dogs?" he said.

"You're the mayor. This is your city. Don't you have the balls to stand up for it?"

Jason seethed with fury. He couldn't come up with an answer thanks to his scrambled brains.

"I guess I'm not the only person to call you ball-less, huh, Mr. Mayor," said Muldoon. "You and worms got something in common. Neither of you can stand up."

"You're the nightclub boss," said Jason, white-faced. "Why don't you stand up for yourself? It's your club getting flushed down the toilet."

Muldoon laughed.

What was so funny? wondered Jason, caught off guard.

"I guess you don't want to run for reelection," said Muldoon.

244

"Do I look like I'm wearing a crown? I can't solve everybody's problems."

I can't even solve my own.

"How did a worm ever get elected mayor?" said Muldoon.

"If they harm my wife, I'm holding you to blame. That's your part of town."

"Your reputation for being incorruptible is going down the tubes when I give the media an earful."

Jason's ear canal was itching like crazy. Grimacing, he stuck his pinky into it and scratched it. He inspected his pinky, half expecting to see blood on it.

"I got dirt on you that you wouldn't like to get out," said Muldoon.

"I'm dealing with stuff."

"Well, deal with this. Val's been talking to me. I know about you and her."

Jason started.

"Nobody will believe you," he said. "Your reputation is mud. You're nothing more than a jumped-up crime boss. And everybody knows it, no matter how fancy your car is."

Despite the courage of his words, Jason found his nerves tightening. Having his relationship with Val exposed would dynamite his career. It was the reason he had hired Hardy to remove Jones. Removing Muldoon would be a whole lot harder. The guy was surrounded by beefed-up bodyguards with itchy trigger fingers.

Val needed to go, he decided. It would be a lot easier removing *her* than removing Muldoon. Val was causing too many problems. What was wrong with him? Why couldn't he think straight? Val wasn't a problem anymore. She was infected and had become a vegetable. She couldn't testify against him. She couldn't even talk. She was a gibbering maniac hanging from chains. She hadn't even recognized him when he was watching her through the biolab's bulletproof glass.

"Are you there, *Mr. Mayor*?" said Muldoon, his voice laced with sarcasm.

"Val won't back up your story."

"We'll see about that. A little 'friendly' persuasion can work wonders if you get my drift."

It was Jason's turn to laugh because Val had her brains scrambled with virus and couldn't talk about anything, but he couldn't make a sound because his head was killing him. He could feel the earwig/virus gobbling his brain tissue.

No matter how hard he tried, he couldn't escape the hellscape of his own mind.

Chapter 79

It was a matter of trust, decided Phoebe.

She had trusted Jason was being faithful to her. And then she had seen him soliciting the hooker Val. Was cheating with a hooker as bad as cheating with a friend? What difference did it make? Cheating was cheating. It was a betrayal of her trust in him.

"We need to come up with an alternative plan," said Hardy. "I don't want to drag this tub of lard"—he pointed his Beretta at Beer Belly—"out onto the street and get wasted."

"His corpse is infectious," said Phoebe. "We could get infected since we're in the same room with it. We need to burn it."

"We'll die of smoke inhalation."

"That's why we dragged the other stiff out onto the street," said Courtney.

"I got a better idea," said Hardy. "Let's make a run for it."

"We're dead meat if we go outside."

Phoebe didn't want to think about it. She kept thinking about Jason cheating on her. It galled her that he would choose a common streetwalker to betray her. How could he pick a cheap tramp over her?

She had trusted Jason. And look where she was now. In the middle of an outbreak of a deadly virus. All because she wanted to save her marriage and get rid of Val the Homewrecker.

"We need to work together," said Phoebe.

"What?" said Hardy.

"Either we hang together or we hang separately," said Phoebe, remembering Ben Franklin's words.

"I say burn the dead guy," said Courtney.

"I say we beat it," said Hardy.

"In the end you have to trust someone, don't you?" said Phoebe, her thoughts obsessed with Jason. "Otherwise, we're islands cut off from each other."

"That's my problem," said Courtney. "I keep trusting the wrong person, and here I am stuck in the ass end of the world. I got hooked up with the wrong boyfriend, a dirty lying drug-dealing pimp who doesn't care about anybody but himself and fattening his wallet using me as his moneymaker."

"You shouldn't put yourself down like that."

"Then why do I keep picking Mr. Wrong? There must be something *wrong* with me."

"Why kick yourself when the world will kick you every minute of the day?"

Talk about picking Mr. Wrong, decided Phoebe. Who was she to give anybody advice about a relationship? Her husband was turning out to be Mr. Wrong. But you had to trust someone. How could you get through life without trusting someone? Not everybody was a lying cheat. Or were they, and it was just a matter of degree?

"What do *you* know?" said Courtney. "Are *you* some kind of expert?"

"An expert I'm not," said Phoebe. "I've made my share of mistakes."

I'm a walking compendium of bad decision-making. I was going to file for bankruptcy thanks to my failed start-up when I met Jason who bailed me out—and proceeded to betray me after we got married.

"That's your problem," chimed in Hardy. "You *trust* people. I never trust anyone. You live longer that way. My advice: Never trust a soul."

"You can't live like that. They'll bury you in an unmarked grave in potter's field because nobody gave a damn about you."

"They can bury me in a tub of shit when I'm dead, for all I care. Trust no one and carry a gun," said Hardy, brandishing his Beretta. "It's the only way to live. You keep trusting people, they'll double-cross you sooner or later."

"I'm beginning to think you're right," said Courtney, her tone bitter.

"Of course, I am." Hardy paused. "Standing here chitchatting isn't the answer. We need to hatch a plan before we catch Beer Belly's disease. I say let's bug out."

"How will we get past the choppers?" said Phoebe.

Hardy mulled it over. "We stage a diversion to keep the choppers occupied. Then we escape under their noses."

"What kind of diversion?" said Courtney.

"I'm thinking about it."
The three of them stood in silence.

Chapter 80

"I'll be the diversion," said Courtney, her face gloomy.

"What are you talking about, Courtney?" said Phoebe.

"I'm not going anywhere in life. My life's a train wreck. I can't escape what I am."

"That's not true. If you want out of this place, you can up and leave—well, when this quarantine is over anyway."

"I doubt it. This is where I belong. I haven't got any skills or talents, so this is where I ended up. Loserville. It couldn't happen any other way. There's no escape for me."

"You need to stop thinking like that."

"If I leave here, I'll probably end up in a trailer park or hitching rides at truck stops. The only thing I got to sell that anyone wants is my body."

Was there much difference between her and Courtney? wondered Phoebe. They were both losers even if they came from opposite sides of the tracks. Neither of them could make a right decision.

"At least you never had to file for Chapter 7," she said.

"What's that?" said Courtney.

"Bankruptcy."

"Why should I do that? I don't even have a bank account."

"Courtney's right," said Hardy. "She would make a good diversion. And she's the logical choice for the job."

"You don't care about anyone but yourself," said Phoebe, in a pet. "Why should we listen to anything you say?"

Hardy trained his Beretta on her face. "I can think of one reason. What I say goes."

"I'm gonna do something decent for once in my life," said Courtney.

"He can't force you to do it," said Phoebe.

"Nobody's forcing me."

"You're young, Courtney. Your life is just beginning. You'll have plenty of opportunities coming your way as you get older."

"I don't have the skills or the brains for opportunities."

"You can learn a skill."

"Look, I believe now that you're the mayor's wife. You're important to this town. I'm not. I'd just as soon end my life now. Nothing's ever gonna work out for me. This will save me from waking up one morning and slashing my wrists."

"You're only saying that because we're trapped here and you're bummed out."

"I'm trapped here forever, not like you. I'll be the diversion so you two can escape."

"There must be a way for all three of us to get out," said Phoebe, knitting her brows in thought.

"There isn't," said Hardy. "We need a diversion, or they'll cut down the three of us with a hail of bullets."

"If I don't do this, I'll end up OD'ing on drugs this year or the next," said Courtney. "Let me do one good thing in my life."

"Now you're talking," said Hardy. "You're the bomb in my book. Listen to me. You run to the right and draw their fire when we leave. We'll run to the left to the cul-de-sac."

"Let's all run to the left," said Phoebe. "One of us is bound to escape."

Phoebe had never met Courtney before today, but during the hours they had spent together she had grown to like Courtney even though she wore a cynical shell around her and hadn't been easy to like at first blush.

Tears welling in her eyes, Phoebe walked over to Courtney and hugged her.

"You don't need to do this," said Phoebe.

"It's our only choice."

"No, it isn't. We can think of a different diversion."

"Like what?"

Phoebe couldn't think of one offhand. "We can think of one. It'll just take a while."

"Meanwhile, the stiff infects us," said Courtney, cutting her eyes toward Beer Belly.

"We have no idea how long that takes. It could take a week, for all we know."

"Then why did the choppers torch all the corpses right after they shot them?"

"We'll think of something," said Phoebe, staring with commiseration into Courtney's burned-out eyes.

"We don't have time. We're getting infected. We have to leave."

"I got an idea," said Phoebe, her face brightening a little. "Let's choose straws. Whoever loses is the diversion."

She knew she might lose, but it seemed fairer than asking for volunteers. Otherwise, she would feel responsible for Courtney's death.

"My mind's made up," said Courtney. "I have nothing to look forward to in my rotten life. I have no future."

"You don't know that. Your luck might change."

"The only luck I have is bad luck. I'll be the diversion. We all can't get out alive. You know I'm right."

"Everybody happy now?" said Hardy. "It's time to shit or get off the pot. Let's make our move."

"Who knows?" said Courtney with a crooked smile and a faraway look. "Maybe I'll be the one that escapes while you two get shot."

Chapter 81

His jaw set, Muldoon strode out onto his casino balcony, his satphone to his mouth.

"With all due respect, Mr. Governor, your cops are wasting my town," he said. "Call 'em off, or your presidential prospects are slim and none."

"Your town is the hotbed of the virus," said Vitti. "My men aren't going anywhere till the virus is eradicated. We cannot let it spread. If it spreads beyond your town, nobody will be able to stop it."

"I feel fine. Not everyone here is infected," said Muldoon, glancing up at one of the choppers hovering in the cloud-dappled sky.

"You could be infected and not know it. This virus is a bastard."

"You need my money, Vitti. Your political aspirations are a pipe dream without it."

"I don't take orders from you. I suggest you surrender to the authorities, or I guarantee they'll take sterner measures."

"Sterner measures? They're already gunning down everybody on the street. That's your idea of curing a virus?"

"You have no idea what you're up against. This virus makes Covid look like the common cold."

Muldoon was becoming concerned for his health. Could he be infected? he wondered. Was the virus airborne? He sniffed the air. He couldn't smell anything except residual smoke wisping from the fire-gutted Mustang and from the cremated corpses strewn on the street. His right eyelid twitched.

"If I surrender, will your maniac cops let me live?" he said.

"If they know you're not infected, they have orders to let you live."

"How the hell do I prove I'm not infected?"

Vitti hung fire.

The delay in Vitti's answer boded ill, decided Muldoon. It was catch-22. In the quarantine zone you couldn't prove you weren't infected. If you were in the quarantine zone, you were considered infected. Which explained why they were shooting everybody on the Strip.

He should never have come here. He should have stayed off the Strip. But his business was dying because of the virus. If his business died, he died, the way he saw it. How could he make a living without his business?

"We're working on tests for that," said Vitti at last.

"Until you find a test, are your boys gonna keep blowing away everybody they see?"

Vitti launched into his gubernatorial tone. "The greatest state of the union is at stake. I will not let any force on earth take down California. This is the American dream. California is the vanguard and what the entire nation strives to be. It will never besmirch my administration's record that I was the one who led California to the brink of disaster. That is not gonna happen. This great state will never perish from the face of the earth, not while I'm governor."

Muldoon wondered if Vitti was standing in front of a mirror as he gave his pompous speech.

"If your boys whack me out, my donations to your campaign will dry up faster than a witch's wizened tit," said Muldoon, pacing around the balcony. "Think of all those millions gone from your coffers. You and Albright are history without me. You better do everything you can to save my life. Your power will wither up and die without my support."

"I will not hesitate to make sacrifices to save the fate of California."

"You better not be including me on your list of sacrifices. That would be a mistake you would never live down."

"You have no idea how difficult my job is, Muldoon. I'll do whatever has to be done to save California, no matter how difficult my decision, no matter how deep my sacrifice."

This was sounding worse and worse for him, decided Muldoon. The words *my sacrifice* bothered him. They meant Vitti was going to hang backers out to dry, the nearest Muldoon could determine. Politicians went out of their way to obscure the true meaning of their words.

"Where are you?" said Vitti.

"On my balcony," said Muldoon, digesting Vitti's words.

"Thank you."

Absorbed in his thoughts, Muldoon didn't notice the chopper flying toward him.

The bullets that sprayed his face alerted him. They severed his jaw from his face and replaced it with blood that gushed like a water fountain from his hacked carotid artery.

Freed from his thoughts, Muldoon dropped dead.

Chapter 82

Rising to a sitting position on the sofa, Jason winced and squinted in the brightness of his office. The overhead lights were off. Why was it so bright in here? he wondered.

It was the sun in the picture window. Holding his hand like a visor on his forehead, he shielded his eyes from the glaring sun.

He thought he had closed the drapes. Had Yvette come in to open them while he was dozing?

He crossed to the window and drew the drapes shut in irritation.

No sooner had he returned to the sofa and lay on his back then his cell phone chimed.

The pain in the neck, Muldoon, Jason decided. He had a good mind not to answer it. But the cell kept chiming like it would never stop. The sound vibrated in his head bouncing back and forth between his eardrums like a ping-pong ball studded with needles.

Jason bolted to his feet and reached his desk in two strides. He scoffed up his cell phone from the desktop.

"Stop calling me, you greedy bastard," he said. "It's out of my hands."

"What?" said Vincent Zandorf, aghast.

"Oh—uh—I—uh—thought you were someone else," said Jason, realizing his mistake.

"This is Vincent Zandorf. We met earlier."

"Yes. I remember. How can I help you?"

"Are you all right?"

My brain feels like it's doused with lighter fluid and blazing out of control.

"I'm—fine," he managed to say through the pain.

"I need you to come to the lab."

"The lab? What for?"

"It has to do with the virus."

"I don't see how I can help," said Jason, dreading going anywhere in his condition. "I have work to do."

"We don't understand why the infected patient Val Lewton has been repeating your name."

"*My* name," said Jason, taken aback.

"We heard her say your name several times. In fact, she was screaming it."

Pale as he was from his headache, Jason became even paler. "You—uh—must have misunderstood her. I don't know the woman. I never met her."

"I suppose that's possible. After all, you *are* the mayor. Maybe she saw you on TV."

"Right. That must be it," said Jason, relieved Zandorf had bought his lie.

"But we need to make sure. You see, we can't take chances with this virus. It spreads like nothing we've ever seen. We have to stop it dead in its tracks. If we suspect anybody of being infected, we must examine them."

"I don't understand. What has that got to do with me?"

"If she knows you and has met you, we need to examine you."

"How could I possibly know her? I've never been to the Strip in my life. You're talking hookers and drug addicts down there. I'm the mayor and I'm happily married. Why would I, of all people, go there?"

"All the same, we would be remiss in our job if we didn't examine you. We have to know for sure about you one way or the other. Are you feeling OK?"

"I'm fine," said Jason through gritted teeth, his face contorted with pain.

"No headache or lightheadedness?"

"Not me," said Jason, trying to sound calm.

Every time he talked, his head rang with pain, Jason noticed, baring his teeth and squinting. Zandorf's voice was just as grating, triggering waves of agony when Jason heard it.

"Then you shouldn't mind coming down to my biolab so we can inspect you," said Zandorf.

Jason had to think fast. If he returned to the biolab, Val might recognize him and yell his name. He was lucky she hadn't done so the first time he went there. Unfortunately, she must have yelled his name afterward, according to Zandorf.

Could Val have recognized him at the biolab in her advanced diseased state but wasn't able to acknowledge him? wondered Jason. Maybe part of her mind wasn't infected, was in fact coherent. But she had looked like a raving lunatic when he had seen her hanging from chains.

His career was hitting the skids. If anyone found out he had patronized a hooker, he was finished as mayor. But what if Zandorf was right? wondered Jason. What if Val *had* infected him with the earwig/virus when they had had sex? *This was what he got for getting a couple of blowjobs from Val?* The idea that he was infected staggered him. *It could not be.*

Appalled at the thought, Jason reeled backward, unable to cope with the realization.

It *would* explain the fire rampaging in his brain, he decided, trying to steady himself.

Could he risk going to the biolab again and having Val recognize him?

There was too much at stake. On the other hand, if he didn't go, Zandorf might become suspicious of him and think he was infected. Then Zandorf would send feds to escort him back to the biolab. If Zandorf saw Jason in his present condition, he would conclude Jason was infected.

Maybe he should flee the city while he could, decided Jason. He dreaded the idea of Zandorf hanging him from chains next to Val in the biolab. His picture would be splashed all over the papers if someone with a smartphone saw him in such a condition. His career shot down in flames.

He could see the tabloid headlines now:
Infected Mayor Raves Like a Lunatic in Chains
Hooker Infects Mayor with Deadly Virus
Adulterous Mayor Writhes in Agony

How had he got into this mess? he wondered. Because he had too much money, so he thought he could do whatever he wanted? Like bedding any woman who put out for a price? If he had stayed loyal to Phoebe, none of this would have happened. By the same token, if he was broke, none of this would have happened. He wouldn't have been able to afford a hooker.

He cursed Val for tempting him with her skintight miniskirts and low-cut blouses. At the same time, he knew he could have resisted her if he had tried harder. But he hadn't wanted to try. Why should he resist her? What was so awful about going to a hooker?

Phoebe, he decided. He should have thought of Phoebe.

258

What difference did it make how he had got into this? The problem was he was in it up to his neck, and he could see no way out of it. *And the pain was intolerable.*

He tore open the drapes and squinted in the sun. Its brightness stung his eyeballs, which were already boiling in their sockets and pulsating with agony.

How much pain did a man have to take? he wondered, his brain a furnace as the earwig/virus gnawed it. The body had its limits. It could withstand only so much pain . . . until . . . until . . . it couldn't.

Screaming his lungs out, he picked up the steel and leather chair behind his desk and hurled it out the picture window shattering it.

Three seconds later he threw himself out the window.

It was a long way down.

And he howled in pain all the way.

Chapter 83

Courtney psyched herself up to make a mad dash out the hotel lobby door. She took long slow breaths, steadying her heartbeat.

"I got everything to live for," said Hardy. "I got a cool million waiting for me courtesy of our creepy mayor when I get out of here. And another cool million bonus on top of that when he hears I have his wife."

"Why would he give you so much money?" said Phoebe.

"I gave him a lot of reasons," said Hardy, chuckling. "You have pride of place on the short list."

"Me? I don't understand. I never met you before."

"He sent me here to save you."

"I don't believe that for a minute."

"I'm a fixer. I deal with a lot of people I've never met. That doesn't stop me from fixing things."

"I'm ready," said Courtney, tired of listening to them. "We can't take the chance of staying any longer with the infected stiff."

"We're ready when you are," said Hardy. "Remember. You run to the right. We run to the left."

Courtney nodded yes.

"There's still time to change your mind," said Phoebe.

"No," said Courtney. "I'm doing the right thing for once in my life. I don't deserve to go on living. I messed up my life too bad."

Phoebe's eyes welled with tears. "You don't have to do this. It's never too late to change your life around."

"My life is a mess. I want to set it straight."

"You don't have to make up for your past," said Phoebe, her voice tight. "Why do you feel like you have to punish yourself?"

"I'm not punishing myself. I'm helping you."

Courtney would not be denied the one moment of glory in her life, her one moment of doing something meaningful.

She burst out the door and dashed to her right.

She could run fast, she knew. She had the eyes of a cheetah, her mother had once told her. Her mother was part Cherokee, her father Scottish. Courtney had Indian blood running in her veins. Indians could run like the wind. Like Jim Thorpe, one of the greatest runners of all time. He was an Indian, a member of the Sac and Fox Nation.

Churning her legs she raced down the sidewalk, only dimly aware of the choppers hovering overhead. She banished everything from her mind except for the will to run as fast as she could. She felt the blood rushing through her veins as she ran, her lungs burning.

She felt exhilarated. She was going to make it. She was going to escape. No bullets would find her.

Maybe the chopper crewmen would see how healthy she was when she ran, and they would not shoot her, knowing she must not be infected.

She was running like a cheetah, the fastest animal. Nobody could catch her, she decided, flinging her head back and breathing lustily.

It came as something of a shock to her when she heard a burst of gunfire from the choppers above.

Couldn't they see she was healthy from the way she was running? she wondered. She wanted to yell at them to stop, but she knew she didn't have time to stop and talk. She had to keep running. She remembered what they had done to Meredith when she had tried to talk to them.

There was no talking to them, Courtney decided.

She would outrace their bullets. She could do it. She heard her mother calling her. *Run, Cheetah Eyes, run. You can run faster than the wind in a hurricane.*

If she had listened to her mother more often when she was younger, she wouldn't have ended up a drug-addicted hooker with no future, Courtney decided.

She couldn't think about it. She had to keep running. She was going to beat the odds. She was going to escape.

The AR-15 Parabellum bullets that struck her in the back turned her into a ragdoll with crimson splotches on it that sprawled motionless and askew face down on the sidewalk.

Chapter 84

Before the gunfire erupted, Phoebe and Hardy stormed out of the hotel lobby and turned left.

Phoebe couldn't help but glance in Courtney's direction to see how she was faring. Courtney was running almost as fast as the infected, decided Phoebe in amazement. Maybe she would escape.

Phoebe sprang after Hardy in the opposite direction. She could see that the six choppers hovering in the sky were converging on Courtney. The diversion was working. Maybe there was hope she and Hardy could escape unharmed, decided Phoebe. Maybe all three of them would escape.

The bursts of gunfire from the AR-15s in the choppers helped dispel that illusion.

They were killing Courtney, Phoebe decided in dismay. She dared not look back at the sobering carnage. She had to keep running. The chopper crewmen would pick up on her and Hardy any minute.

Crazed with fear, she barreled down the sidewalk after Hardy.

The choppers were going to come after them. It wouldn't be long, Phoebe decided.

"We're almost at the cul-de-sac," said Hardy over his shoulder to her, gun in hand.

She realized she could run away from him now that he wasn't looking at her. But where would she go? She didn't know the way out. Hardy did. Following him she might escape. It was her only chance.

It was *her* decision. Even if it was the wrong decision, *she* was making it. It felt good to make a decision. It made her feel free.

She listened for the whump-whump of the choppers flying in her direction, knowing she wouldn't have to wait long. They had stopped shooting.

Courtney must be dead, Phoebe decided.

She must keep running, thrusting her legs for all she was worth.

Hardy whipped his head around and eyed her with malevolence.

262

"Don't try anything," he said. "I can hear you running behind me. When I can't, I'll turn around and whack you out."

He snapped his head forward and kept running.

Phoebe didn't doubt him. The guy oozed evil. There was no telling how many people he had killed.

She tried as best she could to keep up with him. She didn't want him to turn around and blast her. But he was faster. She couldn't keep up.

He whipped his head around to check on her. Seeing her running after him he looked up into the sky and saw a chopper bearing down on him. Continuing to run, he trained his Baretta on the chopper's cockpit and let loose two rounds. He faced forward and belted toward the cul-de-sac that led to a way out.

Phoebe could hear the choppers flying in her direction from behind.

An AR-15 opened fire on her. She heard the bullets ricocheting off the cement sidewalk at her feet.

Her heart in her mouth, she tried to run faster.

She had to keep up with Hardy.

He was yelling something at her. She couldn't make out what.

Following him she listened to the choppers bearing down on her, wielding death. She wondered if they had killed Courtney. She was tempted to look back, but she had no time. She had to keep running till she dropped from exhaustion.

Chapter 85

Dressed in his white Tyvek hazmat uniform, Zandorf couldn't believe how fast Val was pumping her legs as she hung by her arms from the chains bolted to the ceiling of the biolab.

"There's no way she can keep running at that fantastic rate, Celia," Zandorf told his aide, a tall black woman in her thirties with a narrow, vulpine chin that accentuated the fullness of her lips.

Celia's brown eyes widened behind her tortoiseshell-framed glasses as she gazed through the Plexiglas shield of her hazmat helmet at Val's gyrations.

"How can she survive with her metabolism rate so high?" she said.

Zandorf faced Celia. "She can't. It's physically impossible. Something's got to give."

Val screamed.

Even through the thick Plexiglas of the picture window that shielded Zandorf and Celia from Val, Zandorf could hear the nerve-shredding shriek of pain. Zandorf jerked his gaze back toward Val.

Val rolled her eyes. Her face was flushed. Her pain-racked features contorted at a hectic rate.

"She can't sustain this," said Zandorf, concern rucking his brow. "Her heart will burst."

Her feet suspended two yards above the floor, Val continued to run in place, furiously thrusting her legs.

"I can't imagine the pain she's in," said Celia.

"The infected must run thinking they can escape the pain by running from it," said Zandorf. "The irony is they can't. You can't run from something attacking you from the inside."

"Why do they feel the urge to consume living human flesh?"

"They need to keep eating to fuel their raging metabolisms. Who knows? Maybe in their infected minds they think they can assuage the pain racking their bodies by eating another body—a human body like their own. I can only theorize. I've never seen anything like this."

"Can you imagine if this virus spread from Costaguana?" said Celia, her eyes bulging with anxiety.

"We can't let that happen under any circumstances. My orders are to prevent it from happening, no matter what. The president has given me the power to take every means necessary to eradicate the virus."

Val began screaming a name.

"What is she saying?" said Celia.

"It sounds like Jason Albright. The mayor. She called out his full name before. She must know him somehow."

"Maybe from his appearances on TV."

"Maybe. But we need to make sure he's not infected. If he had contact with her, he could be infected. We need to examine him."

"Do you have the authority to make him come here?"

"The president has given me the authority to have him arrested, if need me."

"The mayor?" said Celia with disbelief. "You can arrest the mayor?"

Zandorf nodded yes, his face grave. "This is a catastrophic virus we're dealing with. All precautions must be taken to stop its spread."

A noise from within Val's chamber distracted him.

Val's eyes popped out of her head—literally. Her face turned a vibrant scarlet before her head exploded.

Chapter 86

Zandorf drew back from the Plexiglas picture window in stupefaction, grimacing at the stomach-turning sight.

Globs of Val's honeycombed brain thumped and splattered against the Plexiglas.

Zandorf could discern white worms squirming inside the oozing, porous brain matter which was sliding down the Plexiglass, leaving behind a wake of slime.

The worms must be the virus, he decided. Hundreds of worms burrowed holes through the victim's brain, igniting an inferno of pain inside the victim's head as the virus took root inside its hapless host gorging on their brain cells.

Zandorf tried to imagine the pain of hundreds of worms boring through his brain. The image revolted him.

He grimaced in revulsion and horror at the worm-infested pieces of Val's brain that slithered down the Plexiglas.

Celia couldn't stand the sight. She turned away, gagging.

Incredibly, Val's body continued to run in place, minus her head, arterial blood fountaining out from her severed throat at a slower rate as she died. Even after she died and ceased bleeding, her legs continued to pump.

It must be a reflex, like a twitch after death, decided Zandorf.

He watched Val's brain matter slide down the Plexiglas and reach the white linoleum floor. When the moist, spongelike brains landed on the floor, the worms emerged from the brain matter and slithered along the linoleum. At first, he thought there had been hundreds of worms, but as more and more blobs of brain reached the floor, he could see there were thousands of the revolting creatures—some long, some short. The shorter ones must be offspring of the longer ones, he surmised, as the virus reproduced inside the brain matter.

On one section of the floor, a bolus of brain matter seemed to be moving along the linoleum. On closer inspection Zandorf could make out scores of worms acting like caterpillar legs, propelling the bolus forward. He could barely suppress his urge to retch.

He couldn't imagine the pain the infected suffered as the vermiculate disease progressed, eating them alive and forcing the victim to eat as a result. Not only was the food nourishing the infected, it was nourishing the all-consuming virus blazing through their system and burning them alive.

"No one must enter that room," he said, his face stricken, watching blood-smeared worms wriggle across the floor seeking a new host.

"Isn't it airtight?" said Celia, turning toward him, but shying away from looking at Val.

"Yes. Thank God."

Zandorf wasn't a religious man, but he couldn't think of anything else to say to fit the enormity of the crisis confronting him—*confronting the world.*

"If one of those virus worms escapes, we're doomed," he went on. "We must incinerate Val's corpse and all living matter inside that cell."

"Can a fire burn inside an airtight chamber?"

"It can until all of the oxygen is depleted," said Zandorf, musing.

"What if all of the virus hasn't been eradicated by that time?"

"We'll have to pump more oxygen into the chamber until the fire consumes every last remnant of the virus."

"What if the virus escapes when we open the air ducts to pump more oxygen into the chamber?"

Zandorf shut his eyes in pained thought. "We can't let that happen."

But he knew Celia was right. Some of the virus might escape if the biolab chamber's air ducts were opened. He couldn't afford to let any of it escape. For the sake of humanity all traces of the virus had to be annihilated.

"Some of those worms are tiny," she said. "What's to prevent them from escaping through the open ducts?"

Zandorf heaved a sigh of frustration.

"Jesus. We need to torch the entire building," he said, surveying the ceiling, thinking of the floors above him.

He stared ahead of him in consternation.

"What?" said Celia, picking up on his concern.

"The city. The entire city."

"What?" said Celia, not understanding.

"We need to get out of here."

"How can we? We must continue our virological studies."

Zandorf stepped toward the console in front of the picture window and flicked on the speakerphone switch.

"This is Zandorf," he said into the speaker. "Initiate incineration inside the airtight chamber."

"Say again," said a surprised man's voice.

"You heard me."

"Patient zero will be destroyed."

"Her remains must be incinerated, burned to ash."

"The oxygen will be depleted by the fire before the entire contents of the chamber are incinerated."

Zandorf racked his brains. If he gave the order to open the air ducts to the chamber, the virus could escape via them, and he would be responsible for the spread of the virus and for the deaths of countless lives. He saw no other alternative. He would have to order the incineration of the entire building—and then, though he hated to contemplate it, the entire city.

"After you set the fire in the chamber, you and everyone here are to evacuate the building," he said.

"Sir? All of our studies of the virus will be destroyed in the flames."

Zandorf cleared his throat and tried to sound self-assured, though he could feel the crippling effects of fear undermining him.

"That's a direct order," he said, and flicked off the speakerphone switch.

"Is it *that* bad?" said Celia.

"I must call the president at once."

Celia rolled her eyes, on the verge of fainting.

The chamber containing Val burst into flames, which fell to consuming Val's churning headless torso that remained suspended from chains. Flames also engulfed the blobs of brain matter infested with worms that were inching along the window and across the floor.

Startled, Zandorf reflexively backed away from the Plexiglas window, which remained intact. He swore he could hear the creatures screaming in pain as they ignited.

"Will the window hold?" asked Celia.

"It's bulletproof and can withstand intense heat," answered Zandorf.

268

"Can you hear screaming?" she said, aghast.

"Come," said Zandorf. "We have no time to waste. This building must be incinerated without leaving a trace."

He bolted out of the biolab through the exit door, Celia in tow.

Chapter 87

As Phoebe watched Hardy running in front of her, she felt drops of liquid falling on her arms from above.

Was it starting to rain? she wondered. How could it? The only clouds in the sky were fluffy white cumulus ones.

A racketing chopper hovered over her.

She could smell gasoline.

She could hear Hardy's voice ahead of her but couldn't make out what he was saying.

Was the chopper leaking fuel? she wondered.

Bullets chipped the sidewalk a few inches away from her right foot. She had to keep running. If she stopped, she was dead. Another shot of adrenaline burst through her system.

She saw Hardy hang a left down the cul-de-sac.

The escape route, she decided. She had to make it to the cul-de-sac.

Another chopper was flying over the buildings on her left. She could see liquid pouring from the chopper. Hardy hadn't shot at that chopper, she decided. Why was it leaking fuel? She didn't understand. She had no time to think about it.

Hardy had disappeared from view in front of her.

She could run away in a different direction and escape him without his noticing, she decided. If she couldn't see him, he couldn't see her. Did she want to take her chances by herself and find another escape route?

She didn't trust Hardy. He called himself a fixer, but he sounded like a hit man. Or why was he carrying a gun? He said he was working for Jason. Could Jason have sent him to kill her? Why would Jason do that? Because he had found out she knew about his tryst with Val? How could he have found out?

Phoebe didn't know what was going on with Hardy. The only thing she knew about him was that he had a gun and was prepared to use it. She didn't trust him. But, realistically, did she have any chance if she ran in a different direction without Hardy?

No way, she decided. She didn't know a way out. Hardy did. Hardy was her only chance despite her misgivings about him.

Her lungs bursting, she charged down the cul-de-sac after him. She could see him nearing the end of it.

He craned his head around, saw her, and beckoned to her.

Bullets from a chopper chewed up the alley tarmac, casting a shower of golden sparks.

She had to watch out for ricochets, she knew. She couldn't stand still for a moment and catch her breath. The chopper AR-15s would zero in on her.

He knew the way out. She had to follow him. Feeling more gasoline drip on her arms, she bolted after him. *Gasoline and sparks*, she thought. A bad mix.

She gulped air and ran, her lungs scorching from overwork.

She saw Hardy disappear to her left. She wondered where he had gone. He hadn't entered a building entrance in the alley. The only way to find out was to keep running. In a few strides she would reach the cinder-block noise barrier that ended the cul-de-sac. She would have to turn left in front of the barrier, but as yet she couldn't see an entrance to the mattress store on her left.

Hardy popped out of nowhere on her left and snatched her arm.

She realized there was a narrow gap about a foot wide, if that, between the end of the mattress store and the cinder-block wall in front of her. You couldn't see the gap from the mouth of the cul-de-sac. No wonder black-and-whites weren't barricading the alley. Only a neighborhood denizen would know of the secret entrance to the Strip.

Hardy led her into the gap.

Gasping for breath she shoehorned herself into it behind him.

The choppers couldn't see her, she realized, looking up and spotting on top of the noise barrier a cement coping that blocked an aerial view of the gap. The chopper spotlight beam swung over the gap but didn't see her and Hardy thanks to the coping. The chopper crew must have decided she and Hardy had escaped into the mattress store, she decided.

Hardy led the way as they squeezed through the gap.

"They spilled gas on me," she said.

"I know," said Hardy. "Me too."

"Did you shoot their fuel tank?"

"I might have hit it. I wasn't aiming at it. I was aiming at the cockpit."

"It makes no sense."

"It does if I'm right about what they're gonna do."

"Which is?"

"I hope I'm wrong. We need to beat it."

Phoebe shook her head in confusion.

They threaded their way through the gap and exited it. A chopper was hovering overhead, but it was over the Strip out of their sight.

"All right," said Hardy, letting her see the gun in his hand, reminding her he was in charge. "We walk briskly to my car. But we don't run. We don't want to draw attention to ourselves. We're just residents of this peaceful neighborhood."

"Do you think Courtney made it?"

"No."

"She was running really fast."

"It doesn't matter how fast she ran. There's no exit in that direction. It's blocked by a police barricade."

She and Hardy made for his car, he with his peculiar bowlegged gait.

The choppers remained on station over the Strip.

"Take it easy," he said, concealing his Beretta 92 Compact in his trouser pocket to prevent nosy neighbors from seeing it. "We're gonna make it."

Chapter 88

When Phoebe and Hardy reached his Honda Civic, she heard a deafening explosion behind them which rumbled through her body.

She whipped her head around to see the Strip burst into flames.

"That's what I thought they were getting ready to do," said Hardy. "The avgas the choppers were spilling was meant as an accelerant. They're probably gonna drop thermite bombs next."

"What's the point?"

"They're razing the quarantine zone to the ground to eradicate the virus."

"My husband would never allow them to torch his city."

"I doubt he had any say in the matter. The feds are running the show. Let's get outa here."

They clambered into his Honda as curious, startled neighbors emerged from their houses to find out what had caused the explosion that had rocked their neighborhood.

Hardy fired the ignition and peeled away from the curb.

Riding shotgun Phoebe saw that he hadn't withdrawn his pistol from his pocket. Maybe she would get a chance to escape him, she decided, waiting for her opportunity.

Even though she had escaped the quarantine zone, she felt like her life was going down the drain. She had gone to the Strip out of love for Jason. She wanted him to return her love for him. With Val in the picture, that was impossible. Phoebe had felt compelled to remove the threat that Val posed to her marriage.

"All I wanted was love," she said.

"What?" said Hardy, puzzled.

"That's why I went to the Strip. Not for any other reason. Val was destroying my marriage. I'm too selfish to share him with anyone else."

"That love stuff is overrated. It's all based on money anyway."

"The world is a cruel place if nobody cares for you."

"It's a damn jungle. But love doesn't change it. It's still a jungle, and you can't count on anyone but yourself in the end."

"Jason can't love me with all his heart with Val around," said Phoebe, her voice breaking. "Val has to go. I have to get her to leave town."

"If you expect other people to look out for you, you're an idiot. They're only looking out for themselves—even when they say they're in love."

Phoebe eyed him. "How can you live like that? You can't go around trusting no one. Eventually you have to trust someone, or you'll end up alone and dead."

"I got news for you. We all end up alone and dead."

"I guess nobody ever loved you."

"Do you really think anybody loves you? Or do they have a selfish reason for saying they do?"

"I care for Jason. All I ask is that he care for me. I refuse to believe he was using me solely to advance his political career and didn't love me."

"You were living in a dreamworld. Reality has disabused you. The truth is nobody cares about anybody but themselves."

"That's not the truth. What about Courtney? She sacrificed her life, so we could live."

"She was suicidal to begin with. With all her booze and drugs. She's been trying to kill herself her whole life. She finally got her wish."

Phoebe shook her head. "You just hate everybody."

"Nobody ever game a damn about me. I'm returning the favor. Which reminds me."

"What?"

"You're my prisoner. I'm holding you hostage till your husband pays me." Hardy laughed. "Now we'll see if he really loves you."

"Shut up."

"If he doesn't care for you, he won't pony up."

"You're a sociopath. I can't believe people as evil as you exist."

"People like me exist all over the place. We tend to be rich and successful," said Hardy, puffing out his chest.

Should she sit back and count on Jason's love to free her by his paying the ransom money that Hardy demanded? Phoebe wondered. Half of her wanted to believe in his love. The other half remained skeptical. Even if Jason paid the ransom, Hardy might still kill her to prevent her from ID'ing him to the cops.

She had to escape Hardy using her wits, she decided. Her life depended on it. She harbored doubts about Jason. She couldn't count on him, no matter how hard she wanted to believe he would rescue her in the nick of time. She had to rescue herself.

Chapter 89

Phoebe watched Hardy slow the Honda and stop at a traffic light.

She considered flinging open her door and fleeing.

He must have been reading her thoughts, she decided. Glancing at her he reached toward the Beretta stuck half inside his trouser pocket. The pistol grip was exposed. He could reach it in a matter of seconds even as she tried to open her door, she realized.

She heard a fleet of helicopters above.

Hardy observed them through the Honda's windshield as they flew above the traffic like giant maleficent grasshoppers.

"They're gonna napalm the Strip," he said. "Like they napalmed Nam. They're gonna wipe it off the face of the earth."

"That's insane. What about all the people there?"

"They're toast."

"Wholesale slaughter of fellow human beings is their idea of a cure?"

"It's the only sure way to eradicate the virus. Firebomb it. Burn it into extinction." Hardy tapped his temple with his forefinger. "I know how their minds work."

"I'm sure it wasn't Jason's idea."

"Did you ever smell burning flesh?"

"Yes," she muttered. "On the Strip." She didn't want to think about it.

Hardy grimaced. "Not good. The whole Strip is gonna reek of it."

"If we had left a minute later, we'd have been cremated."

"Even so, your life hangs in the balance. If Jason doesn't pay the ransom . . . well, you get the picture."

She didn't doubt his words. He might have looked like an accountant, but his harmless appearance belied his actions and talk. Killing her wouldn't keep him awake at night, she knew.

She needed to think of a way out. She thought of movies she had seen. How did the hero escape such a situation? Scenes from action movies flashed through her mind. Of course, the movies were fake. Did any of those escape methods work in real life?

Hardy accelerated as the light turned green.

Traffic was slowing down as rubberneckers peered out their windows at the conflagration ravaging the Strip. Teed off at the slow traffic, Hardy cursed and tried to pass it.

He floored the gas and crossed a double yellow line in his eagerness to pass a slow Volkswagen.

Phoebe widened her eyes. She saw her chance. She lunged to her left and, seizing the steering wheel, shoved it to Hardy's left, sending the Honda hurtling toward a grassy median strip lined with coral trees. The Honda jumped the concrete curb, sped across the grass, and crashed into a coral tree before Hardy could regain control of the steering wheel.

The Honda struck a glancing blow against the tree trunk, smashing the driver's-side door. The metal door wheezed under the impact of the collision and caved in. Hardy's head snapped forward and to its left through his open window and against the tree trunk.

Phoebe's head also snapped forward and to the left. But it didn't strike anything.

The airbags began to deploy.

Dazed, Phoebe noticed Hardy slumping forward, unconscious with blood streaming from his forehead. The driver's-side airbag pushed his head back. Her airbag sprouted in front of her on the dashboard.

Collecting herself, she shoved open the passenger's-side door and bounded out of the Honda.

Sprinting along the median strip she heard and saw three helicopters overhead bound for the Strip. Or were there two? She continued to feel dazed from the car crash. Maybe she was seeing double. She shook her head to clear out the cobwebs. Now there were two choppers. What difference did it make?

She had to keep running. Hardy might be alive. If he was, he'd come for her. The whir of the chopper rotor blades reverberated between her ears. She almost tripped on the uneven ground of the grassy median strip.

If anyone saw her, they would think she was running from the fire. Nothing suspicious about that. Nobody would give her a second thought.

She felt rather than heard something sing past her head from behind. She glanced behind her.

Gun in hand, Hardy was running after her awkwardly like a newborn colt trying to find his legs. A sheet of blood was pouring down his forehead into his eyes, throwing off his aim. Groggy from the car collision, he wiped the blood away from his brow with the back of his hand and blinked his eyes trying to see through the blood that had dripped into them, stinging them.

Phoebe figured Hardy must at least have a concussion as a result of the impact of the collision of his head with the coral tree, and yet he was able to run, albeit clumsily.

He threw up on his chest as he ran, confirming her view that he had sustained a concussion.

He fired another shot at her, which went wide of its mark.

She didn't think he could hit her in his present condition. But when his head cleared, which could occur any moment, his aim would improve.

Her options flashed through her mind. She decided her best bet might be to confront him while he was rattled from the crash.

She stopped running, faced him, and held her hands up in surrender.

"Don't shoot," she said.

A half smile creased Hardy's mouth.

"You would've been dead in a matter of minutes if you hadn't got smart and surrendered," he said. "You saved your life by giving up."

He lurched toward her and spat blood out of his mouth onto the grass. She saw her chance and kicked him in the groin without telegraphing her move. She was glad she had taken lessons in self-defense from the retired cop Gus. Never telegraph your move, he had instructed her.

When Hardy groaned and doubled over in pain, she kneed his face with all the strength she could muster. He groaned again and fell. She hoped she had knocked him unconscious. Since he already had a concussion, it shouldn't be that difficult to knock him out. She wasn't going to wait around to find out if she had succeeded.

She wheeled away from him and broke into a run.

Maybe she should have taken his gun, but he might be conscious, she decided and kept running. She wasn't going to return to get it now. He might come to while she was near him.

As she fled, she half expected him to start firing at her back. She had no idea how long he would stay unconscious. Maybe he wasn't unconscious. He could have been stunned momentarily, for all she knew.

She kept running.

Not good, she decided, played out, her strides slowing. She couldn't keep this up. She needed to get a ride.

Chapter 90

At the next intersection, she crossed the street, and, sticking her thumb out, tried to hitch a ride. Ordinarily she would never risk hitching a ride what with all the weirdos in California. But this was an emergency.

A grey-haired lady driving a little red Fiat passed her, pulled over to the side of the road, and honked her car horn.

Smiling, Phoebe scampered toward her.

The woman was wearing a purple blouse and blue jeans.

"Are you OK?" she said with concern, noticing Phoebe's disheveled hair and flushed face.

"I've been running, is all," said Phoebe, deciding not to mention her car accident as she poked her head through the open passenger's-side window. "I come here to jog on the median strip."

She could hear the radio on the dashboard playing an all-news station in the background.

"How far are you headed?" said the woman.

"The Burger King about five miles west of here. Do you know it?"

"Oh, sure."

"My girlfriend's waiting for me there."

The woman smiled with her chapped lips. Her faded denim eyes twinkled genially.

"Hop in," she said.

Glancing in the woman's direction Phoebe tried to open the Fiat door.

"It's locked," she said.

"Oh, sorry."

The woman unlocked the door from the control panel on her armrest on the driver's-side door.

Phoebe clambered in.

"What's all the commotion on the Strip?" said the woman. "I'm Margaret, by the way. What's your name?"

"Phoebe. There's a big fire on the Strip."

"There are a bunch of helicopters flying over it making a racket. I guess they're helping put out the fire."

"Yeah, must be," said Phoebe, deciding not to tell Margaret the choppers were the ones that had set the fire in the first place.

"Government aircraft by the looks of them," said Margaret, eyeballing her side-view mirror.

Margaret smelled of talcum powder, Phoebe realized. Better by far than the reek of burning flesh emanating from the Strip.

"Authorities are searching for the mayor's wife Phoebe Albright," said the newscaster on the radio.

Uh-oh, decided Phoebe. Margaret must have heard. Would she recognize her? What the hell did the authorities want with her anyway?

"Why do they want the mayor's wife?" Phoebe asked Margaret.

"Who knows? I don't even know who the mayor is," said Margaret with a chuckle.

"You don't?" said Phoebe with surprise and relief.

Considering her situation she felt glad so many people were ignorant of politics.

She decided Courtney hadn't been alone in her ignorance. Poor Courtney. If it wasn't for Courtney, she'd be dead by now, gunned down by the sadistic crewmen in the choppers. Now those same crewmen were burning people alive on the Strip. It was unthinkable. How could the government hire such maniacs? Didn't the personnel department have any standards? Or—and the thought sent a frisson down her spine—maybe they were just carrying out orders. In which case, *they* weren't the sadistic maniacs. It was their *bosses*.

"I don't follow politics," said Margaret. "Politicians are a pack of lying crooks. Why should I waste my time caring about lying crooks?"

"What about his wife?" said Phoebe, wondering if Margaret recognized her.

"What about her? I'd be lying if I said I knew her name, let alone what she looks like."

Good, decided Phoebe. She didn't know what the authorities wanted with her, but if they were the same authorities that had ordered the Strip razed to the ground, she didn't want anything to do with them.

She decided to call Jason. Maybe he could enlighten her.

She withdrew her cell phone from her trouser pocket.

"I guess I'm the only one in this country who doesn't have one of those," said Margaret, catching sight of Phoebe putting the cell phone to her mouth after using speed dial to call Jason.

The call went straight to voicemail.

"Hello, dear, call me back ASAP," she said after the beep, and terminated the call.

"Your husband?"

"Yeah."

At least her cell phone was working now, decided Phoebe. But where was Jason? She pocketed her phone.

"Where's your purse, by the way?" said Margaret.

"Oh—I—uh never carry one when I go jogging."

Margaret nodded yes. "I guess it *would* get in the way."

"Do you know what the authorities want with Ja—, I mean, the mayor's wife?" said Phoebe.

"No idea. I don't normally listen to the news, but I was wondering what's going on at the Strip with all that fire and smoke and helicopters over there, so I turned it on. It looks like the whole shebang is on fire," she said, sneaking a cursory glance in her side-view mirror at the conflagration behind her. "If you ask me, it's burning out of control. Those helicopters aren't doing a bit of good."

They're the ones who started it, thought Phoebe, dumbfounded at the thought and still finding it hard to believe. But she was there when they had started the fire. How could she not believe her own eyes?

The government needed to be called to account for this debacle. Was that why they wanted her? she wondered. Because they knew she had been on the Strip when they had firebombed it? If that was the case, she couldn't let them catch her. They would no doubt do everything they could to keep her from talking if they caught her.

She thought she had escaped, but she hadn't. She was a wanted woman. Wanted by the government no less. The government had all of its resources at its disposal while she had none. All she had on her side were her own wits. Unfortunately, her track record making decisions was spotty at best—which was putting it mildly.

Truth be told, her decisions sucked. They had got her here—at the nadir of her life. Having to file for bankruptcy, choosing a deceitful husband, trying and failing to scare away his hooker girlfriend, and now running for her life from the most powerful force on earth—the government, a government that was immolating people like they were so much trash in a landfill.

"We're almost there," said Margaret.

Where? wondered Phoebe. Where would she be safe—if anywhere—in a world gone mad?

Chapter 91

"Did you hear?" said Margaret.

"Hear what?" said Phoebe.

"Before I picked you up, the commentator on the radio was saying the Strip is quarantined because of a virus with a hundred percent kill ratio."

"There are a lot of viruses going around," said Phoebe, not wanting to reveal the horrors she had learned from firsthand experience in the quarantine zone.

"He said they were getting ready to drop an H-bomb on the Strip and wipe out Costaguana," she said.

"What?" said Phoebe with alarm.

Jason would never allow them to bomb his city, she decided. Where was Jason? Why didn't he answer his cell phone?

"He said it was the only way to stop the spread of the virus," said Margaret.

"That's insane. They would never kill all those people to stop a virus from spreading."

And yet they were torching the Strip even now, decided Phoebe. Could it be that what Margaret had heard the radio commentator say was true? It beggared belief.

"That's why I picked you up," said Margaret.

"I don't understand."

"I wanted to talk to someone before I made my decision."

"What decision?" said Phoebe, bewildered.

"I don't know about you, but I'm not gonna let them blow me up," said Margaret.

"You can't believe everything you hear on the radio."

"The radio's more reliable than the TV."

"It doesn't sound believable that our own country would bomb us."

"They're not gonna bomb *me*."

"What are you gonna do? Drive across the border into Nevada?"

"There's no time." Margaret braked for a red light. "He said the bomb could fall on us any minute."

"I—"

Before Phoebe could finish her sentence, Margaret withdrew a handgun from her purse, trained the muzzle up at her jaw, and blew the roof of her skull off. Blood and bone shards splattered the vinyl headliner and the windshield in a pattern that looked like the missing piece of a jigsaw puzzle.

Deafened by the pistol blast, Phoebe started in shock. The sight of Margaret's corpse slumping against the steering wheel sickened her. She flung her door open, unbuckled her seat belt, and clambered out of the Fiat.

She barely dodged a black Camaro that thundered past her. She couldn't hear the traffic around her thanks to the pistol shot ringing in her ears.

Trying to pull herself together she lurched across the road to the safety of the sidewalk and made for the Burger King the better part of a mile away. She couldn't run very fast in her stunned condition. Her balance was off as she jogged on the sidewalk.

Maybe Margaret was right, Phoebe decided. Maybe suicide was the only escape from a government running amok in fear of a virus.

No, she wasn't going to take Margaret's way out. Phoebe was a fighter. She wasn't going to give up and blow her brains out. She might have been a loser, but she wasn't a defeatist.

Sure, she made bad choices. But they were *her* choices. Choosing was an exercise of her freedom—even if it meant choosing wrong. She wasn't going to let the government, or anyone else for that matter, make her choices for her.

She was going to fight to the bitter end no matter who tried to kill her. Whether they came at her with H-bombs or napalm, she would keep fighting. Which reminded her—where was Hardy? She glanced behind her and didn't see him. She continued jogging.

Maybe the commentator Margaret had heard on the radio had been wrong about the H-bomb, Phoebe decided.

She heard the scream of an F-16 Fighting Falcon flying above her. Couldn't an F-16 drop an H-bomb?

She broke into a run.

They wouldn't dare, she decided. They wouldn't.

ABOUT THE AUTHOR

Multi-award-winning author Bryan Cassiday writes thrillers and horror fiction. His postapocalyptic horror thriller *Horde (Zombie Apocalypse: The Chad Halverson Series Book 6)* won the Independent Press Award for Best Horror Novel 2022 and the American Fiction Award for Best Horror Novel 2021. His Scott Brody thriller *Threads* won the Independent Press Award for Best Thriller Novel 2023 and the American Fiction Award for Best Hard-Boiled Crime Novel 2022. He lives in Southern California.

www.ingramcontent.com/pod-product-compliance
Lightning Source LLC
Chambersburg PA
CBHW020306200626
46814CB00006BA/2103